I0671301

Secrets of a Baby Mama

By

D T Pollard

Essence Bestselling Author

Follow D T Pollard https://twitter.com/dtpollard

http://DTPollard.com

This is a work of fiction. All of the characters, names, incidents, organizations and dialogue in this novel are either the products of the author's imagination or are used fictitiously.
Based upon Ratchet Woman by D T Pollard

Original non-text Image used on cover Школа Синди

"I asked one of the other girls about you. You interest me. She said you have two young kids at home," the man sitting on a couch in a dimly lit room said.

"What business is it of yours to ask about my private life? I don't know you. You just paid for a VIP suite lap dance and that's it," Lindsay said.

"I just like to know who I'm doing business with. What do your children think about their mother bending over and showing her pussy for a living? You're just another thot baby mama stripping because that's all you know how to do to make a living. I can throw in a few more Benjamins for some special services, if you know what I mean. I know you could use that extra cash and maybe buy your kids some new clothes or something," the man said as he tossed several one hundred dollar bills onto the table in front of the sofa he was sitting on.

"I'm not for sale," Lindsay informed.

"Come here bitch!" the man demanded.

"Get your hands off me! You know the rules," Lindsay said as she pushed the man's hands away from her hips.

"Come on! You ratchet little ho. I paid a lot of money for this VIP suite and with that extra cash on top, I want my money's worth!" the man said as he tried to pull Lindsay down onto his lap.

Lindsay decided she was not calling security that night. This man had called her a ratchet ho one time too many and before she realized it, Lindsay grabbed the neck of a wine bottle that was sitting on the table in front of her. With one swing of the bottle Lindsay made contact with the head of her overly aggressive customer just above his left ear. The wine bottle shattered against the side of the man's skull as a mixture of red wine and blood spilled onto his white shirt.

"Who's the ratchet ho now, bitch?! I'm not a fucking hooker and you don't have enough money to buy me motherfucker," Lindsay screamed at the man who was now spread out on the couch.

Before Lindsay could make another move the man sprung up from the couch and lunged at her throat.

"You fucking bitch!" the man screamed in anger.

This man weighed over two hundred pounds and soon had both of his hands around Lindsay's neck as she tumbled backwards to the floor with her clear soled platform heels flying into the air. All Lindsay could see was the blood streaming down his scowling face and bulging eyes as he tried to choke the life out of her.

Lindsay Wilson was not some shrinking violet and this was not her first fight with a man. Lindsay knew where his weak spots were. While this man had huge advantages in strength and size over a five-foot four inch tall woman who weighed one hundred and thirty pounds, he underestimated his opponent. While she was gasping for breath, Lindsay thrust her right knee upward as forcefully as she could. Lindsay's knee made contact with her target area between her assailant's legs. The man made an audible grunting sound and the grip he had around Lindsay's neck loosened immediately. Lindsay scrambled away from him and sat up against the wall in order to catch her breath.

The commotion in the VIP room attracted the attention of Darrius Jones who was a bouncer and head of security for The Secret Island Club. Darrius was a massive three hundred pound black man and amateur bodybuilder who stood over six feet tall.

"Lindsay, what the fuck is going on in here?!" Darrius asked.

"This asshole put his hands on me. I told him to stop. Then he grabbed me again and tried to pull me down on his lap," Lindsay explained.

"Well, how the hell did he end up on the floor holding his nuts with his head busted wide open?" Darrius quizzed.

"He jumped me and was choking the shit out of me! I kneed him in the balls to get him off me," Lindsay replied.

"Was that before or after you busted him up side the head with the wine bottle?" Darrius asked.

Lindsay just starred at Darrius with her mouth open.

"That's what I thought. You should have pushed the alert button and let me know what the fuck was going on. No, you had to take shit into your own hands again. This ain't gonna sit well with Jacob. You better hope this asshole stretched out on the floor here has too much to lose to make a big stink about this. You know Jacob's gonna be on your ass about this shit," Darrius said.

"Get your ass up!" Darrius said to the man as he grabbed him by the shoulders and pulled him upright.

The man stumbled to his feet and looked over at Lindsay.

"I want that whore put in jail for assault!" the man said.

"What do you do for a living?" Darrius asked.

"I'm a doctor," the man replied.

"Really, you're a doctor?" Darrius responded.

"Now, what if that young lady over there filed charges of attempted rape against you for trying to force her into a sex act? That would not be good for your reputation as a doctor, would it?" Darrius asked.

"What! I never tried to rape her," the doctor replied.

"You piece of shit! You thought you had bought some pussy for a few hundred dollars you threw on the floor. When that didn't work you tried to force me to do something with you. Sick bastard!" Lindsay informed.

"Oh, so you go around soliciting strange women for sex. When that didn't work, you put your hands on her and she told you to stop? Then, didn't you try to pull her onto your lap against her will after she told you to stop the first time?" Darrius asked.

"What the hell are you talking about? She hit me in the head with a bottle. That's assault," the man said.

"I don't know. It sounds like self defense to me. It seems like she was fighting off some pervert trying to force her to have sex with him against her will. How does attempted sexual assault sound to you? Are you sure you want to press charges? I suggest you get your ass out of here and take a few days off to patch yourself up and keep your mouth shut," Darrius asked.

"I want him to apologize to me," Lindsay said as she stood to face the man.

"What!" Darrius said as he turned to face Lindsay.

"I want him to say he's sorry for putting his hands on me and calling me a ratchet ho," Lindsay said.

Darrius looked at Lindsay and made a facial expression to her indicating that she might be pushing things too far.

"Miss, I don't know your name, but I apologize for getting out of line. I'm sorry," the man said.

"Look, could I get some paper towels and clean myself up a little before I leave?" the doctor requested.

Darrius looked at Lindsay and took the man to the bathroom and watched him as he wiped the blood and wine from his face. Although it looked worse, it seemed that the cuts on his head were superficial and covered by his hair. The man left and nodded to Lindsay on the way out of the club.

It was two o'clock in the morning and Lindsay Wilson went to the dressing room in the back to change before going home. Lindsay paused

7

and looked at her naked body in a full length mirror mounted on a wall. Lindsay felt that she still held her own in terms of attractiveness. Lindsay kept a tan that she felt enhanced her tips when she danced. Her curves had always been rather noticeable compared to other White women. Lindsay turned to the side and her flat abdomen and protruding butt combined with an ample bust line were her moneymakers. Lindsay stood on her tip toes and flexed her calf muscles. Lindsay wanted to make sure her calf muscle definition was still there and popped out when she wore her heels. Lindsay walked up near the mirror and saw that her blue eyes were still vibrant, but she did notice somewhat dark circles under her eyes from a lack of sleep and nonstop schedule. Lindsay also noticed the fading red imprints of her attacker's hands on her neck. Lindsay went to her dressing area to put on her top and skirt. It had been a good night for Lindsay in the form of tips as she danced on the main stage on a Saturday night. Just then Darrius stepped into the dressing room and Lindsay was the last dancer there as everyone else had left.

"Lindsay, are you okay?" Darrius asked.

"I'm fine, but Jacob is going to be pissed if he finds out what happened with that guy tonight. I'll either be taken off the schedule altogether or have to work shitty day shifts. I can't afford for that to happen. I've got two kids to take care of. He's out of town tonight and won't know what happened unless you tell him. I'm begging you please don't tell him!" Lindsay pleaded.

8

"Look, you got lucky tonight in more ways than one. That guy could have hurt you bad before I came in. Just look at the marks he left on your neck. The other thing is how the hell do you ask for an apology after I've talked that motherfucka into leaving and not pressing charges against you for busting his head open with a wine bottle? What, so your fucking feelings got hurt because he called you a name. You dance in a totally nude strip club. Men call you all kinds of names every day while you shake your ass in their faces, so what was so different about tonight?" Darrius asked.

"That's different. When I'm on stage it's not one on one and it's a show. I dance and they can say whatever they want. It's not personal. Tonight that guy assumed that I would just let him do whatever he wanted, because he thought I was nothing but a ratchet ho and a few hundred dollars had bought me for him to do as he pleased. He was asking other dancers about me and my personal life and thought I would do anything for money since I was a single mother with two kids. It made it worse to find out he was a doctor. He thinks he's a god and I'm just a slutty baby mama turned stripper," Lindsay said.

"Look, why are you surprised that some men think that way. That's why half of them come here in the first place. Here, they can look at and think about a woman any way they want. They know that even in this strip club it is a fantasy, because these women are not here for them to have their way with either. That guy that was fucking with you found that out the hard way," Darrius said.

"Okay, back to what happened tonight. Please do me a favor and don't tell Jacob. I'm begging you. I need my job to support my children," Lindsay said looking at Darrius pleadingly.

Darrius stood there in deep thought for a minute. Before Darrius could speak, Lindsay looked at him while slowly spreading her legs apart and pulling her skirt up to her waist while sitting in her dressing room chair. Lindsay ran her hands up the inside of her thighs to her exposed genital area and looked at Darrius with a beckoning look in her eyes.

"Darrius, there's nobody here but you and me right now," Lindsay said as she licked her lips.

"Lindsay, put your panties on and go home. I won't tell Jacob what happened because I like you, but not because of what your just tried. I see you naked in here all the time. Lindsay, I'm thirty-five years old and a grown ass man. I don't get excited by pussy anymore. I don't mean it that way. I meant that sex is not going to make me do something I wouldn't do anyway. When I was younger, I got into a lot of trouble by thinking with my dick. I've got three children by three different women that I wouldn't deal with now for any reason at all if I met them today for the first time. When I met them back then I was hitting the clubs and each one of them was bangin and ready for anything. I was all hopped up, cocky and thought running up my score on gettin ass was what made me a man. Three kids later it didn't seem like it was such a good move. Now I'm paying child support to three baby mamas that I can't stand to be in the same room with now.

10

That's why I'm working in this shithole club at night," Darrius said.

"Darrius, I didn't mean to piss you off or anything. I mean, well I don't know what I mean," Lindsay said.

"Lindsay, I guess you're about twenty-five or so. You're still young enough to learn a few things about life. My old man always told me not to think with the wrong head and I thought he was crazy. Let me tell you something. I met an older guy one day and he was a businessman. We struck up a conversation and he told me, after I laid out my situation, that the definition of insanity was to keep doing the same things and expecting to get a different result. I finally figured out what he meant. That move you made on me a few minutes ago, that was a ratchet ho move. If you don't want to be called a ratchet ho, then stop acting like one," Darrius said.

Lindsay felt a flash of anger and almost exploded like she normally does when frustrated by life situations, but this was different. This man had just turned down the most valuable and powerful thing she felt she had to offer a man while giving her a piece of advice.

"You've got two kids now. Don't wake up at age thirty with six. Try using what is between your ears to get what you want instead of what's between your legs. Every woman can compete with you if it's a combat waged based upon what you tried earlier tonight and some will be younger and better at it than you are. Using what is between your ears and improving that can separate you from

11

everyone else. Just look around your own neighborhood and look at those old former dime pieces that are past their prime. They can't compete using what they used before after they became old, tired and worn out. Men will use you up and throw you away. They don't give a fuck!" Darrius said.

"Why didn't you just do like most other men and take what I offered and move on. I mean, is something wrong with me?" Lindsay asked.

Darrius looked at her in disbelief and rubbed his forehead.

"Lindsay, I'm trying to be a better man for my kids' sake and I have someone special I'm seeing and I don't want to fuck that up. Lindsay, go home and think about what I said," Darrius advised

They closed the place down and Darrius watched Lindsay walk away. Lindsay was a woman that could bring any man to his knees. Darrius had to use all of his willpower that night because his body told him to do what came naturally. Her long blond hair, tanned skin and those calf muscles in heels earned her the highest tips in the club. Jacob would not let her go anyway, because she had a loyal following that spent a lot of money in that club. Darrius waited until she drove off in her old beat up economy car. He thought that maybe he was the insane one for giving her a pass when she willingly offered herself to him. The next man would have been all over her.

"Fuck! I should have hit that ass!" Darius said as he armed the alarm system and left the club.

Lindsay's life offered very few moments of solitude when she could be alone with just her thoughts and her solitary drives to and from the club were two of those occasions. In the span of those few minutes Lindsay thought about her life in more carefree times before she had to be the responsible adult. All manner of thoughts ran through Lindsay's mind. In spite of the chaos at the club just moments before a smile came to Lindsay's face when thoughts of her high school years in rural east Texas played in the theater of her mind. Lindsay felt she was still that teenage girl deep down inside in spite of the unexpected detours life had thrown her way.

Lindsay made it home to the apartment she shared with her best friend. At this time of morning there should have been no one outside, but this part of town seemed to be active at all hours of the day. Lindsay always kept a watchful eye out for those involved in what could be classified as less than wholesome pursuits during those early morning hours when she got home.

A long shift of dancing always left Lindsay bone tired. Her platform heels looked good, but left her with aching feet. Lindsay's first inclination would be to fall across her bed and go to sleep, but she always took a shower to wash the strip club essence off her body. A combination of cigarette smoke, perspiration and perfume would be in her clothes, on her skin and in her hair. After cleaning up Lindsay would look in on her two children because she didn't want them to smell their mother with the scent of her occupation all over her person. Lindsay's children only knew she worked at night, but had no idea about what she did for a living. All Lindsay's kids knew was that their mother loved them, took care of them and was with them as much as possible. Lindsay's felt like she was asleep before her head hit the pillow on most nights after getting home early in the mornings.

2

"Hey bitch. Why you just sittin there starring out the window?" Lindsay's roommate Tameka asked.

"I don't know what's going on anymore. A lot of shit went down at the club last night and my fucking head is spinning," Lindsay replied.

"What the hell happened?" Tameka quizzed.

"Well, shit kind of got out of hand when this asshole started grabbing me in one of the VIP rooms. He was a creep who was asking other women at the club about me. Somebody told him I had kids and called me a thot, ho and baby mama stripping to make a living. He even tried to pay me to turn a trick with him. I busted his ass upside the head with a wine bottled and then he started choking the shit out of me. I kneed him in the nuts to get him off me?" Lindsay said.

"What the fuck! You're such a crazy bitch. That man could have hurt you. Why didn't you call that big fine ass bouncer, what's his name, Darrius?" Tameka asked.

"I just snapped on his ass and lost it," Lindsay said.

"Yeah, but what if you had got hurt. You've got two kids to think about. You know how fucked up your relationship is with your folks. I mean, I love your kids like my own, but I can barley take care of me and my three kids. You need to check that temper shit, for real. So what happened after you got him off you?" Tameka asked.

"Darrius came in and smoothed everything out and got the guy to leave. I was scared as hell that Jacob was going to find out and boot my ass out of there. I begged Darrius not to tell him," Lindsay said.

"What did he say?" Tameka asked.

"He said he wouldn't tell Jacob because he liked me, but something else happened," Lindsay said.

"Come on with it. Why you gonna make me have to drag it out of your ass," Tameka asked.

"Well I was so scared that Darrius would tell Jacob that I kind of offered to fuck him if he wouldn't," Lindsay said.

"What! Are you fucking serious? That's nasty. What, did you just come out and say, here's the pussy, come and get it? Come on. I want details. I've been watching that big, fine ass nigga for a long time. Girl, did he knock your back out?" Tameka asked while laughing loudly.

"No. I didn't just tell him to just dive in. I kind of just pulled my dress up and showed him what he could have if he wanted it. You know how it is when you put that shit on display," Lindsay said.

"Whaaat. So you just showed him your white chocolate trap, as you call it," Tameka asked.

"Well, I also reminded him that it was just us there at the club. You know letting him know that only we would know what happened," Lindsay admitted.

"Did it work?" Tameka quizzed.

"No. He told me to put my clothes back on," Lindsay said.

"Hold the fuck up! You showed that man your coochie with a welcome sign on it and he turned you down. I guess that's why I can't get his attention. That motherfucka must have some sugar in his tank. How a grown ass man gone turn down pussy. Shit if I was into women I'd be all over your ass. I mean I'm not, but I'm just saying. Did he say why he didn't want to do it?" Tameka asked.

"He told me about how that kind of thing got him in trouble before and he ended up with three kids by three different baby mamas. Plus, he said if he met those women now he wouldn't have anything to do with them," Lindsay said.

"Hold up. That nigga just called you a thot on the sly. Did you go off on his ass! That's some foul shit," Tameka observed.

"Here's the thing. I told Darrius that one of the things that pissed me off so much about that guy was that he called me a ratchet ho. After I tried to bribe Darrius with sex he told me if I didn't want to be called a ratchet ho then I shouldn't act like one. He said I made a ratchet ho move on him," Lindsay said.

For once Tameka sat there with a stunned look on her face.

"I don't even have a comeback for that," Tameka said.

"Darrius also said some shit about being insane is to keep doing the same things over and over while expecting something different to happen," Lindsay said.

"What the fuck is that supposed to mean. I mean he's a bouncer in a fucking strip club. Is he supposed to be some kind of head doctor? What the fuck does he know?" Tameka said.

"I know what he meant. He meant that if you keep doing fucked up shit. You will keep getting fucked up results. So, if I keep doing ratchet ho shit, then I will still be called a ratchet ho. It's simple, but I can't hardly think of myself that way. It makes me feel like shit. Like I'm worthless," Lindsay said.

"Why you taking that kind of advice from a fucking strip club bouncer. This is about surviving in this fucked up world out here! We both got kids from niggas that ain't doing shit to help us out. I do what I gotta to survive in this motherfucka and you do too! Your own family disowned you when they found out you were pregnant by a black man and you moved in with us so you could finish high school. Now look at us! We moved to Dallas and now we got five kids between us by smooth talking, sorry ass niggas that ain't doing a damn thing to help us out. I saw Joquan's trifling ass daddy yesterday rolling around in that damned car he spends all of his money on instead of helping to feed his son. He was Mr. lovey dovey until after he got in my panties. Mr. 'I don't use a condom because I want to feel you.' Then when I told that nigga I was pregnant, you know what he said. He said 'It ain't mine'. I'll bet Darrius said the same thing to his baby mamas when they told him they were pregnant, so a nigga like that can't tell women like me or you shit about life!" Tameka ranted.

18

"Tameka! Calm down. He said that to me, not you. He also said that he worked at the club to pay child support for his kids, so I guess he grew up some. Shit, my three-year olds' daddy, Trey, is locked up in the state pen in Huntsville for slinging crack. He was a fine motherfucker when I met him at that club. I was banging when we went there. You remember that night. You had your weave together with some new real human hair, the good shit, not that imitation stuff that will break you out. I had those heels on that made my calves pop. The brothers love that shit. I was getting the eye from every black woman in the spot," Lindsay said.

"Yeah, I remember that night. I thought we was gonna have to fight our way outta that bitch. Those hos were ready to jump your white ass. Those bitches didn't want you up in there taking their men. You left my ass up in there after Trey stepped to you. I was looking around and was like, no this bitch didn't just leave my ass up in here chasing some dick. Then I went outside and saw this tall, fine nigga with some white bitch trying to pull his tongue out of his skull while sitting on the back of his Mercedes and it was you. Then you let that nigga slip his hand under your dress and the next thing I knew you jumped into the passenger seat of his car and were gone. Just left my ass at the spot," Tameka said.

"You saw that? Well it's not like you haven't left me somewhere either. Shit, we both took the bus to the club anyway," Lindsay said.

"What happened between you two anyway? You don't talk about it much," Tameka said.

19

"Well the obvious happened and that's how I ended up with Jasmine, but a lot of other crazy shit went down when I was with him. He's the one that I started getting high with. I thought I was on top of the world when I was rolling around with him in his Benz. I became his ride or die chick and was ready to drop any other bitch putting her ass in his face. Then one day we were stopped at this traffic light on Malcolm X and I'm chillin and sitting back with my sunglasses on. I looked over to the side and I'm starring right into the barrel of a gun. Some guy told me to get the fuck out of the car and there was another guy on the other side of the car with a gun to Trey's head. We got out and they took off in his Benz. I'm standing there feeling like the biggest fool on earth. I've got on a short white dress, heels and my titties were damn near about to fall out of the top I had on. There I was standing in the middle of the street with people blowing their horns at us. I was so embarrassed, but I tried to play it off.

I was pregnant at the time and didn't know it. That's when he told me he was a drug dealer and those guys worked for his supplier. They took Trey's car and money because he was holding back on him. I broke down crying right there on side of the road at the bus stop. My dumb ass bought into the lie he told me that he made his money flipping houses or some bullshit. I was out. I could have been killed and my son ended up lord knows where. Trey never recovered and started selling crack on the streets until he got busted," Lindsay said.

"You were with Trey for a while and you didn't know he was dealing drugs?" Tameka asked.

"You know the game. He was giving me money, buying me nice things and paying my bills so you kinda act like you don't know, but you do know," Lindsay said.

"Yeah, I know what you mean. Just like I was pretending that I didn't know that my lawyer friend Calvin was married," Tameka said.

"Tameka, are you serious?" Lindsay asked.

"Look, I'm not stupid. He never took me around any of his friends. We only saw each other at night and that was usually at some hotel or something. I didn't even know where he lived and he called me and not the other way around. I finally told him that I knew he was married. He freaked out a little, but I told him that we were both grown and may as well be honest about it. I'm basically his side chick, jumpoff or whatever you want to call it. As long as he is paying some of my bills, I may as well fuck him instead of some broke ass nigga out there that won't do nothing for me, but get me pregnant with a kid he won't take care of" Tameka said.

"How long have you known?" Lindsay asked.

"It didn't take me long to figure it out, but with three kids to take care of, I'll play the role. I feel like shit sometimes, but I'll go along as long as he pays to play, but I think I'm getting hooked on him. I can't let myself fall in love with a man that belongs to someone else? That ain't gonna happen," Tameka said as she wiped away a tear.

"Mama what's wrong with Aunt Tameka?" Lindsay's son Riley asked when he walked into the room.

"Nothing's wrong with her baby. She just got something in her eyes," Lindsay answered as all five of their kids came flooding into the room.

3

There is something about July in Dallas that brings everyone out to the malls and it is those scorching 100-degree plus temperatures. Tameka's cousin volunteered to watch the children to give the two young women a break from their constant cycle of work and child care. As they walked across the scorching concrete parking lot to Lindsay's car, Latron Williams decided that he needed to make his presence known.

"Ya'll ladies are looking nice today. Hey Lindsay, when are you going come holler at a brother? You know we could have a good time together. I got what you need," Latron said.

"Latron, didn't you just drop out of school last year? Are you going to support me and my two children? I see you hanging around here every day, do you even have a job," Lindsay asked.

"Well, I'm looking for a job now. It's a little hard out there right now," Latron answered.

Lindsay walked over to Latron and stood about two inches from his body. Latron was about three inches taller than Lindsay and his tan pants were hanging below his exposed underwear. A solid white t-shirt and white sneakers completed his attire. Latron smelled Lindsay's perfume as she invaded his personal space. Lindsay looked up at Latron.

"When I moved in here you were in junior high school and now you want to holler at me. I don't think you could handle what I could put on you. Stick to girls your own age. Plus I don't like sagging. You need to pull your pants up and you smell like weed," Lindsay said as she looked him up and down.

"Yes ma'am," Latron said as Lindsay walked off.

Latron looked on as the object of his fantasies ass swayed as she walked away.

"Why did you do that boy like that? You gonna give him a complex," Tameka said.

"Well he decided to put it out there, so I told him what kind of resume he needed to step to me," Lindsay said.

They ventured out to The Parks Mall in Arlington, Texas which amounted to a field trip given their usual travel radius. Lindsay's car was beat up externally, but the drive train was sound.

These two women didn't have a lot of money to spend, but they used what they had to look as good a possible. It was doubtful that the jeans Lindsay wore could be any tighter and she was showcasing what earned her the description of being a wooty, a white girl with a big booty. Tameka was still keeping it tight even after having three children. Their lipstick, nails and heels were all designed to attract attention from the opposite sex and it was mission accomplished as they swayed down the mall concourses.

Lindsay wore jeans that stopped above her calves so she could show off those legs that had brought many men to their knees. Their dark sunglasses allowed them to see without being seen.

"Look at these men walking with their wives and girlfriends giving us the side eye. You see,

24

that's what I'm talking about. They wife up those boring heifers and see women like us and their minds go wild. If they had half a chance they would be all over us if they could do it and not get caught," Tameka said.

"I'm hungry. Let's hit the food court," Lindsay said.

They ordered pizza and found a table in the middle of the eating area.

"Tameka, do you ever just get tired of being tired?" Lindsay asked.

"What do you mean?" Tameka replied.

"I mean. Okay I'm 25, but I feel like I'm 52. I don't see an end to the bullshit cycle I'm stuck in. I'm dancing at a strip club, got two kids and I don't have a college degree or any other skills to offer so I can make a living doing something else. I feel trapped. I don't see how things will ever change. These men just look at me for what they want and you know what that is. Sometimes I don't even want to get out of bed," Lindsay confessed.

"Look, I'm not fooling myself. I don't want to end up like Miss Robinson in apartment 2C. She called me over there one day and asked about us. Well at first she thought were together, you know like lesbian lovers," Tameka said.

"You're fucking with me, right?" Lindsay said laughing.

"Well, I straightened her out on that and told her I was strictly dickly, okay. She said that she had been watching us and thought we seemed a little different than some of the younger women in the complex. She made a point of saying that we weren't outside raising hell all the time and men didn't parade in and out of our place. She even noticed that our kids seemed to be well behaved and weren't running all over the apartment complex unsupervised. Then she told me to be careful not to end up like her when we got old. This woman has to be sixty and she told me that trying to get through life based upon your looks and body could only work so long. Then she said something that I couldn't believe came out of her mouth. She said that your pussy and body gonna get old like everything else and if that's all you got going for you, then it's just a matter of time before you are thrown away for something younger and tighter. She told me to think about that because that's what happened to her. Now she is all alone and most of her kids were dead or in prison," Tameka said.

"I don't know what to even say about that, but that is some real shit. Maybe that's why I've been having these scary thoughts lately about what's next for me. I'm twenty-five, I don't want to be dancing in a strip club when I'm thirty-five. I don't want my son's friends coming into a club seeing his mother dancing naked. I don't even know how to change anything. Tameka, do you want things to change in your life?" Lindsay asked.

"Where would I even begin? I'm in too deep to even see a way out. I was hard headed and wouldn't listen to my parents. They wanted me to go to college, but I wanted to be free and have a good time, but freedom had a fucking high price. I came up here with you and before I knew it I was pregnant. You were my excuse to escape from what

I thought were my parents trying to control my life. Now I've got three kids by three different men. What the fuck! What man wants a woman with three kids except to use as a side chick? I don't want to be in a situation where that's my only option," Tameka said.

"Hey you ran away from your parents. They didn't throw you out like mine did. Your folks took me in, why do you think they wouldn't help you get back on track now?" Lindsay asked.

"You mean go back home. I would be so ashamed. Those people back there don't know how I'm living up here. My daddy was telling everyone that he wanted me to be a doctor. He worked for the postal service and had saved enough money to send me to college, but I didn't want any part of it. Mama told me when I left like I did that he cried like a baby and I've never seen my daddy cry," Tameka said.

"Sounds like to me, you're just too proud to ask for help, but this shit we're doing up here ain't working. Darrius said something to me the other night that sent chills down my spine. He said told me to be careful not to wake up in five years and have six kids instead of two," Lindsay said.

"I'm halfway there already," Tameka said.

"You know it can happen. There are women in the complex we live in with four or five already and they haven't hit thirty yet. This is a bullshit road we're on. How do we get off?" Lindsay asked.

"When was the last time you talked to your folks," Tameka asked.

"It's been a while, over two years ago. My daddy said some terrible things to me when I got pregnant and when he found out it was by a black man, he lost it" Lindsay said.

"What did he say?" Tameka asked.

"Well, he called me a nigger lover, whore and a Jezebel. He said that he wished I was never born and said I had tainted the bloodline. My sister called me a mudshark," Lindsay said with tears welling up in her eyes.

"What about your mom, what did she say?" Tameka asked.

"Mama just sat there. She would never stand up to him. He's my daddy, but he is a mean old bastard. He doesn't know it, but I saw him knock mama down to the ground with a backhand slap when she talked back to him when I was little. My parents have never even seen my kids, their own grandchildren. I guess because they're half black, my daddy probably hates them," Lindsay said.

Just then two young men pulled chairs up to their table and tried to strike up a conversation.

"Look guys. Not now," Tameka said giving them a back off look.

The two walked away while talking loudly.

"Fuck those thots," one of the men said.

"Oh my God! Let's get out of here," Lindsay said.

During the drive back to Dallas Tameka said something that surprised Lindsay.

"Okay Lindsay. We've known each other a long time. Since we're laying all our shit out here on the line, I'm not gonna bite my tongue. I've

28

always wondered why you stayed in the situation you're in now. At first, I figured that maybe you're were one of those white girls that wanted to play around with black guys to see what it was like and then you would go back to your own world. I mean you're white. Couldn't you just walk into a different life? I really don't know how to explain what I'm trying to say. I mean, I'm black and figure if I change the way I look and dress I wouldn't get as far in getting a break to do something else as you would. Most of the big companies around here are run by white men. Do you understand what I'm saying?" Tameka said.

Lindsay didn't say anything for at least two minutes.

"Tameka, I do understand what you're saying, but it is just not the way you think it is. Just because I'm white doesn't mean that I can just put on a business outfit and get a job downtown in some lawyer's office. I don't know shit. I don't have any more education, skills or job training than you do," Lindsay replied.

"I know, but people would look at you for a job before they would me. I know that sounds racist, but I have seen too many white women in jobs because they looked the part and sometimes they were dumb as fuck. Even in some of those bullshit fast food places I've worked in it happened. I worked a one place where this white girl was there six months and she was promoted to assistant manager over some black folks that had been there for two or three years," Tameka said.

"Tameka. Let me tell you something about white people. They can be worse than black people when it comes to looking down on each other. I'm sure you've heard white people call other white folks white trash. Some white people look at each other based on how much money they make, where they live and what family they come from. I'm on the bottom. I'm a white trash stripper with a tramp stamp tattoo on my back and two half black babies. You know how it goes. My children are black. It doesn't matter than their mother is white. If they've got any black blood in them they're black as far as most white folks see it and it might make it worse that they are mixed, so what kind of future do my kids have?" Lindsay said.

"Maybe they can become President," Tameka said.

Lindsay glanced over at Tameka.

"I'm just saying," Tameka said.

"I know, but his grandparents raised him. My kids' grandparents don't even know or give a shit about them," Lindsay replied.

4

Lindsay Wilson and Tameka Davis had known each other since they met in Junior High School in rural eastern Texas. These girls were drawn to each other and became friends although they mostly only saw each other at school and during school sponsored events. They tended to push each other and when one tried out for the cheerleading squad, so did the other. These friends shared a lot of experiences together as they matured including their interest in the opposite sex.

Lindsay was drawn to the music and style of the African American culture. The way the black girls dressed, danced and talked was exciting to her. Lindsay's father, Clyde Wilson, was more of a traditionalist; he liked country music, hunting and bible study. Lindsay's older sister, Karen, was his prize and did everything her parents suggested while Lindsay preferred to cut her own path in the world. Lindsay would often leave home in one set of clothes and change when she got to school into what she really wanted to wear.

Since Lindsay hung around with Tameka, it was natural that when boys were around they were black and they took an interest in Lindsay. Lindsay's first kiss was on a double date with Tameka with two black football players from their high school team. Tameka and Lindsay were sophomores and these guys were seniors, but kissing was as far as it went that night.

Lindsay knew that her father would be furious if he found out she was going out with black boys and she kept it quiet, but her older sister knew about it. Karen confronted Lindsay and gave her a stern warning.

"Lindsay, you had better watch your ass. If daddy finds out that you have been hanging around and going out with niggers, he would beat the shit out of you and you know it," Karen said.

"They're not niggers. They are my friends. They don't call me names like you call them," Lindsay responded.

"Don't be so stupid. They just want some of your white meat. You see how many of those black girls get pregnant before they finish high school, so you know what they want so they can brag about fucking the white girl. If you keep this up none of the white boys will want to touch you with a ten-foot pole. I have already heard some of them talking about you and calling you a nigger lover. No white man wants a white woman that's been sleeping around with niggers because she's damaged goods. A proper white woman will stick with her own race," Karen said.

"Karen, for your information there is only one race of people and it's called human. We might come in different colors and have different cultures, but we are all the same inside. You're standing there acting all high and mighty like your some angel, but you're not. At least I wasn't down on my hands and knees in the barn with ugly ass Timmy Anderson humping me like a bull in heat like you were last week! I saw you, but you didn't think I noticed when you went out back with him. I followed you and saw it all. You did every filthy thing he asked. You were on your knees in front of him using your mouth while he held the back of your head. I heard Timmy when he said 'suck it bitch' and you were gagging on him. Then Timmy told you to get down on your hands and knees. You did just like he asked and got down there with your ass stuck up in the air. He mounted you like a dog in heat and pulled your head back using your ponytail and rode you like he was riding a goddamned horse. He even slapped your boney ass with his hand like he was telling you to giddy up and go faster. You were grunting like a stuck pig. Bitch, I even found your birth control pills too. You ain't fooling me. So you can't tell me shit about who to go out with!" Lindsay snapped.

"Well at least he's white! His daddy owns a construction company! It will be his one day!" Karen said.

"He ain't gonna marry you. He thinks we're white trash. I heard him bragging to his friends that he humped you like a fucking dog, but he really wants to go out with Stephanie Mitchell because her family is in business like his family. That's what those kind of white guys do with girls like us. They think we're white trash. They will fuck us in the barn or in some oil field at night in the back of their pickup trucks while they take their little princesses out on dates and to the prom. Their parents don't want girls like us messing up their family trees. The guys I'm going out with don't look down on me. You're just easy pussy to him," Lindsay said.

"You're a fucking liar! At least he's white!" Karen screamed as she ran off crying.

"Stupid bitch," Lindsay muttered as she walked off.

Tameka had her own unique journey to adulthood. Tameka was bright and her father was able to provide her and her two other younger brothers a solid middle class upbringing through his career with the postal service. Tameka had a free ride to college waiting for her and her father, Gregory Davis, could not wait to get his first child into college which was something he was never able to experience himself. Tameka had other ideas about her future, she could not wait to get out of high school and experience what she thought was true freedom. Tameka had the notion that the lifestyle she enjoyed at home would somehow magically continue if she left and lived on her own. Thoughts of what it took to pay for the amenities that her parents provided for the family never crossed her mind.

When Lindsay got pregnant during their last year in school her world fell apart around her Tameka stepped into the void. Tameka asked her parents if Lindsay could move in with them so she could finish school and they agreed. Tameka never thought about how big a risk she was asking her parents to take by bringing a pregnant white teenager into their home in an area where racial lines still existed, but Tameka's parents would not turn their backs on a young woman in need.

Lindsay's father was not pleased that Tameka's parents took his daughter into their home. Lindsay's mother had arranged for Lindsay to stay with her aunt in Houston until after the baby was born. Lindsay's father thought he had come up with the perfect solution to spare him the supreme embarrassment of having his daughter parade around with her pregnant belly on full display for all of his friends to see. The fact that she was pregnant by a black man made things even worse from Clyde Wilson's point of view.

Clyde thought that Lindsay had no choice but to go to Houston because he had made it clear that she was not saying in his home and raising a half-black baby under his roof. Lindsay summoned all of her teenage courage, packed her clothes in her old car that she bought from working summer jobs and prepared to go to Tameka's house. Clyde told her that since she was pregnant by a nigger and going to live with niggers, then he considered her to be a nigger. Lindsay heard the ultimate rejection when her own father told her she was dead to him. Lindsay cried the whole time as she drove to Tameka's house and had not stepped a foot back in the house she grew up in since the moment she left.

Tameka thought that it was strange that Lindsay never told her who the father of her first child was and she had stopped asking over the years.

Lindsay's transition to living as a member of the Davis household was surprisingly smooth because she was welcomed with open arms. Tameka's mother knew that Lindsay would be somewhat of a social outcast in local white society, so she was immersed in black culture from family gatherings to church. Lindsay became like another daughter to Tameka's parents and she was thankful to not feel judged by those closest around her.

After Lindsay's baby was born, the two teenage friends decided it was time to leave their small town for the big city. Tameka's parents were not pleased as they desperately wanted her to go to college, but she was ready to call her own shots in the world. No amount of pleading and reasoning could change Tameka's mind, so her parents relented and watched their daughter make what they thought would be the biggest mistake of her life. Tameka was not banished from her childhood home or her parent's lives and she was told repeatedly that help was only a phone call away.

Tameka had saved a couple of thousand dollars over the years and felt like she was rich. With nothing, but optimistic thoughts in their heads, Lindsay and Tameka struck out for Dallas together. Initially the two young women stayed with one of Tameka's cousins until they found an apartment and that was the beginning of their journey in the real world. The road to reality was a bumpy one for two naïve country girls and the big city proved to be a cruel teacher of life's lessons.

After almost seven years and with five children between them, the grind of their daily existence was wearing them down. The wide eyed enthusiasm they possessed when they first moved in together on their own was a very distant memory. There was also a space developing between them as they felt something was either pulling them apart or maybe they thought they could do better separately than they could together. For the last four years they had been living in the drab brown hued confines of the apartment complex they rented near the Fair Park area of Dallas. This property was far from luxury accommodations as this facility was of older construction and had declined along with the neighborhood in general. This apartment building complex was of the style with the unit entry doors positioned along a walkway that allowed access to all the apartments on each level of the three story building. Greenery was in short supply on the grounds of the complex as concrete dominated the landscape. Five children needed room to roam and that was in short supply compounded by safety concerns given crime in the area. Multiple forces were coming together to force Lindsay and Tameka to a decision crossroad on their young families' future directions.

Lindsay and Tameka had reached a tipping point of either going all in with the lifestyle they were flirting with to materially improve their situations or trying to find a way out to do better by going in a different direction. Tameka was really struggling with supporting three children with little help, except she had a sugar daddy, but he was another woman's husband. Lindsay was caught between frustration and a moral dilemma. Lindsay knew she could earn more money by doing things she didn't want to do at the strip club, as evidenced by the man she had the fight with literally throwing money at her for sexual favors, but something else was weighing on her conscience.

Lindsay had a secret that she had been hiding for years. Lindsay would soon drop a bombshell on Tameka that she would never forget, but something had to force her to a breaking point in order to bring it out.

5

On the way back to Dallas Tameka received a text message from Calvin, her benefactor.

"It seems that Calvin has a client emergency and wants me to meet him at the ZW Hotel tonight. He already has a room reserved," Tameka said.

"No problem. I'll watch the kids. That's a fancy place," Lindsay said.

"Yeah we always meet at nice places. All I usually get to see is the inside of hotel rooms. I get great room service food and he always leaves me a nice gift, but then he's gone. He's back with his wife and kids. I mean, I know the deal. I guess I'm his private little hooker," Tameka said.

"Do you think of yourself as a hooker when you're with him?" Lindsay asked.

"Well we don't just meet to talk about what's going on in the world. He's a big time lawyer and helps companies buy each other. I'm a high school educated baby mama who works at a store. What kind of shit am I going to talk to him about? I mean he tells me about all of his problems and bitches about his wife," Tameka said.

"He complains about his wife to you. That's fucked up. I mean he's meeting you and having sex with you, but talks about his wife," Lindsay said.

"I guess he thinks that he can impress me because, you know, he's a lawyer and I'm just a stupid ho or something. I don't know," Tameka said.

"What! You are so crazy," Lindsay remarked.

"Come on! He didn't just text me to discuss politics. He wants to get fucked. I know that and he knows that. Hell, you even know that," Tameka said while laughing.

"You know what? It is what it is," Lindsay said.

"Maybe his wife won't give him any pussy anymore or I'm maybe I'm just a bigger freak than she is. Hell, I don't know. Just keep the cash coming and I'll keep him coming. Cha'ching!" Tameka said with tears of laughter rolling down her face.

"Oh my God. You're a crazy bitch," Lindsay said.

"This ain't free no more. Pay to play is my new motto. He's already married, so I'm not dumb enough to think he's leaving his wife for me. With me he gets what he wants and doesn't have to deal with other drama at home when we're done. No. I'm not one of those silly heifers thinking a man's is leaving his wife and family for them. Some of those hoes have told me they been fucking dudes on the side for two or three years thinking they were going to leave their wives for them. Those assholes are stringing along two or three other silly bitches on the side thinking the same thing. I'm not that chick," Tameka said.

Tameka came home after midnight and Lindsay heard her bedroom door close. They shared a three bedroom apartment and the kids slept in the other bedroom and some slept on a sofa bed in the living room. Their children had grown up like brothers and sisters from the time they were small.

If they were to part and go their separate ways it would be like breaking up a family after a divorce. Tameka stared up at the ceiling in the darkness and one thought kept running through her head. How did she end up in her situation given how she was raised and the opportunities she walked away from after she finished high school? It dawned on Tameka how one decision could change the entire trajectory of someone's life as a tear rolled out of her right eye before she fell asleep.

Lindsay dreaded going back to the club for her first
day of work after her latest altercation. The main
thing that Lindsay thought about was encountering
Darrius after he had rejected her two days earlier.
As much as Lindsay hated to admit it, Darrius
inflicted a blow to her ego by blowing her off so
easily.

Lindsay walked into the club and the first
person she saw was Darrius. Darrius acted like
nothing was different between them. Lindsay said
hello to Darrius and he gestured for her to come
over to him.

"Jacob came in this afternoon and told me to
tell you to come to his office when you came in.
Look, I don't know what he wants, but I didn't tell
him shit about what happened Saturday night,"
Darrius said.

"Is he in his office now?" Lindsay asked.

"Yeah. He's in there," Darrius said.

"Fuck!" Lindsay said as she turned to go
upstairs to Jacobs's office.

When Lindsay walked to the stairs she
noticed another dancer, Latasha Cole watching her.
Latasha hated Lindsay with a passion and would
love to get her out of the club. Latasha felt that
Lindsay was the main roadblock keeping her from
the featured dancer slot and she would not be upset
at all if she was out of the picture.

Jacob Rossman was the club's owner and he
had warned Lindsay before about her temper when
dealing with customers that got out of line. In the

final analysis the Secret Island Club made its profits from alcohol sales. The strippers were simply a draw to bring customers into the place and keep them there while they consumed round after round of profitable drinks. Jacob seemed to be a straight forward businessman. He knew that Lindsay had her fans and they spent a lot of money on liquor, but Jacob knew that would be outweighed by someone filing a claim against the club because of her actions. Lindsay was a bundle of nerves as she knocked on Jacob's office door.

"Come in," Jacob said.

Lindsay opened the door and walked inside and closed it behind her.

"You wanted to see me?" Lindsay said.

"Yeah. Lindsay, have a seat," Jacob instructed.

Jacob was forty-five years old, married and had three children. Jacob carried himself as an entrepreneur who just happened to own a strip club and didn't want to be defined by the business he was conducting. Operating an adult entertainment venue was not easy given restrictions regarding where they could be located in relation to schools and neighborhoods. There was always some politician trying to build a reputation by ridding the city of an adult cabaret because it was an easy target and created opportunities for political grandstanding. Jacob's wife, Rebecca, acted as a counterbalance by being active in civic organizations and charities. Rebecca rarely set foot in the club and left running the business to Jacob. Rebecca never felt threatened by Jacob being around so many women because she told him if she ever caught him cheating then he would never see his children again and she would ruin him financially. Jacob had abstained from becoming sexually involved with any of the female workers at the club and that was quite a feat in that business.

Lindsay sat down. Jacob took a television remote control and turned on a flat screen television and asked Lindsay to watch as a video played.

"Lindsay can you tell me why that man is walking with Darrius with a wad of napkins held up against his head that seem to be soaked with blood? He just came from that VIP room and look, isn't that you coming out of that same room?" Jacob asked.

Lindsay looked at Jacob with eyes as big as twin moons, but could not utter a word.

"Darrius didn't tell me about this situation so I'm assuming that it wasn't a big deal, but I was reviewing the security videos and this caught my attention. Can you tell what went on in there?" Jacob asked.

Lindsay decided to be up front and told Jacob what took place and didn't try to leave anything out.

"Lindsay, I like you. You're dependable and you show up for your shifts on time. You have created a good fan base of customers that are repeat visitors and that's good for your bank account and the business, but you have an anger problem. Look, you work in a fucking strip club. When you mix alcohol with men and naked women, somebody's judgment is going to be off and they will cross the

44

line every once in a while. We have Darrius and other security guys around for a reason. Hitting a customer in the head with a bottle is totally unacceptable behavior. This is not the first time something like this has come up. Remember when you slapped that guy at the edge of the stage during a lap dance?" Jacob asked.

"He tried to put his hand between my legs and touch me, you know, there," Lindsay said.

"Okay, I know you don't want guys putting their hands where they shouldn't be. I'm in a tough situation. You bring in a lot of money for me. When you are on stage guys spend a lot of money on drinks and hang around for a long time. On the other hand I got the city council looking for an opportunity to shut me down. A new school is being built just inside the restricted distance of where a business like this can operate, but since we were here first I've got what is called a grandfather clause and can remain open. If something happens that shows we are a public nuisance, then we could be put out of business. If that guy had gone to the police or called a lawyer they would have gone after me because I've got deeper pockets than you do," Jacob said.

"I didn't think about any of that and didn't mean to put your business in danger. I just didn't like being treated that way. I'm sorry and it won't happen again," Lindsay said.

"I know you didn't think about that. You have made an impact here for a long period of time. You are popular with customers, work the best shifts and other girls want your spot, especially

45

Latasha. Latasha does well here and also has a good fan base. Latasha has been working hard to convince me that she could bring in as much money as you do if she had your shift on the main stage. She also said she wouldn't cause me any trouble. Lindsay what makes you worth the extra risk?" Jacob asked.

Jacob was about six feet tall, with black hair and kept himself in good physical shape. Jacob just starred at Lindsay waiting for an answer with an expressionless look on his face as he sat behind a large mahogany desk.

It is often true that the winner in any negotiation is the person that first dictates the terms of the agreement and Lindsay decided it was time for her to win. Without saying a word, Lindsay walked over to Jacob's desk and climbed on top.

"What the hell are you doing? This is a custom built desk," Jacob remarked.

Lindsay ignored his protests and went into her dance routine to the sounds of the music she could hear coming from downstairs. Lindsay didn't have her usual dance costume on but she slowly peeled out of her white cotton top and was not wearing a bra underneath. Next she gradually slid her jeans down her waist and as she stretched out on the cool surface of the desk. Lindsay slowly pulled her jeans off one leg at a time. The only thing that prevented Lindsay from being completely naked was the small pair of thong panties she wore and they covered very little. It took over three minutes for the minute piece of underwear Lindsay had on to be removed as she danced and gyrated around

Jacob's desk. Lindsay was a feast of smooth tanned flesh and except for the long blond hair on her head, the rest of her body was an even expanse of unblemished skin.

Jacob was transfixed with his face within a fraction of an inch from Lindsay's womanhood and his head was framed on both sides by her muscular thighs. Lindsay had lifted her entire body with her hands planted flat on the desk while her toes gripped the edge of the credenza behind Jacob's office chair with her calf muscles bulging. Lindsay looked at the ceiling while Jacob was encased in a prison composed of succulent female flesh, a leather chair and rich mahogany wood. The scent of Lindsay was a cocktail of female essence, sweat and lavender perfume and it was invading Jacobs mind. Lindsay lifted her head and fixed her penetrating blue eyes on Jacob, but she really had her gaze fixated on a framed photo of Jacob's wife Rebecca that was sitting on his credenza.

Jacob was a strong willed man, but even he had his breaking point. Jacob slid his hands across his desk with his palms facing upwards. Jacob lifted his hands and made contact with Lindsay's toned buttock's and caressed them. Jacob suddenly pulled Lindsay's body to his face and initially sampled and then bathed himself in her juices. Lindsay lowered her body down to the desk and felt the cold wood on her back as Jacob pleasured her while still seated in his chair. Lindsay didn't emotionally feel anything in particular for this man, but this was a business move. Jacob was enjoying this feast that seemed to indicate to Lindsay that he was not accustomed to what she had to offer.

Jacob soon pulled Lindsay to his body and it was apparent to her that he had lowered his pants and underwear. The office chair that Jacob was sitting in was sturdy and it reclined back against the credenza as Lindsay lowered herself onto Jacob's lap. The next few seconds signaled a power shift in a relationship that was previously one sided. Jacob gasped as Lindsay's body made first contact with his throbbing manhood. Inch by pleasurable inch Lindsay welcomed Jacob into her smoldering core.

"Oh my God!" Jacob exclaimed.

Lindsay wrapped her legs around the back of his chair while she gripped the top of the back of the chair with her hands. Jacob was trapped between her body and the chair. With Lindsay's hot body on one side of his and the leather seat back on the other, Jacob found himself wedged with little room to move but that was not a problem. Lindsay put her exquisite buttocks muscles into motion in combination with her thighs and the grip she had on the chair, Jacob was just along for the ride of his life. Jacob's face was pressed between Lindsay's sized 36D breasts and at this point he only thought about the sensations running through his body. Lindsay locked her gaze on the eyes of Jacob's wife in the photo as she pleasured her husband.

"Oh, shit!" Jacob said as his body shuddered several minutes later.

Jacob held tightly onto Lindsay's body as she pressed into him. It was not long before Jacob had exhausted himself and Lindsay slowly and

48

calmly disengaged herself from his body. They never kissed or had a verbal exchange between each other during their sexual tryst.

"Am I worth the trouble?" Lindsay asked.

Jacob just looked at Lindsay.

"What? Why did you do that?" Jacob asked.

"I didn't do anything. I was showing you why I should still keep my spot in the rotation. You decided that you wanted more than that. You're my boss. I figured if I still wanted my job then I need to give you what you wanted," Lindsay said.

"That's bullshit. You threw yourself at me. I didn't come after you," Jacob protested.

"What are you talking about? That's the same routine I do in the VIP room for the platinum package, except for the last part. I don't do that with my customers," Lindsay replied.

"What? What does that mean? I don't do that with the other girls here. Are you trying to tell me that you're saying I pressured you into this? I didn't force you into anything," Jacob said.

"I work here and you're my boss. I need my job to take care of my kids, so I did what you wanted," Lindsay said.

"What do we do now?" Jacob said.

"Look. This can be between us. Nobody else has to know. It was a one-time thing and you got a little excited. It's not like we are in love or anything. I mean you're married with kids. We wouldn't want your wife to find out about this. Would we?" Lindsay said while looking directly at Jacob.

"No, we wouldn't," Jacob said.

"Are we okay with everything else?" Lindsay asked.

"Yeah. We're fine. You keep your spot and nothing changes. Just try to watch your temper," Jacob said.

"Okay. Thanks for understanding," Lindsay said as she left.

Jacob stood there with his pants and underwear still down around his ankles and knew that he had had underestimated Lindsay.

"Fuck!" he said loudly as he pounded on the desk with his fist and pulled his pants up.

Lindsay walked downstairs with a smile on her face knowing that she didn't have to worry about her job security at the club any longer. Latasha was in the dressing room when Lindsay walked in.

"What did Jacob want with you?" Latasha asked.

"Nothing. He just wanted to talk and told me what a great job I was doing. I'm going to take a shower," Lindsay said.

Latasha was furious. Latasha had secretly told Jacob that something had gone on in the VIP room with Lindsay Saturday night and thought that would get her out of the way. If she didn't know any better she would have thought Lindsay had sex with Jacob but Latasha knew Jacob didn't roll that way since he had rejected her before when she made advances towards him and threatened to fire her if she did it again.

Lindsay didn't feel great about what happened with Jacob, but she didn't feel bad either.

50

She knew about the business she was in. Women that work in strip clubs are not strangers to club owners and managers demanding sex for employment. Lindsay had managed to avoid the sex for work trap up until the situation with Jacob. Lindsay figured that at least she pulled the trigger on her encounter with Jacob in order to get a strategic advantage and secure her position at the club. Many in society would frown upon what Lindsay did as a despicable move that was below the dignity of a woman, but none of those people were paying her bills so their opinions held no weight with her. Lindsay had the attitude that many women whored themselves out in different ways in this world and felt that women that remained in a loveless marriage for money were doing the same thing she did earlier under a false cloak of legitimacy. Everyone has to have some justification for when they take actions that would otherwise make them question their morality and Lindsay was no different. On the plus side, Jacob turned out to be a good fuck and Lindsay hadn't had one in a while given her circumstances.

The rest of Lindsay's shift went as usual. She danced with good energy and was well rewarded with tips, at least good enough for a Tuesday night. Lindsay had cemented her place as queen of the strip club, but that was a crown she never thought she would wear.

Lindsay made her way home again and saw a figure standing out by the street at the edge of the apartment parking lot leaning into a car that had pulled up and stopped. As the car pulled away she could tell it was Latron Williams. It was past 2 o'clock in the morning. Latron spotted her looking at him and walked over to Lindsay.

"Latron, what are you doing out here this time of day?" Lindsay asked.

"I'm getting paid. I'm a businessman now," Latron said.

"What kind of business operates at two in the morning in an apartment complex parking lot?" Lindsay asked.

"I'm in distribution," Latron said.

"Do you mean selling drugs?" Lindsay asked.

"I just meet the demands of the public," Latron said.

"You'd better be careful. My daughter's father is in prison in Huntsville for distribution," Lindsay warned.

"Yeah, but I'm too smart to go out like that. I've got a system and I'm getting paid," Latron said.

"You couldn't find some other job?" Lindsay asked.

"I can't make this kind of money flipping burgers," Latron said as he flashed a folded up wad of one hundred dollars bills he pulled from his pockets.

"All money is not good money," Lindsay said.

"I'm not broke anymore. You want to talk to me now?" Latron asked.

"No Latron. I'm going home to my children upstairs," Lindsay said.

"Alright, I'll holler at you later. I've got a customer," Latron said as he walked out to a car parked at the edge of the parking lot.

Lindsay looked back at Latron as she turned the key to enter her apartment.

6

Tameka worked at a twenty-four hour big box retail store with long hours and low pay. Lindsay and Tameka had worked out their schedules so that one of them could be at home with the children while the other was working. When Lindsay would be dragging in from work early in the morning Tameka would be leaving a couple of hours later to work an early morning shift. They would usually spend an hour catching up on events of the day and what needed to be taken care of in regards to their children.

"Hey girl. You look   like you're really dragging ass tonight," Tameka said as she entered Lindsay's room after she got home.

"You don't know the half of it. Hey, did you know that Latron Williams is selling drugs right out there in the parking lot? He was there when I got home. He was just a kid when we moved in here," Lindsay said.

"I'm not surprised. He dropped out of school and thinks that is his way out. What can you do, it's the same old story. Well the kids are fine and there's nothing special on the schedule tomorrow. Now, did something happen at the club? I can tell by the look on your face that something went down. Was it something with Darrius again?" Tameka asked.

"No. It wasn't Darrius. It was Jacob, the owner. He found out about the shit that went down last Saturday and called me into his office," Lindsay said.

"Oh shit girl! What did he say?" Tameka asked.

"Well he showed me the security video of the man walking out of the VIP room holding bloody napkins to his head with me coming out behind him, so I told him everything that happened. I thought I was out of there for sure. Then he starts talking about how much money I made for the club and how much trouble I was. He even said that bitch Latasha had talked to him about taking my place as the featured dancer," Lindsay said.

"Latasha. I met her at the club one day. She's a nasty, sneaky ho. I can tell. What else happened?" Tameka asked.

"He asked me if I was worth all the trouble I caused," Lindsay said.

"Did you tell how much money you brought in and how many customers came just to see you?" Tameka said.

"No. I climbed on top of his desk and started dancing and stripped all of my clothes off. I put it right in his face and he went for it," Lindsay said.

"What? What do you mean by he went for it?" Tameka asked with a tremble in her voice.

"He grabbed me and I put it on his ass?" Lindsay said.

"You fucked him! Oh my God. What kind of shit was that? Why did you do that? I'm confused" Tameka asked.

"He made the first move. I was just demonstrating my dance skills and doing the same routine I do for my platinum paying VIP customers," Lindsay said.

"You didn't tell him to stop like you did those other guys?" Tameka asked.

"Look, he's the boss. Now I've got him by the balls. He doesn't want his wife to find out and I don't have to worry about being kicked out of the club or losing my spot that brings in the money I need to support my kids," Lindsay said.

Lindsay saw the look of bewilderment that spread across Tameka's face.

"Tameka, don't look at me that way. I did what I thought I needed to do to keep my job," Lindsay explained.

"Okay. I understand you did what you felt you had to do. I've got to get out of here to go to work. I'll see you later," Tameka said as she got up and walked away.

Lindsay was a little taken aback that Tameka seemed to be disappointed at what she heard. Lindsay went to bed and thought about what had taken place and soon tears began to run down her face and wet her pillow.

Tameka drove to work and after she arrived in the massive parking lot she rested her forehead on her steering wheel and cried. Tameka felt she was starting to lose her long time friend to a world that was slowly consuming her. The Lindsay she once knew would have never taken the actions she told her about in the past. Tameka wondered where the bottom was for Lindsay, herself, and their children. How many compromises would they make in the name of survival? Tameka thought about how she was sleeping with a married man to help make ends meet and Lindsay had just used her body to help secure her job. Tameka looked in her rear view mirror, cleaned her face and proceeded to walk into her job for a full shift of work with a thousand thoughts running through her head. Tameka was a desirable woman in her own right with a cocoa brown skin tone. Tameka still maintained a trim figure after having three children and her legs were long, shapely and trim. The crowning feature that gained more attention than anything concerning Tameka's physique was the way her legs and rear end came together. Tameka had a unique shape to her butt that almost brought tears to the eyes of men. Tameka's body was that of a much younger woman as she was very thin as a child, as she matured and had children she became better proportioned. Instead of being more of a bombshell body type like Lindsay, Tameka was tall, lean and had a decidedly protruding rear end that seemed even more noticeable on her slender frame. At five-feet eight inches tall her bust size was proportionate to her frame. One of Tameka's favorite outfits was a tight form fitting dress made out of stretch material that was mid-thigh in length. The thin material of the dress would cling to her buttocks as she walked and it would have men snapping their heads around as she passed. With her high cheekbones and slicked back shoulder length hairstyle she knew when she was attracting attention.

As Tameka was working her area in the home department, she spotted her red-haired department manager, Kristen, coming down the aisle. Kristen Ross was a twenty-one year old manager trainee fresh out of community college and this store was her training ground for store operations. Kristen was one of the reasons that Tameka told Lindsay that she could better herself simply because she was white. Tameka had a low opinion of Kristen and thought she was getting ahead because of her connections and race. Tameka pretended that she did not see Kristen and hoped that she would keep walking. Tameka felt that Kristen had targeted her for some reason and she didn't like it.

"Tameka, how are you," Kristen asked.

"Kristen, I didn't see you coming. I'm doing fine how about you?" Tameka asked.

"I'm doing great. I wanted to talk to you about something. I did a review of your area yesterday and, although it's not a big deal, it seemed that there were some items that should have been restocked before you left and the next person that came on shift after you had to do it. Do you think that was fair to them?" Kristen asked.

"Well we had a big sale on bath wares that day and people were pulling towels off the shelf as fast as I could stock them. Then we ran out of the full sized towels and the truck didn't come in until after I was off. You can check the inventory and delivery log because I updated it and made a note of the out of stock condition," Tameka said.

Kristen made some notes on her tablet computer and did an inventory check.

"Oh yes. I see it now. Sorry, my mistake. Hey, were those your children I saw you with the other day when you came in?" Kristen asked.

"Yes those were my kids. I was buying a few things to get them ready for school to start," Tameka said.

"They are so cute and well behaved. You and your husband must be proud," Kristen said.

"I don't have a husband," Tameka replied.

"Oh. I'm sorry. I just assumed," Kristen said.

"That's okay. There's nothing to be sorry about. You know I've got to get back to work restocking these shelves. We want everything looking good for our customers," Tameka said.

"Oh, sure. Let me know if you need anything," Kristen said as she walked off.

Tameka looked across the aisle and her coworker Janice, a black woman about thirty years old beckoned for her to come over to her department and she walked across to the kitchenware section.

"What was that all about," Janice asked.

"She is just on my ass all of the time and it's always nitpicking type shit. She just said something about my kids and me having a husband," Tameka said.

"Don't worry about it. She won't be around long. They will either send her to another store or send her home. She's just trying to impress the big wigs. She acts like she knows more than she does and is picking on you to make the point. I don't know whose dick she sucked to get in here in the first place," Janice said.

"What! Girl you a mess. I better get back over to my side before she comes back around," Tameka said.

"Well you know that kind of shit goes on all the time," Janice said under her breath as Tameka walked away laughing.

Tameka finally left the store with tired feet and a sore back. She was bringing two precooked roasted chickens home and the whole group would sit down for a rare meal together as a family. Lindsay had a few hours to go before she had to be at the club for another long shift. Their lives were a never ending treadmill of work, raising children and anything else that came up in between. The grind of keeping everything afloat was wearing the two young women down and they knew it better than anyone because they lived it every day.

7

Lindsay and Tameka looked on in amazement at how fast five hungry children could demolish two chickens and the side dishes that Lindsay cooked before Tameka came home from work.

"These children are really growing up fast. We might have to get out of this place before too long to get more room," Lindsay said.

"Hey! Joquan and Riley. Ya'll stop leaving the leaving the smaller kids behind. You know they can't keep up with you when ya'll run like that," Tameka said.

"Good lord. Hey, I got something to tell you. It's been bothering me for a long time. Are the kids up front?" Lindsay asked.

"Yeah, they're up front. What is it?" Tameka asked.

"Well you know when I got pregnant with Riley during my last year in high school. I never told you who his father was," Lindsay said.

"As far as I know you didn't tell anybody. I always wondered why you kept it to yourself," Tameka said.

"Well I was too ashamed because of how it happened. You remember Cindy Emerson. She graduated two years before we did. We were pretty good friends and she went to college in Nacogdoches. Well it was football season and a major college was coming to town to play her school's team. She told me there would be a lot of parties going on. She had an extra game ticket and asked me if I wanted to go. I was curious about what college parties were like and went with her," Lindsay said.

"How did you get your parents to let you go?" Tameka asked.

"They were visiting my aunt in Houston. She had an operation and they went to be with her. I didn't go with them because school was going on and they went during the week. Anyway we went to the game and I was so excited to be around all of those college people. There was this player on the visiting team and he was the star running back. I didn't really know who he was but they were calling his name all night long for touchdowns and long runs.

After the game we went to a party at this place off campus and some of the football players were there. You know I looked a little older than my age and I dressed as grown up as I could so I was fitting in. I started dancing and drinking. I was having a blast when this guy came up to be and asked me to dance. He was built like a rock and over six feet tall. While we were dancing he asked me my name and I asked him his name. When he told me who he was it took me a minute to realize that his name was the one being announced all night during the game. I said something about it and he said yes it was him," Lindsay said.

"Wait a minute. Why was he there? He played for the out of town team," Tameka asked.

Just then Tameka's two year old daughter came around the corner and said she had to use the bathroom. Tameka took her to the bathroom and soon returned.

"Okay. He told me that he was from the area and was staying one extra night and leaving the next morning. Anyway, he was spending all of this time with me and I was flattered. A lot of the other girls in the club were giving me the evil eye," Lindsay said.

"Where was Cindy all of that time?" Tameka asked.

"She was hugged up in the corner with some guy that played on her school's team. So I'm with this guy and it never crossed my mind about why he is spending so much time with me. Well I'd been drinking the whole time and he was bringing me mixed drinks. I wasn't used to drinking liquor and was getting drunk. Well we danced again to a slow song and he had me all heated up and asked me to go outside with him. The next thing I know we got into a car and drove somewhere not too far from the school and pulled up to an apartment building. By this time I wasn't thinking straight. We went upstairs to an apartment door and he had a key. We went in and the next thing I know he had me in bed and we had sex. I don't even remember much about it because I was drunk by then," Lindsay said.

"Did he take you back to the party?" Tameka said.

"No. I woke up the next morning still in the apartment, but I was on the couch in the living room with a blanket pulled over me and a pillow under my head," Lindsay said.

"Let me go check on these kids. They are getting a little too quiet," Tameka said as she walked up front.

"They're watching television. Jasmine and Tasha are asleep on the floor," Tameka said as she returned.

Okay. I woke up totally confused. You know when you wake up someplace new and are not sure where you are? My head was pounding and I heard this voice behind me and it was Cindy," Lindsay said.

"Cindy was in the apartment that the guy took you to. What was she doing there? I'm confused," Tameka said.

"Look, I was totally lost. I asked her what was going on. She said that it was her boyfriend's apartment. I was freaking out. I told her to take me home right then. I had to get home before my parents found out I had been gone. On the way back I found out that Cindy's boyfriend and the guy I was with were friends. Cindy had set me up. Her boyfriend asked her to get a girl for his buddy who was coming in to play a game and I was the unlucky victim. Those two guys went to high school together. Cindy knew I wasn't used to that kind of environment with alcohol flowing like water. I didn't stand a chance. Then I missed my period and felt like the world was falling in on me," Lindsay said.

"Did you ever hear from him again?" Tameka asked.

"No. I was a kid. I didn't know what to do. My head was spinning. When I told my parents I was pregnant, I was thrown out of the house. I was mad at the world. I never heard from or saw him again, but I watch him play football every Sunday. He plays for the Oklahoma Buffalos pro football team. It's RJ Jefferson. His first name is Riley and I named my son after his father," Lindsay said.

"You've got to be fucking kidding me. RJ Jefferson is one of the biggest pro football stars in the country. Does he even know he has a son?" Tameka asked.

"No. He probably never even thought about me again. I was just some dumb little country girl he fucked and forgot. I wouldn't be surprised if he didn't do that all of the time. Who knows how many baby mamas he has scattered all over the country," Lindsay said.

"I don't know about that. He's not one of those idiots that you see on the news that are always in trouble or making it rain at the strip clubs," Tameka said.

"I guess you're right," Lindsay said.

"Didn't he marry some girl a few years ago that was like one of those rap video dancers? She called herself Super Stacked when she was doing her video stuff. I read she was just a straight up freak that was passed around by rappers and athletes. Monica Monroe, that's her name. I hear she's trying to act all sophisticated now since she hit the jackpot with RJ, but she can't get away from her past," Tameka said.

"Yeah, I read about that. Supposedly that's one reason he signed with Oklahoma so he could get her away from the temptation that was everywhere in Los Angeles. She still didn't want to come to Oklahoma and leave Los Angeles, but he put his foot down," Lindsay said.

"That shit ain't gone last. She's addicted to the spotlight. If she's a ho, she just a ho, case closed. So why are you talking about this now?" Tameka said.

"Riley is in school and it's just been me with him the whole time. That man is his father and he needs to know he has a son. Riley should know who his father is. I don't want my son to end up like Latron Williams. When I saw him standing there selling drugs I had an image of Riley ending up the same way," Lindsay said.

"Why are you worried about that? You're raising him to know right from wrong," Tameka said.

"Latron's mother didn't raise him to be a drug dealer. She was taking him to church every Sunday. I saw them coming home every Sunday with their church clothes on. When he was about sixteen, he stopped going to church and started hanging around with some older guys. I saw them come around and pick him up. A parent can only do so much and she was by herself with Latron, his younger sister and brother. The world started to have a stronger influence on him than she did. I don't want that to happen to my son. Look at what's happening with all of these shootings and young black men dying. They're killing each other, dying in police custody or just walking home from a convenience store with snacks. One kid was killed when he was sitting in a car because some guy with a gun thought the music was too loud. I might be white, but Riley is seen as being black and I'm scared of what could happen to him. This is not about me anymore. Riley has a father and it's time he found out about his son and has some part in his life. I don't want to end up burying my baby," Lindsay said with fear in her eyes.

"I hear you and I feel the same way about my two boys. I think you are doing the right thing, but how are you going to reach him?" Tameka asked.

"I have no idea. I don't even know where to start," Lindsay said when she looked at her watch.

"I've got to get out of here and go to work," Lindsay said.

Lindsay went up front to say goodbye to her children and told them to mind their aunt Tameka while she was gone.

Tameka's head was spinning. Her friend had a son by a multimillionaire football player and had been struggling to raise him alone for years. She shook her head and went up front to make sure the children were not getting into something. It was nap time for the two youngest and Tameka needed some rest herself. Tameka told Riley and Joquan to watch some videos and keep an eye on her four year old son Malik. Tameka took her two-year old daughter and Lindsay's three year old daughter to her bedroom. Tameka placed the two children on the bed between her and the wall and before she knew it they were all asleep.

8

Lindsay came home from work and hadn't thought about RJ Jefferson much at all for the past few hours. Tameka was sitting at the kitchen table drinking coffee before she went to work. Lindsay went and looked in on her children who were both sound asleep before sitting down at the table with Tameka.

"You know there is one way you could get in touch with RJ Jefferson. Get a lawyer," Tameka said.

"A lawyer. I don't want to get a lawyer, then he'll think that I'm after something," Lindsay said.

"Well. I'm always seeing these lawyers on television when women file suit on men for sexual harassment when the men are famous and the women don't have the money to stand up to them," Tameka said.

"I did think about that, but there has to be another way that doesn't seem like I'm some kind of gold digger," Lindsay said.

"What about Cindy," Tameka said.

"Cindy. What could she do?" Lindsay asked.

"Cindy owes you. She pimped you out to this guy when you were a teenager. She could probably get hold of her boyfriend at the time and have him get a message to RJ Jefferson," Tameka said.

"Well he wasn't just her boyfriend at the time. They got married and still live in Nacogdoches. He became a real estate agent and works in his father's real estate company. I kept up with them through a few people I talk to every once and a while from back home," Lindsay said.

"There you go," Tameka said.

"I haven't talked to Cindy in years. I was so pissed at her for setting me up like that. I'm still mad about it and try to block it from my mind. Don't get me wrong, I love Riley, but I wasn't ready to be somebody's mama back then. I don't even know how to get in touch with her," Lindsay said.

"It's time to make that phone call. I'll bet you can find their phone number online at the library," Tameka said.

Lindsay thought about what Tameka said and took that thought to bed with her.

The next day Lindsay left for work an hour early and stopped by the local public library branch. Lindsay entered a search for the name of Cindy Kirkland in Texas and one of the results was Mark and Cindy Kirkland in Nacogdoches, TX. Lindsay wrote the number down and hurried out so she would not be late for her shift at the club.

Lindsay danced with her usual energy that night, but she was distracted by the prospect of revisiting something that had been buried in the back of her mind for a long time. Over the years Lindsay had occasionally felt bitterness towards everyone involved in what was a minor incident for them that changed the course of her entire life. Lindsay loved her son dearly, but becoming a teenage mother was not something she planned for or even thought about. The idea that everyone else involved simply moved on with their lives while she dealt with the devastating effects of the estrangement from her family as a pregnant teenager. Lindsay was swinging around the pole on the main stage and the faces of the men shouting to her, the music and lights seemed to all blend together as she pulled herself upside down and wrapped her legs around the pole and slowly descended downward to the stage in a slow spin. Lindsay thought this was a metaphor for her life as she slowly spiraled down to the floor to a pulsating bass beat blasting from the speakers from the song Darling Nikki by the late musician Prince.

After finally exiting from the main stage, Lindsay retreated to the back room to get a drink and refresh herself. Lindsay opened her locker to check her cell phone to see if Tameka had left any messages concerning the children. There was a missed call and message on the phone, but it wasn't from Tameka, it was from her sister Karen with a midnight time stamp. If it was one thing Lindsay knew, it was that a midnight phone call from her sister was not going to be good news. Her first thought was that something had happened to her mother. Lindsay put her pants and top on as fast as possible and went out to her car to call her sister back in private. Once in the car, Lindsay pressed the return call button on her phone.

When Karen answered, she informed Lindsay that their father had suffered a stroke and was in a hospital in Tyler, Texas. It wasn't a fatal stroke, but it was serious. Lindsay told her sister that she would call her back. Lindsay needed to figure a few things out before she decided when she would be leaving to visit her father in the hospital. Lindsay went in and told the club manager what happened and he told her to take as much time as she needed. Lindsay rushed home as quickly as she could.

"What are you doing back home so early?" Tameka asked when Lindsay walked into the apartment.

"My sister called. My daddy had a stroke," Lindsay said.

"Oh no! Was it bad?" Tameka asked.

"Well, she said it wasn't fatal, but he's in the hospital in Tyler," Lindsay said.

"You are going to see him, aren't you?" Tamkea asked.

"Yes. I'm going. How are we going work out the thing with the kids? I'll take Riley and Jasmine with me, but what will you do?" Lindsay answered.

"My cousin Andrea will help me out. Don't worry about that. You need to focus on your family right now," Tameka answered.

"I hope my car will hold up," Lindsay said.

"Look, you shouldn't drive your car. It's fine for driving around here, but you don't want it to break down on side of the road with just you and two kids out there by yourselves. There are too many crazy people out there. You should rent a car. I saw a Universal Car Rental commercial saying they have unlimited miles for in-state driving. I'll feel a lot better if you did that. You can't be stranded on side of the road being a single woman with kids these days," Tameka said.

"I do have that credit card that I saved for emergencies. That's what I'll do. Thanks Tameka, I'm not thinking straight right now," Lindsay said.

Lindsay checked on her children and went to bed so she could be fresh enough to drive the next day.

The next day Lindsay arranged for a rental car and after an hour she was on the road with her smallest child in the back seat in a carrier. Her son Riley kept his little sister company while strapped into a booster seat. The miles soon melted away all traces of the city. Riley was taking in the rolling scenery as Lindsay drove eastward on Interstate Highway 20. Lindsay began to notice that it was quiet in the back seat and she took a quick glance back. Both children were asleep while slumping in opposite directions. Lindsay turned the radio off and just listened to the hum of the tires against the road. Lindsay suddenly realized how few times she was able to be alone with her thoughts without other sounds making an intrusion, but her reflection time was short lived as someone called her from the back seat.

"Mama, I need to use the bathroom," Jasmine said from the back seat.

"Okay baby," Lindsay replied.

Lindsay knew her window to stop was short and luckily she was driving through Canton, TX and took the next exit. Lindsay pulled the small subcompact car up to a fast food restaurant in order for all of them to use the bathroom and get something to eat in one stop. After everyone had used the bathroom they ordered food and sat down to eat. Lindsay decided that it would be too risky to allow two children to eat while she was driving because she didn't want be charged an additional fee for cleaning the interior of the vehicle. As Lindsay and her children sat down to eat she noticed an older white woman about sixty years old starring at her from the table next to hers. Lindsay looked up and she was looking the woman right in the eyes.

"Ma'am you have some lovely children," the woman said.

"Why, thank you," Lindsay said as she thought the woman was starring at her because her children were biracial.

When Lindsay looked up again a black man about sixty-years old came and sat across from the woman that had complemented her children.

"This is my husband, Herbert," the woman said as she turned to Lindsay again.

"Nice to meet you. I'm Lindsay and these are my children Riley and Jasmine," Lindsay said.

"I told Herbert that your children reminded me of our children when they were young. They are all grown and married now. My name is Maggie," the woman said.

"How long have you been married?" Lindsay asked.

"Thirty-five years. We met when I was in the service and stationed in San Diego. I'm originally from Shreveport and we're going there to visit my folks. I guess we better get on the road. It was nice to meet you," Herbert said.

"Is it just you and your children traveling today?" Maggie asked.

"Yeah ma'am, it's just us," Lindsay replied.

"You be careful and watch where you stop," Maggie said as she leaned over and talked in a low voice.

The older couple left the restaurant and Lindsay felt guilty for thinking that Maggie was looking at them with a motivation totally opposite of what she really intended. Lindsay left the restaurant feeling a little better about people and the world in general.

About one hour later Lindsay was pulling into the parking lot of the hospital where her father was being cared for.

"Riley and Jasmine, we're going to see your aunt, grandmother and grandfather. This is a hospital so you can't run and you have to be quiet, okay," Lindsay advised before taking the children into the hospital lobby.

Lindsay was a bundle of nerves. Given how raw emotions were when she last spoke with her father, Lindsay's emotions were best described as dreadful anticipation. Lindsay made her way to the hospital room that she was informed her father was in by the information desk attendant. Lindsay paused, swallowed and slowly pushed the door open with the name Clyde Wilson on the nameplate.

Lindsay's sister Karen and mother Martha were in the room with her father. Lindsay's mother walked over to her and hugged her.

"Oh my baby. I've missed you," Martha said with tears in her eyes.

"I've missed you too mama. Mama, this is Riley and Jasmine. Babies, this is your grandma," Lindsay said.

Lindsay's mother squatted down and hugged her grandchildren for the first time

"Oh you beautiful little babies. Lindsay, you brought me some beautiful grandchildren," Martha said.

"How you doing sis?" Karen said as she hugged Lindsay.

"I'm okay. How about you," Lindsay said.

"I'm fine. We can talk later," Karen said.

"How's daddy doing?" Lindsay asked.

"It's not as bad as it could have been. We got him here pretty quick. He was talking and just started slurring his speech. Then he couldn't lift his left arm. We called the ambulance and they rushed him here and said it was a stroke," Karen said.

"Can he talk?" Lindsay asked.

"Yeah, he can talk. It seems like it's his left arm and hand that has been affected the most. Look he's waking up," Karen said.

"Who's that over there?" Clyde Wilson asked.

Lindsay walked over to his bedside.

"It's me daddy, Lindsay," Lindsay answered.

Clyde grasped Lindsay's left hand with his right hand. Lindsay leaned over and hugged her father for the first time in many years. Clyde started sobbing.

"I'm sorry darling for what I did. I was a stubborn old fool. Can you forgive me?" Clyde asked.

"Oh daddy. You can't get all worked up like that. You need to stay calm," Lindsay said.

"Could you raise the head of my bed so I can sit up?" Clyde requested.

Lindsay pressed the control button that caused the head of the bead to elevate and placed Clyde in a sitting position.

"Riley and Jasmine, come over here and saw hello to your grandpa," Lindsay said to her children who were occupied with their grandmother.

The children came over and Lindsay introduced them to their grandfather for the first time. Lindsay watched for his reaction.

"You have some fine looking children Lindsay. Come over here and give your grandpa a hug," Clyde said.

Riley climbed onto the bed and hugged his newly introduced grandfather. Lindsay placed Jasmine on the bed and she was apprehensive until her mother gave her reassurance that it was okay for her to hug her grandfather.

"I've taught her to be careful around strangers, dad, Sorry," Lindsay said.

"That's good. There're a lot of evil people out there today. That's good. Well I won't be a stranger anymore. Will I Lindsay?" Clyde asked.

"No. You won't be a stranger anymore and I won't either," Lindsay said.

"How are you feeling," Lindsay asked.

Clyde proceeded to fill Lindsay in on how everything happened until the nurse came in and told them he needed to get some rest. Lindsay's mother stayed with Clyde and told her daughters that they should go home and get some rest.

"Did you come here by yourself?" Lindsay asked Karen as they walked out of the room.

"Yeah, I came alone. George and I are separated," Karen said.

"Karen, I'm so sorry to hear that," Lindsay said.

"Could I ride back to the house with you? I rode up here with mama and left my car at the house?" Karen asked.

Before Lindsay could get out of the city limits of Tyler, Karen was fast asleep, obviously exhausted from the last day's events. Karen had changed from the tall, thin and awkward flaming red haired girl Lindsay remembered. Karen was a woman now and had blossomed in body and boldness. Karen was three inches taller than Lindsay and had their father's fair skin complexion with a few barely noticeable freckles. Maturity had added a few pounds to Karen's lean frame and it gave her the figure similar to some of those runway models that were far from Lindsay's body makeup. Lindsay figured that Karen was approaching six feet in height in a pair of five-inch heels. Karen had made a transformation from country bumpkin to elegant city dweller over the course of several years. Lindsay had to admit that her sister had become an attractive woman and looked like some of those women of means she saw when she visited upscale shopping centers in Dallas.

When Lindsay finally pulled up to the house she grew up in, she felt a sense of unfamiliarity until she stepped inside. It was like time had stood still. The inside of the house looked almost unchanged from the day she left. Lindsay went back to her old room and it was exactly like it was the day she left home to move in with Tameka's family. That thought reminded her to call Tameka and tell her that they had arrived safely. That house and one acre of land where Lindsay grew up was in an unincorporated part of Rusk County, Texas about thirty miles from Tyler along state highway 64.

Riley and Jasmine were exhausted from the trip from Dallas and being at the hospital so long. It was getting late and Lindsay put the children in her room on a rollaway bed that the family used when people came to visit. Lindsay and Karen walked outside and sat in a swing on the porch.

"I have not set foot on this place in so many years," Lindsay said to Karen.

"Daddy never forgave himself for the way he acted when you got pregnant. He used to mention it all of the time. He was too stubborn to reach out to you. I'm sorry for the awful things I said to you too. I didn't mean it. I was just mad at you for telling me about seeing me with Timmy Anderson and what you heard him say about me," Karen said.

"I know you didn't mean it. No apologies needed," Lindsay said.

"No. Apologies are needed. You were a kid and your family turned their back on you when you needed support. I can't imagine how that felt," Karen said.

"I felt so alone. I didn't know what to do. If it hadn't been for Tameka's folks, I don't know what would have happened to me," Lindsay said as she broke down crying.

Karen held her younger sister in her arms as she released years of pain and frustration.

"They are some good people and I really understand now how much guts it took for them to take you in like that," Karen said.

"It's been really hard since I left, but I'm surviving. Sometimes it's tough to keep going, but I have to for my children," Lindsay said.

"I know, Lindsay. I know," Karen said.

"I'm sorry Karen. You must be going through some rough times yourself. What happened between you and George?" Lindsay asked.

"I guess I wasn't enough of a woman for him," Karen said.

"What do you mean?" Karen said.

"I supported George as he went to school and pursued his law degree. I worked to keep us afloat and put everything I wanted on hold. He finally passed the state bar exam and got hired by a big law firm in Houston. As he rose up the ladder, I started noticing a change in the way he treated me. He started saying that maybe I should dress a certain way or learn more about world events. I felt like he was comparing me to someone else. It was almost like he wanted to say, 'like somebody he knew', but he would stop just short of saying her name," Karen said.

"Was he cheating on you with someone else?" Lindsay asked.

"Well, I think so, but that's not the whole story. I went to an office party with him and this stunning woman was talking with George and he introduced her as a senior partner in the firm. She was about forty-five and just a knockout. She talked to me a long time and seemed nice and very interested in everything I had to say," Karen said.

"Was George sleeping with her," Lindsay asked.

"Who knows? George told me later what a great impression I made on this woman and then he dropped a bombshell on me. She wanted George and me to get together with her," Karen said.

"What for lunch or dinner?" Lindsay said.

"No, for a threesome," Karen said.

"You're fucking kidding me, right?" Lindsay said.

"No. I'm not kidding you," Karen replied.

"Did George tell her no?" Lindsay asked.

"George told her that he would ask me if I wanted to do it, and he asked me," Karen said.

"What! How could your husband ask you to let another woman come and have sex with the two of you?" Lindsay asked.

"It was more like she wanted to have sex with me while George watched," Karen said.

"What, and George wanted you to do that?" Lindsay said.

"He said to think of what it could mean for his career and us financially," Karen said.

"You've got to be kidding me. What did you say?" Lindsay said.

"I told him. 'Fuck your career. I'm your wife and not someone you can whore out to your dyke bitch of a boss.' It's all over, but the singing. I thought about what you said about Timmy Anderson and me in the barn. We'll fucking somebody to get ahead didn't work then and I was not about let this bitch screw me so George's ass could get ahead now. What if I had agreed and he moved up the ladder. What would he ask me to do next? No thanks," Karen said.

"What are you going to do?" Lindsay asked.

"I'll stay here for a while and help mom with dad. She's too old to be trying to take care of him by herself. Plus it'll give me a chance to clear my head," Karen said.

"What about you? How are you doing?" Karen asked.

"Well. It's been a struggle sometimes, but I manage. I still share a place with Tameka to split expenses. It's not in the best part of town, but it's what we can afford. She has three kids now," Lindsay said.

"So, it's seven of you in the same place?" Lindsay quizzed.

"Yeah, but the kids are small so it doesn't feel as crowded as it sounds," Karen asked.

"Well what do you do? Work wise, I mean," Karen asked.

"Well, I'm an exotic dancer. Most people call it being a stripper," Lindsay said as she watched for a reaction.

Karen looked a little stunned for a minute and blinked her eyes for a couple of times as if she was trying to clear her head.

"Are you good at it?" Karen asked.

"Yeah. I would say I'm pretty good at it. I'm the featured dancer at the club I work at," Lindsay replied.

"Daddy always said, if you're going to be a bear, be a grizzly. Do you make decent money?" Karen asked.

"You know I do pretty good for myself. I don't have to ask anybody for anything. I don't have any medical benefits and doctor visits for the kids cost a fortune," Lindsay said.

"I always wondered about strippers. I mean you've got to have confidence in your body to do something like that. I could never get my skinny ass up there. You got all of the curves in this family. The doctor must have left my ass inside mama and you got it and yours when you came along. You've got what they call that donk. You know, donkey booty," Karen said.

"Karen. What's gotten into you? You never used to talk like this," Lindsay said.

"Well I learned a few things since I left home and went to the city. I was just as green as grass when I left here. My attitudes about people who were different from me were so backwards back then. I met George and fell in love with him, but there was another guy after me first. His name was Quinton. When I first got a job with the city, Quinton worked in the same building and he came over and started talking to me in the cafeteria. Quinton was tall, dark and very smart. I acted offended that he thought I would even want to talk to him, but he kept trying. He was so nice to me and I was just an asshole to him. I was actually attracted to him, but I couldn't get past my old racial attitude and just when I was worked my courage up enough to go out with him it was too late. He had moved on. I saw him leave for lunch with a gorgeous black woman one day. Quinton was in the planning department and became the head of the department. Finally, I met George and here I am today," Karen said.

"You actually were going to go out with a black man?" Lindsay asked.

"The thing is, I didn't meet George right away. I went out with a few other guys in between and some of them were black guys," Karen said.

"I hate to ask this, but did you sleep with any of them?" Lindsay asked.

"Well, yeah. I did with a couple of them. I mean it was good, but neither one of them were real serious relationships. I guess I was learning how to have fun as a grown woman with my own mind and experience different things," Karen said.

Lindsay sat there with her mouth hanging open.

"I can't believe what I hearing given the way you felt about black people before I left home," Lindsay said.

"Like I said, I learned a few things in Houston. I found out it wasn't the outside of a person that mattered, it was the inside. I've had a lot of people help me that I wouldn't have spoken to back here. My first boss was a black man and my second boss was a Mexican American woman. Those were some sharp people and they helped me out when I was getting started in my career. That opened my eyes," Karen said.

"That's good to hear," Lindsay said.

"You know Lindsay, there's something I've been wondering about for a long time. You've never told me how you got pregnant. We're sisters and I know we haven't been very close over the years, but I want that to change. I love you and you can tell me anything, so what happened?" Karen asked.

Lindsay proceeded to tell her sister the details of how she became pregnant during her last year of high school. She even told her who Riley's father was.

"Oh my God, I never knew that Cindy was such a self-centered, needy bitch. That was the lowest of the low. You were a teenager in high school. They just didn't give a shit about what happened to you after they had their fun. I tell you what. We're taking a trip to Nacogdoches and paying that bitch a visit. I know where she is. She works in her father-in-law's real estate office as the office manager. She goes around town like she is the queen b of the town. She's nothing more than a pimp. That was statutory rape. You weren't seventeen until November of the year you got pregnant. Remember you were graduating early because you took those summer courses that allowed you to graduate with all of your credits as a junior. You were sixteen when you got pregnant and that's below the age of consent in Texas," Karen said.

"How do you know all that?" Lindsay asked.

"I helped George research a case that involved a high school football star who was eighteen and his sixteen year old girlfriend. They were having sex and the girl's father found out and pressed charges against him. There is also a ten year statute of limitations to press charges against someone after it happens," Karen said.

"That's been so long ago. How could something like that be proved?" Lindsay said.

"Your proof is sleeping in your old room. If your seven-year old son's paternity test proves that RJ Jefferson is his father, case closed," Karen said.

"Wow. I never knew any of this," Lindsay said.

"We need to go see that bitch tomorrow. I might have some more use for George's ass after all," Karen said.

9

Lindsay's mother came back home the next day and agreed to spend time with her grandchildren while her daughters went on an excursion. Martha Wilson didn't much care where her daughters were going because she was concentrating on getting to know and spoil her only grandchildren.

Lindsay and Karen made the forty-eight mile drive from their house to the heart of Nacogdoches, TX. This was a city of about 33,000 residents and considered the oldest city in Texas. Karen directed Lindsay to a building that resembled an old stately home. The sign out front read, 'Kirkland Realty'. Lindsay and Karen walked up the steps and walked in. The heels of the shoes the sisters were wearing made a sound that reverberated off the stained wooden floor. A female voice from the back of the building called out.

"I'll be right with you," and they heard footsteps coming their way.

"Hello ladies can I help you today. I'm Cindy Kirkland," the woman said as she shook their hands.

Lindsay looked Cindy over and could tell that she had been living well for the last few years. Cindy wore an expensive looking clothing ensemble accented by immaculately styled bleached blond hair, diamond ear studs and a pair of designer high heeled shoes with red soles.

"Why yes you could. I'm Lindsay Wilson and this is my sister Karen. Remember us?" Lindsay said.

"Oh my God! What are you guys doing here? It's been forever. How did you know I was here?" Cindy inquired.

"Oh we kept up with what people we grew up with were doing," Karen said.

"Cindy I need to talk to you about something. Do you remember that night you brought me down her for that football game when I was in high school?" Lindsay asked.

"Well yeah. I kind of remember that," Cindy said.

"Is your memory getting fuzzy Cindy? Why don't you refresh her memory Lindsay," Karen said.

"Well I came to the game with you after you asked me if I wanted to use your extra ticket. Remember that?" Lindsay asked.

"Yeah. I remember that. What is this all about? I'm really busy today," Cindy said as she tried to get up.

"Cindy, sit your ass down and listen," Karen said coldly.

"Well, we went to that party after the game was over and the star player for the other team, RJ Jefferson, who was your boyfriend's, who is now your husband, best friend. He got me drunk and took me over to your boyfriend's apartment and had sex with me. I woke up the next morning in that apartment and you were there. That's when you told me it was your boyfriend's apartment. I asked you to take me home and you told me that you brought me to the party as a favor to your boyfriend for his friend RJ Jefferson. Do you remember that Cindy?" Lindsay asked.

"Yeah, I kind of remember that. That was a long time ago. Why are you bringing this up now?" Cindy asked.

"Bitch, I was sixteen years old! That guy must have been twenty or twenty-one. Guess what, I got pregnant that night. It turned my whole life upside down. My son by RJ Jefferson is seven years old now," Lindsay said.

"Just in case you missed that, Lindsay was sixteen years old when you served her up like a pimp to your husband's adult friend. That makes what happened, statutory rape. Can you deny what you did by targeting a teenager so some guy could get his rocks off? Everybody else went on about their business like nothing ever happened while her life went into the shithole," Karen said.

"What do you want from me? That was ages ago. Nobody's going to listen to that now!" Cindy said.

"You ever heard of the term statute of limitations. The statute of limitation for statutory rape is ten years. Lindsay's son is only seven years old. Your boyfriend, who is now your husband, set you up to take the fall if what you did came to light. You brought Lindsay to the party when she was sixteen and she was drinking alcohol which was also against the law. She got drunk and a grown man had sex with her which was against the law. What you did is called contributing to the delinquency of a minor or it could be a case of human trafficking. You enticed my teenage sister to go with you so you could provide her to someone else for sexual purposes. Your husband's hands are clean because he set you up to take the fall if something happened," Karen said.

"What. This is insane. I didn't know you got pregnant," Cindy said as the wiped her hand over her forehead and through her red hair.

"No you didn't know and you didn't care. You just wanted to please your boyfriend. I was used like a piece of meat and thrown aside. You and your husband have your nice little life. RJ Jefferson is a rich pro football hero. I'm just the leftover trash he used to relieve his tensions for one night," Lindsay said.

"So what are you some kind of lawyer, Karen, or is this just a bunch of bullshit from two broke pieces of white trash trying to hit the jackpot off a big time pro football player?!" Cindy quipped.

"No, Cindy. I'm not a lawyer, but my husband is. This kind of thing is his specialty. You know what Lindsay is saying really happened because you set it up and you have the nerve to call us white trash," Karen said.

"What do you expect me to do?" Cindy said.

"I want your husband to get in touch with his friend RJ Jefferson and call the number on this business card. He can ask for George Thomas, that's my husband. He's expecting his call. Don't keep us waiting too long or we may have to go to the press. RJ Jefferson has a lot to lose if he is tagged as a rapist. Companies don't like rapists endorsing their products, do they? Lindsay, let's get out of here," Karen said.

Lindsay and Karen left with Cindy sitting there with her mouth open as they walked out.

"Let's get something to eat. It's lunchtime," Karen said.

They got in their car and started to drive away.

"Karen, I don't know what to say. You are not the same person that left here all those years ago. She was about to piss in her pants. What do I do now?" Lindsay said.

"We just wait. We will hear something in a couple of weeks. If we don't I'll be shocked. That heifer knows that everything we said was true. She'll call a couple of folks that still live around home and they'll confirm that you were pregnant and had a baby. Those people know everything about everybody. They'll even know that your baby was by a black man. She'll be shitting bricks by tonight. Her husband is gonna get his head torn off by Cindy for setting her up to take the fall if something happened. He's not going to be happy at all about this. Until something happens, his ass ain't getting close to getting any pussy from that bitch. That store is closed," Karen said laughing.

"Karen, I thought I had a foul mouth. I'm the one working at a strip club," Lindsay remarked.

"Shit, these assholes in the business world are worse than any strip club customer. You know why they come in. They want to see you shake that donkey butt. You know that when they walk in the door. These business types will smile in your face and stab you in the back the next second if it gets them where they want to go," Karen said.

"What about George? I know you called him and told him what was going on. Why would he do this? I mean you guys are separated," Lindsay said.

"Look I got so much dirt on his ass with that threesome stuff that he wouldn't dare turn me down. Plus, George is a social climber. A case like this with a future Pro Football Legend's Hall member would put him on the map. He would almost pay to do this," Karen said.

They drove and drank in the sights of rural east Texas with the cattle, pastures and pine trees before stopping to eat lunch in the town of Mt. Enterprise at a small family owned restaurant.

10

Lindsay stayed with her family for five days, but she needed to get back to Dallas. Going five days without working was not good for Lindsay's bank account. In the business Lindsay was in, not working meant that no money was coming in while plenty was still going out. Lindsay's father was doing better and had been moved to a rehabilitation center in order to start his recovery from the effects of the stroke he suffered. Lindsay felt that she had found something she lost years ago and did not feel so isolated anymore. More than anything, Lindsay had given her children the sense of what it felt like to have an extended family. Now Lindsay had a sister to reach out to and discuss anything on a woman to woman basis. Out of the tragedy of her father's illness emerged positive changes in Lindsay's family life and support system.

"Hello," Lindsay said as she answered her cell phone.

"Lindsay, it's Karen. A representative of RJ Jefferson called George this morning. They want to meet with you and George," Karen said.

"Karen, I can't go to Houston. I've missed too much time at work already," Lindsay.

"Don't worry about it. George's firm has an office in Dallas and he can have the meeting up there. Give George a call and he will have them work around your schedule. He's expecting your call," Karen said.

Lindsay called George and felt a sense of nervousness at the prospect of moving forward with this process to close a huge hole in her life. Lindsay also felt a flash of fear know that she would be potentially facing off against someone worth millions of dollars when she basically had nothing in comparison.

Lindsay drove the rest of the way back to Dallas with her mind racing from one thought to the other and could hardly contain her emotions. She wanted her son to be acknowledged by his father that he existed. Lindsay also felt that this man needed to recognize how his reckless attitude and actions affected the lives of others.

The skyline of Dallas came into view as Lindsay drove towards her destination. The first task was for Lindsay to return the rental car and have them drop her off at her apartment. Since she had been away for five days in a quiet rural setting it was somewhat jarring for her to get out and walk upstairs to her apartment again.

Lindsay walked in and Tameka's kids rushed up to greet Riley and Jasmine and they ran off to play. Tameka was cooking and Lindsay walked into the kitchen after putting her suitcase in her room.

"Well, hello stranger. How's your dad?" Tameka asked.

"He's doing better than I thought. He's in a rehabilitation center now. You know trying to get some more movement in his left arm and hand," Lindsay said.

"Well how was it getting back together with your family after all of those years?" Tameka asked.

"It was strange. They all hugged me. My daddy, mama and sister all apologized for the way they treated me. They all loved the kids. I feel like I finally have my family back," Lindsay said.

"You don't know how good that makes me feel. I'm so happy for you. Everybody needs their family to have their backs," Tameka said.

"Well something else happened too. I went to visit Cindy with Karen and laid it on the line about what happened to me with RJ Jefferson. You should have seen Karen. She tore into that woman's ass. Karen's husband is a lawyer, well their deal is kind of complicated, but he is going to help me in getting RJ Jefferson to own up to being my son's father. I got a call on the way back that RJ Jefferson's people, whoever they are, want to meet with me and Karen's husband to talk about things," Lindsay said.

"Oh my God. This is really happening. Are you nervous?" Tameka asked.

"Hell yeah, I'm nervous. I mean that guy is rich and famous and I'm a nobody," Lindsay said.

"You're not a nobody. You're the mother of his only child. He doesn't have any other children. Didn't you know that?" Tameka said.

"No I didn't. What if he tries to take my baby?" Lindsay said nervously.

"Why would he do that? He didn't even care enough to use protection when he was with you. He didn't know if you were using birth control or not. He knew what could happen if a man and woman had unprotected sex. He didn't care or even consider if you could get pregnant. They all knew what could happen," Tameka said.

"I guess you're right," Lindsay said.

"Did he call his friends that set you up and ask if that girl he slept with got pregnant or not. Hell no he didn't. You know it's that attitude that is causing so much damage today. Young girls are getting pregnant left and right and the guys that are the fathers just go on about their business like nothing ever happened. These girls don't have a chance. Look at me talking. I've got three kids with daddy's that act like they had nothing to do with it. I was just stupid not to protect myself, but I fell for the same old bullshit lines every time. They were all going to marry me and wanted a family. I know better now, but those were some hard lessons," Tameka said.

"That's the thing that makes me so angry sometimes. They talk about women like us like they had nothing to do with the situation we're in. We are taking care of their children on our own and we are the one's called thots, hoes and everything else under the sun. We're baby mamas and I don't really know what that means. It kind of sounds like when people back home would describe which cow gave birth to which calf. You know they would say the red one over there is the mother of this one. That's what it feels like whenever I hear some guy introduce a woman as his baby mama. It's like there is no emotional connection to the woman, like yeah she had my kid and that's it. It's so cold, like she dropped my kid and that's all she was good for. Tameka, that's how I felt. I felt like I was good enough to fuck and forget. Who I was didn't matter to him, Cindy or her husband," Lindsay said.

"I know. I see people looking at me when I'm out with my children at the store or something. I can see it in their faces. 'There goes another welfare queen with three kids.' I'm not on welfare. I work like everybody else and if I have to do something else they don't approve of to help make ends meet, it's none of their business," Tameka said.

"Preach sister!" Lindsay said.

"Girl, you crazy as hell. You got me all worked up and yo ass just got back in town," Tameka said laughing.

Lindsay's cell phone rang.

"Hello. Yes, that's fine. I'll be there," Lindsay said as she answered her cell phone.

"That was Karen's husband. We're meeting Riley's Jefferson's people next week on Thursday. I can't believe this is really happening," Lindsay said.

11

Lindsay went back to the club for the first time in five days. Latasha had been dancing in the feature slot since Lindsay had been gone. Latasha did a good job and kept the customer's satisfied, but she could tell they really came to see Lindsay.

"Lindsay, welcome back," Latasha said to Lindsay in the dressing room.

"Is everything okay?" Latasha asked.

"Yeah, my dad had a health problem and I went to see how he was doing. He's getting better," Lindsay said.

"That's good. Hey, the feature spot is yours again since you're back. I kept it warm for you, but I think those guys like vanilla better than chocolate. Plus, I want to take the spot straight up, not while you're out for an emergency. You know I don't care for you that much, but I gotta give it to you. You a bad bitch," Latasha said.

Lindsay was taken aback by the complement.

"Well, thanks. I think," Lindsay said.

"I mean you weren't just given the main stage. You worked your butt off and took it, but don't get too comfortable, because I'm on your ass," Latasha said as she walked off.

When Lindsay took the stage that night her loyal fans erupted in applause and rewarded her handsomely with tips and lap dance fees. Although there was an air of excitement surrounding what Lindsay did for a living, for her and others inside the business it was just as routine as any other occupation. The dancers, bartenders and other workers at The Secret Island went about their jobs every day without much thought about how others outside of their industry viewed what they did on a daily basis. Many people made a variety of ethical and moral judgments about the men and women involved in adult entertainment. Lindsay considered taking her costume off while she danced until she was naked was like someone else putting their work uniform on after they clocked in. Her skin was her uniform. Her transparent soled platform heels served the same function as a construction worker's steeled toes boots. The stage was her court and the pole was the way to showcase her creativity just like a basketball player's slam dunk from the free throw line.

Lindsay spoke with her attorney and brother in law, George, often by telephone leading up to her approaching meeting on Thursday with RJ Jefferson's representatives. The day before the meeting George flew into Love Field airport and met with Lindsay at his law firm's Dallas branch in a downtown high rise office building. Lindsay rarely ventured into downtown Dallas, although she lived in close proximity to the city's center. Downtown Dallas seemed to be on another planet to Lindsay that was populated by those operating in the world of commerce that she was not a part of and didn't fully understand. Lindsay honestly felt self conscious as she walked into the lobby of the massive office tower that rose 921 feet and seventy-two stories into the Dallas skyline. Lindsay dressed in what she considered to be appropriate attire with a tight blue form fitting dress that came to just above her knees in length. Lindsay also wore a pair of blue six-inch heels that matched her dress in color and she had a simple pearl necklace around her neck that her mother gave her when she was home in east Texas several days before. The pearls framed her neck and tanned skin. Lindsay's hair was hanging to her shoulders and cut evenly.

Downtown Dallas was no stranger to stunning women, but Lindsay stood out. Lindsay was not a waif thin woman attempting to emulate the popular look of a runway model. Lindsay's ample curves and legs sporting those toned calf muscles attracted the attention of quite a few dark suited men and the cutting stares of some women as she headed for the bank of elevators. Lindsay approached the elevator bank that went to the 45th floor where George's law firm was located. A man of about fifty years old in a dark business suit stepped back and allowed Lindsay to enter the elevator car first. He watched her walk in before he entered.

"What floor are you going to, young lady?" the man asked.

"Forty-five," Lindsay said.

"Are you here on business?" the man asked.

"Well, yes I guess I am," Lindsay said as her floor was approaching.

"What business are you in," the man asked.

"Entertainment," Lindsay replied.

"Look if you ever need any marketing or public relations services, here's my card. That's what I do. I'm Ron," the man said as he shook Lindsay's hand.

Lindsay took the card and exited the elevator.

"Thanks," Lindsay said as she left the elevator.

An older woman was on the elevator with Lindsay and Ron. She made a comment to Ron as Lindsay exited.

"Ron, really!" she said.

"I was just polishing my elevator pitch," he said.

"Pervert. That's not all you want polished," the woman said while shaking her head as the elevator door closed as he released the open door button to catch one more glimpse of Lindsay walking away.

The elevator opened to the reception desk of the law firm and a woman with immaculately styled short platinum blond hair greeted her.

"Hello, ma'am. How can I help you today?" the woman asked Lindsay.

"I'm Lindsay Wilson. I have an appointment to see George Thomas," Lindsay said.

"Alright, I will get him right out here for you. You can have a seat in the waiting area," the woman said as she directed Lindsay to an area with plush leather furniture and a flat screen television.

The walls and floors of the entire area were covered in dark wood trim. Soon a slender man about six-feet tall, with angular features and dark hair walked around the corner with a young woman following him.

"You must be Karen's sister Lindsay. I'm George, Karen's husband, and your brother in law. It's kind of awkward to meet you for the first time under these circumstances. This is my legal assistant, Ashley," he said while introducing the woman.

"Nice to meet you," the woman said.

"Come on back. I've reserved a conference room. You want something to drink? We have water, soda, coffee and juice?" George asked as they walked.

"I could use a bottle of water," Lindsay said.

"I'll go get it," Ashley said.

Lindsay could see why her sister was attracted to George. George was a handsome man and she actually hoped that and Karen could work things out and save their marriage. They entered a conference room with a large window that offered a spectacular view of Dallas from forty five stories up. Lindsay looked out of the window that faced west toward Fort Worth and she could see for miles.

"Have a seat," George said.

Ashley came back with some refreshments and she sat down with her laptop and a digital recorder. Ashley was an attractive young woman slightly younger than Lindsay and she seemed to be very sharp, articulate and professional. Lindsay had thoughts run through her mind that if things had turned out differently in her life then she could possibly be in a situation like Ashley's. Lindsay didn't feel inferior to Ashley because she made her money with her clothes on instead of off. Lindsay just wondered what it would be like to be valued for her thoughts and opinions instead of her ability to make it rain dollars bills inside a strip club.

"Let's get something out of the way. Lindsay this is an agreement that allows me and our firm to represent you in this matter. There is no charge to you unless we make a financial recovery. Now, this part is the brother-in-law deal. If we make a financial settlement our firm is just going to recover an amount that covers our actual expenses. If we recover nothing you own nothing," George said.

"Well, I never thought about getting money from RJ Jefferson," Lindsay said.

"Really. Well why are you doing this?" George asked.

"I want that man to acknowledge my son as his child and I want my son to know that he has a father," Lindsay answered.

"Lindsay let me ask you something. What happened to your life when you got pregnant by RJ Jefferson?" George asked.

"Well everything went crazy. I had to move away from home. I didn't really speak to my family anymore. Then when I had my son, I had to take care of him the best way I could," Lindsay said.

"Were you able to go to college if you wanted to?" George asked.

"No. I had to take care of my son," Lindsay replied.

"So your life was turned upside down because of the careless disregard this man displayed to you as a person. He didn't even care enough for you or himself to use a condom. Suppose either he or you had a sexually transmittable disease? That one sexual encounter could have had lifelong health consequences for you. You didn't know that man or his medical history and how long have you taken care of his son on your own? George asked.

"I've taken care of Riley by myself for seven years," Lindsay said.

"Look, this ball is rolling. If you show weakness, those guys will chew you up and spit you out, except for one thing. You were sixteen when you were with him that night. That's a criminal matter of statutory rape. The last thing those people want is for RJ Jefferson to be convicted of rape," George said.

"What if he said I wanted to do it?" Lindsay asked,

"That doesn't matter. If you were sixteen you could have thrown yourself at him and it still would have been statutory rape. Someone under sixteen years old, by law, can't give consent even if they said they wanted to have sex with that older person. That's why it's call statutory rape, because it's defined by law and not based upon what happened during the encounter. You were sixteen and he was twenty-one when this happened according to our research. In Texas there is a three year age gap required for it to be statutory rape, check. Was there proof that you had sex with him, yes that's your son. Was there proof that he was there where you said the act happened, yes. We have found a copy of the football schedule showing when they played in Nacogdoches and have articles describing what he did in the game. The trump card is a paternity test of RJ Jefferson and your son, if it goes there and it's a match, his ass is grass. Your son's date of birth will validate the time line by counting back nine months. When was your son born?" George asked.

"He was born on June 5, of the year after the game. I was so far along that I didn't even march in my graduation. The doctor said I was a week late when Riley was born," Lindsay said.

"If you count back nine months from your son's birthday, bingo. It lines up with when he was in town for the game that you went to with his buddy's girlfriend. This will be a high profile case. It could end up getting national media and social media attention. People can be vicious when they can hide behind a keyboard. That could affect your ability to make a living going forward. You have to think about the long term financial security of you and your son," George said.

"So, what are we talking about here if we go for some kind of settlement?" Lindsay asked.

"Okay. RJ Jefferson is getting towards the end of his football playing career. He's lasted longer than most running backs in the league and he's trying to set up his post football life. He makes as much in product endorsements as he does playing football. RJ is also trying to move into one of those football analyst positions for one of the major networks once he hangs up his cleats. You see, once RJ Jefferson stops playing football, he will be running on his reputation instead of his legs. What do you think that reputation would be with the tag of convicted rapist hung around his neck? If you've kept up with the news at all, you've seen politicians, athletes and entertainers ruin their careers with their risky sexual behavior. It has happened in all walks of life. RJ Jefferson can't afford to let that happen to him, so what we're talking about is a formula that takes into account your son's current, future and past needs. Money for college has to be put into the equation for your son. Then we come to a settlement for you in order to keep the issue of statutory rape from coming to light in the media and courtroom. We're talking a few million dollars," George said.

"What! A few million dollars. Well what about how everyone finding out about how he had a son he didn't know about? Wouldn't that hurt him also?" Lindsay asked.

"He could have one of those press conferences where he admits to making mistakes in the past and that he is now making up for that, yada, yada, yada. He can survive that. He can't survive being a convicted felon and labeled a rapist. Statutory rape can carry up to a twenty year sentence, but that is not likely in a case like this, but the public wouldn't want to touch him or any product he endorsed," George said.

Lindsay sat there with a concerned look on her face as she processed everything she had just heard.

"Well Lindsay, are we going all the way on this thing?" George asked.

"Well yeah. Yes, we're going all the way," Lindsay said as George placed a pen in her hand to sign the agreement.

"What should I wear tomorrow?" Lindsay asked.

"Wear that again. You look strong and confident. Don't be surprised if they bring up what you do for a living and the fact that you have a second child out of wedlock. Remember, this is about their client's behavior, not yours. Just keep your cool if they take shots at you. We're talking about what happened to the sixteen year old Lindsay Wilson because what happened then had a great effect on where you are now," George said.

"Okay, I'll see you tomorrow. Thank you," Lindsay said.

"Be here at ten, so we can be ready when they walk in," George said.

It barely seemed like she had been home at all before Lindsay was back at the law firm sitting in a meeting room at a massive mahogany conference room table. George and his assistant entered the room. After this group had a short discussion George heard his name come over the paging system asking him to come to the front desk. After a few minutes George came back with two men that were the legal representatives of RJ Jefferson in the matter. Raymond Smith was RJ Jefferson's lead representative and Martin Emerson was his associate.

George and Lindsay were surprised at how smoothly the meeting progressed. George laid out the information he had amassed about the alleged encounter. The last thing RJ Jefferson's attorneys wanted was a public accusation that their client was a rapist. The one thing Jefferson's team hung its case on was the chance that Lindsay's son was not RJ Jefferson's. RJ Jefferson's attorneys demanded a paternity test that was legally admissible in court if required. A DNA testing firm was agreed upon that would collect the DNA from RJ Jefferson, Lindsay and Lindsay's son. The DNA collection would take place within the next week. The samples would be collected and tested and everyone agreed to honor the results.

Lindsay told her son that the place they went to in order to get their cheeks swabbed was for an insurance policy screening. RJ Jefferson gave his DNA sample at a lab in California where his team's training camp was being held. Modern technology had taken paternity DNA testing to a new level. DNA testing kits could be purchased at local drug stores and even big box retailers. Home testing kits allowed samples to be taken and sent to a testing laboratory and the results could often be viewed online. The test that was being used to test the paternity of Lindsay's son was more stringent in regards to the chain of custody of the samples and was deemed legally admissible in court.

Two days later all parties in the dispute were informed that the results of the DNA test were available. It was decided that the results would be announced with everyone involved present, including RJ Jefferson, at George's law firm's office in downtown Dallas. Lindsay wore a red ensemble to the meeting since she had worn blue before. The dresses were identical except for the color.

Lindsay was remarkably calm since she knew the truth about what took place. After being in the room with her team for one half hour, the other side arrived. The same two lawyers arrived and RJ Jefferson walked in behind them. RJ was six-feet three inches tall and weighed two hundred and thirty pounds. Jefferson wore a dark suit and Lindsay had a very vague recognition of this man that she proclaimed to be the father of her son. There was an uneasy tension in the air as everyone exchanged greetings. RJ shook Lindsay's hand which surprised her and George.

"Well let's get this over with," George said.

George called the DNA laboratory and placed the representative on the speaker phone in the middle of the conference table. The lab representative wasted no time before he dispensed the information everyone had gathered together to hear.

"Regarding the results of the DNA test to determine the paternity of Riley Wilson. It is a 99.999 percent probability that this child is the offspring of RJ Jefferson and Lindsay Wilson. There is no doubt. The printed results are in route to everyone involved. Any questions," the lab representative asked.

"No. No questions," George said after checking with everyone in the room.

RJ Jefferson dropped his head in disbelief. He realized his entire football and post playing career was suddenly hanging in the balance. Then RJ Jefferson did something that startled everyone in the room.

"Ma'am. I'm sorry I treated you that way," Riley said as he looked Lindsay in the eyes.

RJ then stood up to leave.

"RJ where are you going? We're not done here," Raymond Smith said.

"Do what you need to do to do right by this woman and her son," Riley said.

"What do you mean this woman and her son? I'm the mother of your son! Your son! Don't you even care about your son? He wears your name. Don't you even want to get to know him?" Lindsay asked.

"Ma'am I accept that I have a child with you, but I don't know you or him. We met once a long time ago, had an encounter and I didn't know anything about the rest. I'll live up to my responsibilities in every way that I can. That's all I have to say about it," RJ said as he turned to leave.

"You son-of-a-bitch! I was sixteen years old," Lindsay said as RJ left the room.

"Where the hell is he going?!" George asked.

"Back to training camp, I guess. He's fighting off a couple of rookies that are after his starting job," Martin Emerson said.

"Where are we with this, guys? Is the fact that RJ Jefferson is the father of Lindsay's son accepted as a settled issue?" George asked

"Look we agreed to abide by the results of the DNA test. We need to pull together the framework for a settlement for this matter," Raymond Smith said.

"Not so fast gentleman. We need to work on a dual agreement and settlement. One portion is a settlement for the paternity issue of Lindsay and RJ Jefferson's son. A package of child support, college fund and recovery of funds for seven years of the absence of support from his father adjusted for interest and inflation. The second part of this package will be directed towards Miss Lindsay Wilson and provide ample motivation for her not to proceed with her right to file statutory rape charges against your client," George said.

"Of course those are valid items that we will pursue with the input of our client, Mr. Jefferson. Naturally if we are able to come to some agreement we will require an ironclad confidentiality agreement signed by Miss Wilson to not disclose the details of the settlement. As for the potential rape charges we can't tell her to not pursue something if it was a legitimate violation of law, but would hope that there would be very little incentive to do so," Raymond Smith said.

"May I say something?" Lindsay asked.

"Of course," Raymond Smith said.

"George, how long did you say the statute of limits was on the statutory rape thing?" Lindsay asked.

"Well if you draw up a rough timeline, there's a couple of years left before it expires," George answered.

"So, for another two years I could file rape charges against that man. I tell you what. As part of my motivation to not file charges until the time runs out, I want him to have to visit his son. I don't know how long or how many times, but the way he walked out of here makes me want to file charges on his ass. I can't make him care about his own son, but if I can make him visit him so my son can see who his daddy is, it will be worth it. George, I want required visits in the deal," Lindsay said.

"Okay, Lindsay this is your show. You guys heard the lady, are we clear on that," George said.

"Yes, we're clear on it," Raymond Smith said.

"When can I expect to hear from you?" George asked.

"You'll hear from us before this time next week," Raymond Smith said as they departed.

"Well, Lindsay how do you feel about what happened?" George asked.

"He doesn't even care that he has a son that he doesn't know. What kind of man is he?" Lindsay said.

"Lindsay. We're dealing with a guy that has been told that he's the greatest thing since sliced bread for a long time because of his athletic ability. Now if you combine that with being wealthy, then he has an ego as big as this building. Once the bright lights go off and everybody's not paying attention to him anymore, reality will start to set in. RJ Jefferson is one concussion away from being retired and he knows it. Now, he has to figure out how to put the best spin on what is about to go public in a week or so to his wife, team and sponsors," George said.

"I guess I never thought about it like that," Lindsay said.

"Lindsay your situation will be totally different in a couple of weeks than it is now. Once this get's out, you may have people parked outside your door trying to get pictures and asking questions. You will have to be careful of what you say because those folks will be digging for a story. Once this is settled, you may have to move," George said.

"I never even thought about all of that. This is kind of scary," Lindsay said.

"Hey, I'll call you. Good job and congratulations," George said.

Lindsay left the office and went home to change before she went to work that night.

"Well what happened?" Tameka asked when Lindsay walked into the apartment.

"Well he's Riley's father, but I already knew that. Tameka you can't say anything until this is over. Promise me, please," Lindsay said.

"I promise. It'll kill me, but I promise not to say a word," Tameka said.

"He was there when we got the results. He just got up and told his people to handle it. He left us all sitting there in that room and walked out. He had no interest in meeting his son. I felt like throwing up. What an asshole," Lindsay said.

"Did he say anything to you at all?" Tameka asked.

"Yeah, he did. After he found out Riley was his son, he said he was sorry he treated me the way he did and then he just walked out. Who does that?" Lindsay said.

12

Lindsay's routine went back to normal with her cycle of working, taking care of her children and occasionally finding time to relax. Lindsay's social life was very limited given her schedule, but she did have a friend with benefits and that worked well for her. She didn't really want to bring a man around her children until they were older. Lindsay was especially wary of exposing her young daughter to different male influences at such a young age. She was not going to be one of those mothers that put some man and her needs above the welfare of her children. There were too many horrid news reports of a boyfriend injuring or killing the child of his girlfriend for Lindsay to take that chance. Many men saw struggling single women with children as easy targets for sexual exploitation. Some men felt that "baby mamas" had few options when it came to male companionship. Single mothers often paid with their dignity and self respect when they decided to mark down their value simply because they had children out of wedlock, but Lindsay was not willing to do that to please a man or to satisfy her own needs.

There was very little time for a serious relationship in Lindsay's life and she met Robert Logan when she was reaching for a can of peas on the top shelf a grocery store two years ago. As Lindsay stood on her tip toes to reach the can, a man's hand reached above her and plucked it off the top shelf. The man took the can and placed it in his shopping basket. Lindsay couldn't believe what had just happened and just stared at the man as he walked away. Lindsay followed him.

"Hey, didn't you see that I was about to grab that can and you just took it from me?" Lindsay said.

"Yes, but your hand hadn't touched the can yet so it was fair game," Robert said.

"What! Are you serious?" Lindsay said.

After engaging with this man for five minutes over a can of peas, Lindsay caught on that she had fell for his conversation starter move.

"Okay, I get it. You wanted to see if I would say something and that was your way to get me to talk to you," Lindsay said.

"Wow. Someone has a very high opinion of themselves, don't they," Robert said.

Lindsay looked embarrassed and thought that maybe she had misread the situation.

"Oh. I'm sorry. I just assumed," Lindsay said before Robert cut her off.

"It worked didn't it?" Robert said.

Robert invited Lindsay to join him for a cup of coffee at a coffee shop in the same strip center as the grocery store and for some strange reason she accepted. These two strangers had a great conversation and he gave Lindsay his phone number. Over time Robert became her sounding board when she needed advice. He was ten years older than Lindsay and she didn't feel particularly attracted to him in a sexual way. They would often talk by phone without having seen each other for weeks at a time. When they did see each other it was just briefly at the same coffee shop they went to initially after they first met. One day Robert invited Lindsay to come to his house and visit. Lindsay was taken aback, but felt obligated due to how familiar they were with each other, yet she didn't really know him at all. Lindsay said yes and went there on day when Tameka was off and agreed to keep the children. When Lindsay pulled up to the address that Robert had given her, she checked it again. This home was in the middle of one of the wealthiest neighborhoods in Dallas.

Lindsay felt self conscious about everything when she parked in the circular driveway. She felt embarrassed about her beat up car, the clothes she wore and even her appearance. How could she have been talking to this man for so long and have no clue he lived in a neighborhood like that.

Lindsay rang the doorbell and before she knew it Robert answered the door and invited her inside.

Robert's home was the most luxurious thing she had ever seen.

"Hey I'm glad you could make it. Welcome to my humble abode," Robert said.

"Robert, I'm shocked. I had no idea you lived in a place like this," Lindsay said.

"Why are you surprised?" Robert asked.

"Well you don't dress or act like you would live in a place like this," Lindsay said.

"Oh, so I'm too nice to live in a place like this. You know what that means. That means that you think that only assholes can live this way and they get there by stepping on everyone else. You are partially right. This place belonged to my parents

115

and I inherited the joint after they died in a plane crash. I loved them, but they were ruthless business people. Come on. Let me show you around," Robert said.

Lindsay's eyes were taking in all of the amenities, such as a heated pool, indoor exercise room and an indoor whirlpool spa. After the tour Lindsay and Robert sat in the living room.

"Robert, do you live here by yourself?" Lindsay asked.

"Yes. I live here by myself. I was married once and it ended very badly, so I don't plan to go down that road again," Robert said.

"When we met, you were shopping closer to where I live. There are stores around here a lot closer to your house. What were you doing over there?" Lindsay asked.

"I used to live over that way and have friends that still live there. I wasn't into the family business and wanted to get as far from all of this as possible. I wasn't fighting with my parents or anything, but I wanted to live around real people. I went to college and graduated with a degree in history," Robert said.

"Why did you want to talk to me?" Lindsay asked.

"You caught my interest," Robert said.

"I caught your interest while I was reaching for a can of peas?" Lindsay asked.

"Yes. It was a riveting sight. I'm not dead yet, you know," Robert said.

Lindsay felt herself blush at Robert's remark.

"Hey. We're friends. I like how you tell it like it is. Most women are trying to hide behind some kind of veil of secrecy and be mysterious. You just laid it all out," Robert said.

"Well. I don't have anything to hide, plus you're too old for me anyway," Lindsay said.

"Ouch," Robert replied.

"The last thing I want is to be pushing an old man around in a wheelchair or having some waiter asking you what your daughter wanted to eat tonight," Lindsay said.

"Hey are you hungry. I've taken up cooking and I've have a dish I just finished," Robert said as he went into the kitchen and Lindsay followed.

There was a platter of food that looked like thick fried onion rings with a red dipping sauce. Robert took one of the rings, dipped it in the sauce and bit into it.

"Oh man, that's good. Try one," Robert said.

"What is that?" Lindsay asked as she picked up a ring, dipped it in the sauce and bit into it.

"Oh. That is good." Lindsay said.

"It's squid," Robert said.

"Squid. You mean like squid in the ocean with the tentacles and suction cups. Oh my God!" Lindsay said as a physical shudder went through her body.

Lindsay spit the squid into her hand, ran water into a glass and washed her mouth out.

"It was good wasn't it, until you found out what it was," Robert said.

117

"Why didn't you tell me what it was before I ate it?" Lindsay asked.

"I want you to think about what you just did. We've talked about this before. You just allowed your mind to limit your ability to experience new things and grow," Robert said.

"Okay. What do mean?" Lindsay said.

"When you first ate the calamari, that's what they call this dish, you said it was good. When I told you what it was, you had a physical reaction and spit it out. You didn't spit it out because you didn't like it. You spit it out because you thought that you weren't supposed to like it. You didn't want to allow yourself to grow. Suppose you were with someone at an important function and this dish was in front of you and everyone ate it except for you. You have to get over your fear of going outside of your comfort zone. Why don't you try the calamari again and pretend it's something you're used to eating," Robert said.

"Okay. I'll try it again," Lindsay said.

Lindsay tried the calamari and just concentrated on how it tasted. She ate three rings without any problem.

"Robert you were right. I don't know why I did that before. It really bothers me," Lindsay said.

"The reason you did that was to stay where you are comfortable. You didn't want to become familiar with something a little outside your normal environment. You thought about how your friends don't eat this and even in that small way you would be different and that made you uncomfortable," Robert said.

"How did you become so smart?" Lindsay asked.

"I'm old, remember," Robert said.

Lindsay left that day with an invitation to come back to escape her world for a few hours the next week.

The next week Lindsay visited Robert and packed her bikini so that she could swim in his pool. When Lindsay arrived Robert came from around the side of the house and beckoned for her to come around to the back. Robert was wearing shorts a long shirt and sandals. When Lindsay came around the corner to the rear patio area she smelled food cooking on a grill.

"I've got some steaks on the grill and they are almost ready. If you want to change into your swimsuit, you can use the pool house" Robert said.

"Great. Those steaks smell good," Lindsay said as she went to change.

Lindsay came out of the pool house wearing a red two-piece bikini that was modest enough for a family day at the beach. Robert definitely noticed Lindsay's s toned, shapely figure when she walked out and sat on the edge of the pool.

"How much time do you have?" Robert asked.

"About four hours and then I'll return the favor for my roommate. I'll keep her kids so that she can go out tonight," Lindsay said.

"Well good. I just asked so I won't keep you too long. I know it's hard for you to get free time alone," Robert said.

"Robert. Thank you for being my friend. You don't know how much a break like this means to me. It's almost like a mini vacation," Lindsay said.

"Don't worry about it. I enjoy your company and I don't socialize with a lot of people, by choice," Robert said.

Lindsay slipped into the pool and felt the cool water wash over her body in contrast to the one hundred degree heat of the day. Robert's backyard was like a tropical retreat with green vegetation planted all around the area. After eating they went inside to escape the relentless sun. Lindsay slipped into the indoor whirlpool spa while Robert retrieved a bottle of wine and two glasses before climbing into the spa with Lindsay.

"Lindsay, I don't mean to pry, but I'm going to anyway. With your children, job and your roommate's children how do find time, you know, for a relationship?" Robert asked.

"I don't make time for that. I've decided that has to wait until later, after my children are older. There just too many risks involved with exposing my kids to different men when they're so young, so I just don't," Lindsay said.

"What about you. You're young. Surely there must be a way for you to have a social life and still protect your children," Robert said.

"I just don't see it right now. Where would I even meet a decent guy? I work at a strip club. I'm not going to date someone I meet there. The rest of the time is spent sleeping and taking care of my kids," Lindsay said.

"What about the grocery store," Robert said.
"I heard you can meet nice men at the grocery store in the canned peas' aisle," Robert said laughing.

"You are so crazy," Lindsay said.

For a while Lindsay forgot about her children, job and where she was in life as she sipped wine in a bubbling spa with her secret friend. After thirty minutes of hot water massaging and wine coursing through her body, Lindsay began to feel warm sensations inside. Lindsay's mind and eyes began to perceive her surroundings in a new way.

Robert was reclining with his back against the edge of the spa and his eyes were half closed. Lindsay looked over at Robert with her eyes squinting. She noticed Robert's long frame, crisply cut black hair, mustache and beard. Lindsay also fixated on the hairy chest of this man that she considered a friend. Hot water, wine and her surroundings had clouded Lindsay's mind. There she was basking in the lap of unaccustomed luxury in the middle of what would normally be another routinely hectic day with a man uniquely different from those she usually encountered right in front of her. Lindsay lightly floated across the short expanse of space seperating them. When Robert opened his eyes he was starring right into Lindsay's face and she had a smile that indicated she was thinking about something other than light conversation.

"Lindsay, what are you..." were all the words that Robert managed to speak before Lindsay planted her lips firmly on his mouth.

Lindsay was in a fog and something had awakened inside her. Although Lindsay worked in a club that flowed with alcohol she rarely indulged and her body was having a swift reaction to the wine in her system. Robert was a little more clear-headed as he would often drink wine while in the whirlpool and was not affected to same degree Lindsay was. Although he had befriended Lindsay, he didn't really know her and felt he needed to take control of the situation. Robert used his strength to pull his body and Lindsay's out of the water while she was still wrapped around his waist. Even though they were dripping wet, Robert managed to walk to his master bedroom with her draped around his torso and he grabbed a large white beach towel along the way. Robert flung the comforter on his bed onto the floor. Robert opened the drawer on his nightstand and retrieved a condom with one hand before lying on the bed with Lindsay still hanging onto his body.

Lindsay sat up and removed her bikini top and Robert for the first time saw what he had only imagined before when her magnificent breasts sprang free. Robert's hands couldn't resist the temptation and felt the bounty before him. Lindsay surprised Robert and lowered her head to his groin area and he soon found himself subject to her oral pleasuring. This man who mostly lived a rather solitary life found himself staring at the ornate ceiling above his massive four poster kind sized bed while a beautiful woman was attending to his most carnal desires. Lindsay brought Robert to the brink of ecstasy, but want things to conclude differently.

Robert was still on his knees when Lindsay sat up and kissed him deeply. Robert assisted with freeing Lindsay from the bottom part of her two piece swimsuit.

Robert quickly placed his condom on before being pulled down by the weight of Lindsay's body as she lay backwards onto the bed with her arms around his neck and lips lock onto his. Lindsay felt the softness of Robert's 2,000 thread count Egyptian cotton sheets caressing her naked body when they made contact with her back. Robert felt the exquisite and erotic warm sensation of welcome into what this woman decided to share with him at that moment in time. Robert gasped and then felt Lindsay wrap those amazing legs around his waist.

With her ankles locked together, Lindsay felt free to unleash whatever pent up sexual tension she had built up with Robert that afternoon. Robert moved beyond being puzzled or confused and enjoyed this bounty of a woman. Lindsay state of mind freed her from all inhibitions and weight of constant responsibility for others. Lindsay gave Robert all she had to offer as she was released from all of usual constraints. Robert was thankful for the insulation and wall thickness of this old home for their sound containment abilities. After thirty minutes Lindsay had exhausted herself and fell into a sound sleep.

Robert felt that he had survived a paramount sexual experience with an extraordinary woman. Stumbling into his bathroom he wiped the perspiration from his body with a towel. Robert estimated that Lindsay had two hours left before she had to be at home. Robert collected the bed comforter from the floor and covered Lindsay. He would wake her an hour later in order to give her time to refresh herself and go home. Robert kissed Lindsay on the forehead and left the room.

"Robert, what happened?" Lindsay asked as she walked into the living room forty minutes later with a sheet wrapped around her body.

"Well, I guess you got a little excited with the wine and all," Robert said.

"Robert, I'm so sorry. I didn't mean to ruin everything. I guess I got a little out of control," Lindsay said crying.

Robert bolted from his chair and hugged Lindsay.

"What are you sorry for? That was fantastic. You didn't do anything wrong," Robert said.

"Look, I won't bother you again," Lindsay said.

"Lindsay. You are my friend. I don't expect anything more than that," Robert said.

"So we can still talk and visit together? Won't that be a little strange after we, you know, just had sex?" Lindsay asked.

"I'm not looking to be in a relationship and you aren't either, so we can still be friends. We can also be friends with benefits, but that's up to you," Robert said.

"You mean have sex like we just did? Wouldn't that be kind of weird?" Lindsay asked.

"No. Not unless you make it weird. I don't have any ties on you and you have none on me. I don't expect anything or demand anything from you, but if you just need to talk or do something more, I'm here and you are something special," Robert said.

Lindsay felt a bit embarrassed and her cheeks turned red. Robert kissed Lindsay on the forehead.

"You can use my bathroom and shower to freshen up," Robert said.

Lindsay walked away with a bit of a puzzled look on her face because she didn't quite remember everything they did together that day.

Over the two years she had known Robert, Lindsay sparingly used her friends with benefits option with him since that first time. Given the anxiety she was feeling awaiting the resolution of the settlement with RJ Jefferson, Lindsay gave Robert a call and asked if she could come over a couple of hours before she went to work. It occurred to Lindsay after she hung up the phone that she had just made a booty-call and felt good about it.

Lindsay stopped at Robert's house on the way to the club and left an hour and a half later feeling much better about the rest of her day.

13

A week had passed since Lindsay met with RJ Jefferson and his legal team and she was wondering what was going on when she got a phone call from her brother-in- law George.

"Lindsay we need to meet. We have a settlement offer on the table. Can you be in my Dallas office at ten in the morning tomorrow?" George asked.

"Sure, I'll be there," Lindsay said.

"Who was that?" Tameka asked.

"That was George. I need to meet him tomorrow at his law firm. We have a settlement offer," Lindsay said.

"I'm off tomorrow and I'll look after the kids. You know this could change your life, don't you?" Tameka said.

"Yeah, and it scary," Lindsay admitted.

"Why are you scared?" Tameka asked.

"I don't know. I feel hot almost like I have a fever. I've never really had much of anything. I don't think I will know what to do. What if I really screw up and lose everything? I've heard about people getting a lot of money at one time and ending up broke," Lindsay said.

"Lindsay, listen. You need to calm down and clear your head. Everything's not over yet and you're the one making the final decisions, not your lawyer. Don't let them run over you in there," Tameka said.

"You're right. I've just got to calm down," Lindsay said as she took a deep breath.

"Damn Lindsay, you almost lost it for a minute," Tameka said.

"I know. I'm sorry, but this is real now. I wish it was over already. Well I've got to work tonight. That will take my mind off some of this for a while, plus by the time I get home and pass out asleep it'll be time to get up and go downtown," Lindsay said.

Lindsay went to work at The Secret Island and managed to get through her shift, but her mind was definitely on something else. Luckily nothing out of the ordinary happened to add to Lindsay's anxiety. Time flew by and before Lindsay knew it the time for her to meet George in his office had arrived. Lindsay walked into that high-rise glass building in Dallas and soon was seated in the conference room when George and his assistant finally walked in and took their seats.

"Well Lindsay, this took a little longer than expected, but they came back with two offers that I rejected out of hand because they were not serious. I went back to them with a formula based upon your age, your son's age and the effects that the reckless actions of their client had on your future. I also hit them with a kicker requirement if they wanted a confidentially agreement. These are the settlement figures," George said as he slid two pieces of paper over to Lindsay who was seated next to him on his right side.

Lindsay looked at the first sheet and she had to blink and refocus her vision. One sheet contained a settlement for her son in the amount of a $420,000.00 one-time payment from the years of his birth up to his current age. There was also a $5,000.00 per month non-court mandated child support payment scheduled to end upon Lindsay's son reaching the age of eighteen years old.

Lindsay's heart rate was already elevated and when she looked at the second sheet that had her name at the top of the page she almost stopped breathing. There was a $3 million lump sum settlement that dealt with the potential harm done to Lindsay and her future prospects due to the reckless actions of RJ Jefferson. The second figure on the page was a $2 million dollar split payment for signing a confidentiality agreement. Lindsay would get $1 million after the agreement was signed and another $1 million dollars after the statute of limitations expired on the statutory rape charge. The second $1 million dollar payment would be placed in escrow and distributed to Lindsay upon expiration of the statute of limitations as a deferred disbursement to be counted as income when received for tax purposes.

Lindsay looked at the figures and looked at George.

"George. Is this fair? I mean this a whole lot of money, but is it fair for what you've seen in this kind of thing," Lindsay asked.

"Well Lindsay. It could have been more if this guy was in the prime of his career as a player. Since he is at the end of his playing days, the odds are that his earning potential will go down substantially. I say let's get this done before the football season starts. If RJ Jefferson goes out on the field and gets injured, it's over. Professional football players in general don't have guaranteed contracts. Suppose he starts off badly this year and gets benched. He could be released from the team. In all of those scenarios his money train stops and they might not be so eager to settle. Get it while the getting is good," George said.

"Okay. What about the visitations with my son?" Lindsay asked.

"Four times a year. That's the best we could get out of Jefferson. It'll be in the terms and conditions," George said.

"What do we do next?" Lindsay answered.

"I'll call his representative and tell them to draw up the paperwork and we will all meet and get it signed, this should be wrapped up early next week. I'll call you. Congratulations," George said and shook Lindsay's hand

"Okay. Thanks," Lindsay said with a nervous smile.

"Lindsay, don't worry this will be painless," George said.

Lindsay left the office and felt very different when she walked out than when she walked in. If she could, Lindsay would not leave the house until everything was signed but she had to go to work because as of that moment she still had to provide for her children just like she always had in the past.

Lindsay came home and Tameka was on pins and needles.

"What happened?" Tameka asked with anticipation.

Lindsay looked around to see if the children were out of earshot.

"It's like $4.5 million dollars," Lindsay said in a whisper.

Tameka just sat down hard in her chair.

"Oh fuck!" she said.

"I know, but It's not done yet. I still have to sign the papers next week, but I feel numb. I'm started to feel kind of strange like other people know what's going on or something," Lindsay said.

"Hell yeah! I feel that way if I've got a $100 bill in my purse. I can imagine how you feel," Tameka.

"Tameka we're going to get out of this place when I get this money. We are all getting out of here. I've still got to go to work tonight. I can hardly think straight," Lindsay said.

Lindsay found that she actually paid attention to more things as she drove to work. She saw cars she might like to own. Lindsay noticed homes that she wouldn't mind living in. It was like her field of vision had widened to include possibilities that she had blocked out of her mind because they seemed so far out of reach. Fear swept across Lindsay once again as thoughts that she would lose everything swept over her again. After she arrived at the club Lindsay went to the bathroom, went into a stall and threw up while she gripped the side of the toilet bowl with her hands. Lindsay made it through the night, but she knew she needed to talk to someone about how she was feeling and she thought about Robert. Robert was rich and had been rich a long time. Lindsay called Robert the next day and said she needed to talk to him as soon as possible. Lindsay went to see Robert the next day as soon as Tameka got home from work.

Robert answered his door and immediately noticed the panicked look on Lindsay's face.

"Lindsay, what's wrong? Your face is telling me something is really bothering you," Robert said.

Lindsay sat down and launched into why she came over to see him.

"Robert. I need to ask you some things about money. I don't want any money, but I may be coming into a lot of money and I am having all kinds of strange feelings that I might really screw everything up if I get this money. I'm seeing all of these things I want and I don't even have it yet. What going on with me? You have been rich for a long time. Why am I feeling this way? It almost feels like a panic attack," Lindsay said.

"Calm down. What you are experiencing is a natural human reaction. When someone goes from having very little to suddenly having a lot, it triggers a desire to make up for all those years of feeling deprived. I watched a television show a few weeks ago about lottery winners that lost everything and ended up with nothing. They tried to financially elevate everyone in their families. People came after them with business ideas and in general they spent money on frivolous things," Robert said.

"That's what I'm afraid I will do and end up right back in the same place I am now or worse. I could be stuck with bills I can't pay or even homeless because it will all be gone," Lindsay admitted.

"First of all, how much money are you talking about? There's a big difference between $50,000 and $5 million. I don't need to know the exact amount, just a ballpark figure," Robert asked.

"Around three million dollars," Lindsay said.

"Wow! That's a lot of money and it's none of my business why you're getting it as long as it's legal. Will you get it all at once or spread out over time," Robert asked.

"Yes it's legal and I'm getting it all at once," Lindsay replied.

"Here's how you need to approach things. If you come into a large lump sum of money the first thing you should do is get your tax situation taken care of. Nothing is worse than spending money that belongs to Uncle Sam, so get that done right off the bat. Secondly, place one forth or one third of the money in something that is difficult to access. It could be government bonds or something like that. The next thing you should do is take the funds you will live off and divide it by twenty years. The number that comes from the twenty year division should be how you live. If you want to buy a home then buy a home that you could afford based upon the twenty year number, not the lump sum. You have to remember, if you can't generate enough income to replace that lump sum, then it's all going out with nothing coming in to replace it," Robert said.

"That's exactly what I'm afraid of. I feel that I want to give everything to my kids and I see all these things I want that I couldn't have before.

So, you're saying to live like a normal person, not like a rich person," Lindsay said.

"Look, a house like mine costs over a million dollars. Then with upkeep, utilities and property tax bills it can drain two or three million dollars pretty quickly. You have to be smart and realize you are trying to live for the rest of your life and not for a few years, so slow down and only do modest things that you think are important in the beginning like getting a nice safe place to live. It doesn't have to be a mansion. Get some good reliable transportation, but it doesn't have to be a luxury car. Once you do that, I recommend that you get the education you didn't get a chance at the first time around. That education will open your eyes to how the world works and give you a lot more confidence about the decisions you are making," Robert said.

"Okay. That's why I wanted to talk to you. I don't really know anyone else that, you know, knows anything about dealing with money. I just don't want to do anything stupid," Lindsay said.

"One of the first things you have to remember is that you can't fix everything or everybody. You'll have people approach you with business ideas and sob stories. What you need to remember is that their situations would be the same if you didn't come into this windfall of money, what would they do then? Their situation had nothing to do with you then and will have nothing to do with you after you get your money," Robert said.

"Robert you have been a good friend to me and you've never asked anything from me. Maybe

that's why whatever we have together works,"
Lindsay said.

"Speaking of work, I suppose you will stop
dancing once your finances improve. If you do,
what will you do with the rest of your life?" Robert
asked.

"I haven't really thought about that. I have
no idea," Lindsay said.

14

George called Lindsay on a Wednesday afternoon while she was in the dressing room at The Secret Island and told her the settlement papers were ready for signature. Lindsay was set to go downtown the next day and sign the paperwork.

Lindsay Wilson walked into the tallest office tower in Dallas as a struggling single mother and walked out two hours later a multi-millionaire. George told Lindsay to bring her bank account information with her so that direct deposit funding could be set up to receive her portion of the settlement. Lindsay also set up a custodial account for her son so that his account could be funded also. The money would reflect in their respective accounts within two business days.

George told Lindsay to find a new place to live temporarily by the next Thursday after her funds were available. RJ Jefferson would be holding a press conference to announce that he had discovered he had a child that was now seven years old and that he would be meeting his son in the near future. George told Lindsay that the media frenzy would begin and it would not take long for them to be on her trail.

Lindsay went home and told Tameka to get ready to vacate the apartment in a few days because they would all be moving to an extended stay hotel until they found a more permanent location. Lindsay found a hotel with room enough for both families. The next Monday Lindsay checked her bank account and tears ran down her face. Her checking account balance was $4,000,450.00. The $450.00 was Lindsay's account balance before the settlement. Lindsay couldn't move or talk. Lindsay made a call to the hotel she had found and paid for two suites for a month. Moving would not be a problem because they were leaving everything in the apartment except their clothes and they had already packed. Lindsay also checked her son's newly established account and it showed a balance of $420,025.00. The $25 was the amount Lindsay used to establish the account. Lindsay then did something that she would tell no one else about.

When Tameka came home they loaded both cars with their belongings and drove to the hotel about ten miles away in a quite area in north Dallas. Lindsay was scheduled to work that night and she thought about calling in and cancelling, but decided that this would literally be her last dance. After almost dumping their belongings in the two adjacent hotel suites Lindsay had an hour to catch her breath and make that last drive to The Secret Island.

Tameka decided to balance her bank account and called to check the balance. The automated voice stated the balance as $250,350.00. Tameka disconnected and called again and got the same result. Tameka then called her bank and got a representative on the line. The bank representative informed Tameka that a transfer from another bank was made into her account in the amount of $250,000.00 that morning. Tameka hung up the phone and started crying. Then she dialed Lindsay's number.

"Hello," Lindsay said.

"What did you do?! I checked my bank account and all of this money is in there," Tameka said excitedly.

Lindsay broke down in tears.

"I don't know where I would be without you. When my own family turned their backs on me you talked your folks into taking me in. You saved my life. I might not even be here. You are like my sister. You are closer than my own sister," Lindsay said.

Both women were crying as they spoke. Tameka looked up and five children were staring her in the face and the two youngest had started crying in sympathy with her although they didn't know why.

"Lindsay, I've got to get off this phone. These kids are looking at me like I'm crazy. Thank you. I love you," Tameka said.

Lindsay put her phone down and thought that was the first time she ever heard her oldest friend tell her that she loved her and she couldn't suppress her smile.

Lindsay went into the club and told Jacob that this would be her last night and thanked him for the opportunity to work there.

The shift seemed to zoom by that night. Right before her last dance, Lindsay took a microphone and announced that this was her last show. Her little cheering section applauded and the music fired up. All of the other dancers exited the side stages and everyone gathered around the main stage. Lindsay had a new move for the crowd from her days as a high school cheerleader. Lindsay did a handstand and mounted the pole upside down by wrapping one of her legs around the pole and then pulling herself upwards. The crowd along the sides of the stage loved it. At the end of her dance Lindsay took the microphone and walked to the edge of the stage.

"This is it, but before I leave I have something for one of my most loyal supporters. Carl has been sitting over here supporting me for years. I've always known that he wanted to get in my panties. So Carl," Lindsay said as she paused to pick up her g-string from the stage.

"This is for you. Now you can get in my panties whenever you want to," Lindsay said as she presented the garment to the man and exited the stage to a roar.

Back in the dressing room Lindsay was preparing to leave the club for the last time.

"So you are really leaving?" Latasha asked.

"Yup. This is it," Lindsay replied.

"Look, I know we haven't always been cool with each other and a lot of that was my fault when I look back on it. I mean you never really did anything to me. So anyway, what's going on? Did you find another job? I know you were making pretty good money here," Latasha asked.

"No. I just needed a change," Lindsay said.

"I guess you found some man to take you away from all of this, huh," Latasha said.

"Latasha, if I had a dime for every time some man said that to me in here, I would have been gone a long time ago," Lindsay said laughing.

"I know that's right. You know what they want before that tired shit even comes out of their mouth. I'll treat you like a queen. Yeah right, until they get what they want. Then it's, bitch get out and turn the light off when you leave," Latasha said laughing.

"Ya'll still got your asses in here. It's time to go home," Darrius said as he walked into the dressing room.

"Alright Latasha, bye. Keep the main stage hot," Lindsay said as she left.

"You know that. Good luck," Latasha said as she continued to get dressed.

"Hey Lindsay, I'm going to miss you. You take care of yourself," Darrius said.

"Oh Darrius. I'm going to miss you too," Lindsay said.

Lindsay walked up to Darrius and gave him a big hug. Lindsay looked into Darrius eyes.

"Thank you for what you did that night when I had that fight with that guy. I know you wanted to do me when I made a fool of myself. I could see it in your eyes, but thank you for turning me down. I never thought I would say that to a man, but thank you," Lindsay said and kissed Darrius on the cheek.

Darrius watched Lindsay walk out of that club one last time and he thought of opportunities lost. Lindsay hopped into her car for one final early morning drive away from the club. After Lindsay drove about one three quarters of a mile away from the club her car lost power and coasted to a stop. She tried to restart the engine, but it would not

139

remain running. Lindsay grabbed her cell phone and during all of the excitement of the day she had allowed the battery to run down. She thought if she plugged in her car charger and left the key on for a few minutes the phone would charge enough for her to call Tameka.

Where Lindsay's car stopped was not a safe place for anyone to be stranded alongside the road after midnight. The area was filled with industrial businesses and warehouses. There were no homes in sight and there was sparse traffic along those streets that early in the morning. A bright light was shinning from the parking lot of a nearby warehouse. Lindsay pulled the release lever for her hood and got out to look under it to see if she saw something obvious like a loose battery cable. Then Lindsay saw a set of car headlights pull up and stop behind her vehicle. She thought that she had lucked out and help had arrived. The headlights went off on the car behind her and a male figure got out.

"Do you need some help?" the man asked as he walked forward.

"Yeah. My car just died while I was driving," Lindsay said.

The man had arrived at the front of the car and Lindsay looked around to see who he was.

"Remember me bitch?!" the man said.

Lindsay looked at his face and suddenly realized it was the man she had hit with the bottle in the VIP room. With one blow of his fist to Lindsay's jaw, he knocked her to the ground. Lindsay looked up at him with her mouth bleeding out of one corner as she sat on the grass near the edge of the road.

"What are you doing here? What do you want?" Lindsay asked.

He reached down to grab Lindsay and she kicked him solidly in the knee and he winched in pain, but that did not stop him. Lindsay did not have the element of surprise this time. He grabbed her and pulled Lindsay up from behind with her feet off the ground. With one arm around her waist and other hand over her mouth, this man literally carried Lindsay to an area between a dumpster and a closed warehouse building hidden from the road.

"You ratchet little slut. You cost me my marriage. The next morning my pillow was soaked with blood and I was forced to tell my wife what happened. She went ballistic. She left me and took my kids. I can't even see my children because of you, but now you're going to pay bitch," he said.

Lindsay was terrified, but she decided if she was going out tonight, she would go out fighting. Her assailant had Lindsay pressed up against the wall of the building and his hot breath was blowing on her neck. Lindsay managed to press against the wall with her arms and thighs to get enough space to allow the toes of her sneakers a small amount of grip on the rough surface of the building. With all of her strength Lindsay propelled her body backwards. Both Lindsay and her attacker went flying, but their momentum was stopped when the man's back impacted the heavy gauge steel of the trash dumpster right where it protruded for the arms of a garbage truck to lift it for emptying.

"Ahhh!" was the sound the man made as he screamed from the pain of the impact.

Lindsay managed to momentarily break free from his grip, but when she tried to run he grabbed her by the ankle and she fell face forward and broke her fall with the palms of her hands. Lindsay turned over and started kicking at the man as he slowly imposed his weight and strength on her. He was now on top of Lindsay attempting to grasp her wrists. Lindsay managed to inflict some deep gouges to his face as she sunk her fingernails deep into his cheeks. Lindsay felt her energy ebbing away as she was simply being physically overpowered. He was able to grasp both her wrists and pin her arms to her side. With his knees on either side of Lindsay's body she was unable to move her arms. With one hand her assailant ripped Lindsay's blouse and bra off in one swift motion. With her top exposed he roughly fondled Lindsay's breasts with his sweaty hands while she struggled to arch her body to throw him off to no avail. Using his strength he flipped Lindsay onto her stomach and pressed the weight of his body down on top of her.

"You're going to give me what I want now, bitch! I already paid and now you are going to deliver," the man said as he proceeded to pull Lindsay's pants down with one hand from the back.

The man then rolled Lindsay's panties down as they were soaked with sweat from the heat and her exertion. Tears were streaming down Lindsay's face and dust from the concrete parking lot would blow upwards each time she exhaled with

142

her face pressed to one side on the paved surface. It was after midnight but the temperature was still hovering around ninety degrees and Lindsay could feel the grit from the hot parking lot sticking to her perspiration coated breasts and face. The exertion from her struggles against her attacker left her clothes soaked with sweat. Lindsay heard this man's belt buckle unsnap as her tormentor loosened the waist of his pants and slowly slid them downwards. Lindsay could not move with the mass of this man pressing her body into the unforgiving concrete surface. Lindsay could smell his pungent odor invade her nostrils. Lindsay then felt the sweaty bare flesh of this man she didn't know on her naked buttocks and she braced for what was to come next as the ultimate violation of a woman was at hand.

"How does that feel baby mama?" the man asked as he probed Lindsay's vaginal opening with one finger before his final assault was to begin.

"No," Lindsay said weakly.

"Get off her or I'll blow your motherfuckin head off!" a voice boomed out of nowhere.

The man turned and was looking down the barrel of a 9 millimeter semiautomatic pistol aimed squarely at his head in the hands of Latasha Cole. The man scrambled to his knees and Lindsay crawled away.

"Get your ass up and sit over there against that dumpster. Don't pull your pants up. Leave your hands where I can see them," Latasha said as she made her way over to Lindsay without taking her eyes off the man.

143

"Lindsay, you ok?" Latasha asked.

"He tried to rape me!" Lindsay said.

"I know. Did he?" Latasha said.

"No. You came just in time. He put his finger in me," Lindsay said through tears

"That sick motherfucka. Here take my phone and call 911. Tell them where we are and that I'm holding a man at gunpoint who tried to rape you so the police will know that I have a gun," Latasha said.

Within ten minutes the police arrived. Latasha raised her hands and placed her gun on the ground. To Lindsay's surprise, Latasha had a concealed weapons permit. An ambulance was dispatched and paramedics treated both Lindsay and the man at the scene for minor injuries. Lindsay had a cut on her chin plus scrapes on her hands and face. Lindsay had also called Tameka so she could take her home since her car would not start.

The women described what happened, but the man, Dr. Elton Fletcher, had a completely different story.

"Those two whores set me up and tried to rob me. They dance at a strip club down the street. I guess they use it to turn tricks and meet men. Well the blond one said both her and her friend would meet me here and do what I wanted. I guess her friend took too long getting here and when I asked her to do what we came here for, she started fighting me. Then her friend showed up with a gun. Then they cooked up this rape story," Dr. Fletcher said.

The detective told Lindsay and Latasha what the man said. They exploded with outrage. Then one of the police officers called the detective over to Lindsay's car and they squatted down behind the vehicle and with a small flashlight, they looked into the rear exhaust pipe of Lindsay's car. The detective called his photographer over to document what they found. Lindsay and Latasha were fascinated by what was going on behind the car.

Tameka finally drove up and ran over to where Lindsay was standing. As everyone looked on, the detective extended a slender device with a clamp on the end into the exhaust pipe of Lindsay's car. Using considerable force he pulled out a tightly wound roll of material. He stopped before he fully extracted it and allowed the photographer to take a series of photographs. He then pulled the material completely out of the pipe and placed it into an evidence collection bag. The detective then walked over to the Doctor and asked him if he knew what the material was and how it ended up in the exhaust pipe of Lindsay's car.

"I want to talk to my lawyer," was the reply from Dr. Fletcher.

The detective called Lindsay over to her car and told her to turn the ignition switch. The car engine started up normally. Lindsay and Latasha were told they could go home, but to be available if any questions came up and for possible trial testimony.

"I can't believe that shit. That guy was stalking you. He put that in your car because he

145

knew it would make it stop running. That gives me the creeps," Latasha said.

"Oh my God. I could have been killed tonight," Lindsay said.

Lindsay turned and hugged Latasha.

"Latasha. Thank you. Thank you. You saved my life," Lindsay said.

"Lindsay. I saw your car and that other one and knew something was wrong. Some people just think we're shit because we work in a strip club. I've got kids myself. I know what it's all about," Latasha said.

"I've got to get home. Take care of yourself Lindsay," Latasha said as she left.

"Let's get out of here before the police look in my car and see all of those kids asleep with not enough seat belts or car seats to go around" Tameka said.

Lindsay and Tameka followed each other back to their hotel and Tameka called in sick to work so that she could get some rest.

The next day Lindsay and Tameka realized that their lives had changed forever, but it takes more than a change of financial circumstances for someone to change their life, it takes a change of mind. Although their bank accounts said otherwise these two women still had the mindset of being perpetually broke and it would take some time for that to change.

The next day at the hotel Lindsay heard a knock on her door and it was Tameka and her children coming over for a visit.

"How are you feeling?" Tameka asked.

"I'm sore all over. I just can't believe that happened to me. It was my last night working there. What if Latasha hadn't come along? He could have killed me," Lindsay said.

"Latasha really surprised me. I don't even know how to use a gun," Tameka said.

"Latasha's pretty tough. She's older than we are and has been dancing a long time. I imagine she's run into some strange characters over the years. Like that guy last night. He's the one I got into that fight a couple of months ago in the VIP room. The idea of a doctor doing that is unbelievable. What a sick bastard," Lindsay said.

"I know you and Latasha didn't get along, but you owe that girl. You should do something nice for her," Tameka said.

"Yeah, I know. She saved my life. I'll think of something," Lindsay said.

"Are you really okay? You said he, you know, put his finger in you," Tameka asked.

"I'll be okay. It was such a helpless feeling to not be able to do anything to stop him, but it would have been much worse if it hadn't been for Latasha. I'm thankful that it didn't go any further than that. I'm good," Lindsay said.

"Thank God. So do you feel any different? I mean with the money you have now compared to before," Tameka asked Lindsay.

"No. I don't feel any different. Maybe it's because the only thing different is where I'm living. I still feel poor. Maybe when I actually buy something that I couldn't afford before, it'll start to sink in. My friend George gave me the name of a financial planner to make sure I don't get in trouble with taxes. I'm seeing him tomorrow. I've never had to even worry about stuff like this. I've always gotten tax refunds every year," Lindsay said.

"Yes, this friend George of yours, who I have never met," Tameka said with a smile.

"Well, I've never met your lawyer friend Calvin either," Lindsay reminded.

"Calvin is not my friend, strictly business, so what's the first thing you want to buy?" Tameka asked.

"A new car. I've never had a new car. I want a car that I can go anywhere in with my kids if I need to without worrying about it breaking down on the road," Lindsay said.

"Lindsay, you can do that now. You don't have to just think about it anymore," Tameka said.

"I guess you're right," Lindsay said when her telephone rang.

"Yeah George. What's up?" Lindsay asked.

"Yes, all of the money is there. Yes, I moved to an extended stay hotel until I find something else. What? Friday afternoon. Okay. Bye," Lindsay said as she ended the call.

"That was George. RJ Jefferson is holding a press conference this Friday at four in the afternoon to announce that he discovered he had a child that he didn't know about before. George said it will be all over social media and television. He also figured that the entertainment shows and websites will be all over it because his wife was in all of those rap videos. He said that he won't mention my name or Riley's," Lindsay said.

148

"Wow. Well, nobody's going to find out and not that many people know you're the mother of his child. You don't have anything to worry about," Tameka said.

Lindsay decided it was time to make her first major purchase and the next day she walked into a car dealership with Tameka and all of their children and bought a new car. It wasn't an expensive luxury brand, but she got a sporty crossover sports utility vehicle. She took Tameka with her because her father taught her how to negotiate when purchasing big ticket items. He told her to be prepared to walk away three times before making a deal and it came in handy in that instance.

Lindsay could hardly believe that she wrote a check for $35,000.00 when she bought her new car.

Friday came around and Lindsay and Tameka were glued to the television when RJ Jefferson held his press conference. He was standing at a podium behind a bank of microphones with his wife, Monica, standing by his side. His agent gave a brief setup to the session. RJ stepped up to the microphones and announced that he had recently discovered that he had a child as the result of a brief relationship in the past when he was in college. RJ stated that he wanted to disclose that information to his fans in the spirit of being honest with those who had supported him throughout the years. RJ also said out of respect for the privacy of the child and the mother there would not be a disclosure of their identities. Jefferson also assured his fans that he was stepping up to the responsibility for supporting his child in a proper manner. He then thanked his wife, sponsors and fans for their continued support and prayers. RJ Jefferson left the room without answering any of the many question shouted in his direction by the media.

"That's just great. He has a child that he doesn't even want to meet. He's such an arrogant asshole," Lindsay said.

"Lindsay, when are you going to tell Riley about his father?" Tameka asked.

"I almost don't know how to tell him," Lindsay said.

"Do you want me to take the rest of the children to my room so you can talk to Riley?" Tameka asked.

"Okay. He does need to know," Lindsay said with a tremble in her voice.

"Riley! Come here baby. Mama needs to talk to you," Lindsay called out to her son.

Tameka took the other children to her room to give Lindsay some privacy.

Riley was a bright and energetic child with a smooth cream colored skin tone, medium length brown curly hair and a bright smile.

"Riley sit down here on the couch on side of me," Lindsay said.

"Mama, why did everybody leave?" Riley asked.

"I needed to talk to you about something," Lindsay said.

"What do you want to talk to me about mama?" Riley asked.

"Well Riley, I want to talk to you about your daddy," Lindsay said.

Riley had a puzzled look on his face.

"My daddy, you never talked about my daddy before," Riley said.

"Well, you know you have a daddy didn't you?" Lindsay said.

"Yeah, I guess. Some of my friends at school talk about their daddies all the time," Riley said.

"Well you do have a daddy. His name is Riley Jefferson," Lindsay said.

"Riley. He has the same name as mine?" Riley said.

"Yes he does. I named you after your father, but everybody calls him RJ Jefferson," Lindsay said.

"RJ Jefferson is the same name as the football player for the Buffalos. You bought me a football jersey with his name on it," Riley said.

"That is your daddy. RJ Jefferson who plays football for the Oklahoma Buffalos is your father," Lindsay said.

Riley has a puzzled look on his face.

"RJ Jefferson is my daddy! How come I've never seen him?" Riley asked.

"Well he didn't know he was your daddy. He just found out a few days ago," Lindsay said.

"Is he coming to see me? Will he come and live with us," Riley asked.

"Well we're working on finding out when he can come see you. You know it's almost football season and he's real busy right now. Since he didn't know he was your daddy, he has another family already so he can't come live with us sweetie," Lindsay said.

"How come he didn't know he was my daddy?" Riley asked.

Lindsay was caught off guard by her son's question and had come up with an answer fast.

"Well, I met your daddy and by the time I found out you were coming, he was gone. I was just able to get hold of him to let him know about you with him playing football in California all those years," Lindsay said.

"Okay mama," Riley said.

"Riley. Why don't we try to keep this our little secret until we can get you and your daddy together to meet each other," Lindsay said.

"Okay mamma. Can I go over to Aunt Tameka's and play?" Riley asked.

"Yeah baby. You can go over to Aunt Tameka's and play," Lindsay said.

Lindsay walked Riley over to Tameka's door and watched him go inside. Lindsay then walked back over to her bed and fell across it face first sobbing with the knowledge that her son's father apparently wanted nothing to do with him.

15

Time moved on and Lindsay and Tameka were adjusting to their new reality. Lindsay found a four bedroom home in a quiet suburban neighborhood outside the city. For the first time since she had been on her own, Lindsay had a front yard, back yard and garage. Tameka and her children moved in with her, but it was just temporary as she had mapped out a shocking change of direction for her life. Tameka decided to move back home to east Texas and fulfill her father's desire for her to go to college. Tameka's parents were ecstatic at the prospect of having their grandchildren around and they would assist greatly in allowing Tameka to concentrate on her studies.

The two women were sad that they would part, but knew they would see each other often. They both realized their time of being perpetual roommates had to end at some point. It was now time for them to truly experience being on their own as adults. Tameka was moving out within two weeks so she could get her children enrolled in school before it started.

Lindsay had one more piece of unfinished business to complete before she could completely put her time at The Secret Island Club behind her. Lindsay pulled into the parking lot of The Secret Island and waited until she saw Latasha's car pull up. Latasha got out and Lindsay lowered her window and called to her. Latasha squinted and walked over to Lindsay's SUV.

"Lindsay, is that you?" Latasha asked.

"Yeah. Get in," Lindsay said.

Latasha opened the door and sat in the front passenger seat.

"This is nice. You seem to be doing well," Latasha remarked.

"I'm sorry. I've been so busy that I haven't had time to thank you for what you did for me that night," Lindsay said as she gave Latasha an envelope with a card inside.

"Don't worry about it," Latasha said as she opened the envelope.

The envelope contained a thank you card and when Latasha opened it, she gasped.

"Oh my God," Latasha said as she looked at a $10,000 cashiers' check with her name on it.

"How did you..." Latasha said before Lindsay cut her off.

"Don't ask. It's my thank you for what you did," Lindsay said.

"Thank you. That's all I know to say," Latasha said.

"That's all that's necessary," Lindsay said.

"You don't know what this do for my family," Latasha said as she hugged Lindsay.

"No, you just don't know what you did means to my family. It allowed my children to still have a mother. That's priceless. Good luck Latasha," Lindsay said.

Latasha got out of the vehicle and watched Lindsay drive away until she disappeared around a corner.

Two weeks passed by much too soon and Tameka was packed and ready to leave for east

Texas. Tears were flowing everywhere. This would be the first time their children would be apart except for the brief time spent at the hotel and even then they often spent the night with each other. Tameka's children didn't understand why they had to go and Lindsay's kids begged for them to stay. Their mothers were of little help because they were hugging each other while sobbing. Tameka loaded her children into the new sports utility vehicle she had purchased and pulled out of the driveway. When Tameka's vehicle disappeared from sight, Lindsay suddenly had the greatest feeling of loneliness she had felt since she first left her parents house as a pregnant teenager. It was then that she realized that she had developed almost no significant relationship connections outside of Tameka and their children. Now Lindsay needed to decide what she would do with the rest of her life.

Being financially secure was far different than Lindsay imagined. She didn't need to work, but she discovered that she missed the routine she had when she was dancing at The Secret Garden. That's when it struck Lindsay that the only thing she knew how to do well was exotic dancing. What kind of experience could she put on a resume if she needed to look for a job? Although Lindsay didn't need to work, a small wave of depression and insecurity swept over her when those thoughts of how limited she was entered her head.

Lindsay enrolled Riley in a new school and he was excited to start the third grade and make new friends. Riley rode the bus every day always had a tale to tell when he got home. Lindsay was home with her now four year old daughter Jasmine every day and they often went on excursions to different venues to pass the time. As much as she enjoyed her daughter's company, Lindsay was in need of some adult conversation.

While Lindsay was sitting at her table eating with Jasmine one morning her telephone rang and it was the detective that was at the scene the night she was attacked by the doctor after she left the club. It seems that he entered a guilty plea after being confronted with video footage from the club's parking lot security camera that captured him walking behind Lindsay's car and stuffing a roll of surgical gauze into its exhaust pipe. It seemed he had been planning how to get revenge on Lindsay for over two months from the time he had his conflict with her in the club. Lindsay thanked the detective for keeping her informed and reflected on that unbelievable episode in her life.

Lindsay put Jasmine down for a nap and went up front to watch television when her phone received an incoming call. It was the principle at Riley's school. Riley was being held in the principal's office for fighting with another boy. Lindsay was shocked. Lindsay couldn't believe that Riley was fighting because he had never been in trouble in school before. Lindsay got Jasmine and drove hurriedly to the school.

The principal of the school was a man by the name of Raymond Tate. Mr. Tate greeted Lindsay as she entered his office where Riley was seated in a chair in front of the principal's desk. Jasmine stayed in the front area with principal's administrative assistant and sat quietly on a couch playing with her favorite doll.

"Miss Wilson, it seems that Riley and another student got into a disagreement during recess and the other boy called Riley a liar. Well, Riley pushed him down and they were about to come to blows when their teacher intervened," Mr. Tate said.

"Riley what's gotten into you? Why did you push that boy down," Lindsay asked.

"He was telling me that his daddy was better than mine. He said his daddy could whip my daddy. I told him that his daddy couldn't beat my daddy because my daddy is RJ Jefferson and he plays football for the Oklahoma Buffalos. He called me a liar, so I pushed him. I'm sorry mama, you told me not to tell anybody," Riley said looking down at the floor.

The principal was a huge football fan and he sat there with his mouth open.

"Miss Wilson could you step in here for a moment with me?" Mr. Tate said.

"Sure," Lindsay said.

Lindsay and Mr. Tate stepped into a meeting room to the side of his office and closed the door.

"Miss Wilson. I follow sports closely. Last summer RJ Jefferson announced that he discovered that he had a child that he didn't know about. Is your son, whose name is Riley, the child he was talking about?" Mr. Tate asked.

Lindsay paused and swallowed.

"Yes sir. He's the child RJ Jefferson was talking about," Lindsay said.

"Miss Wilson, if that other boy tells his parents, and I know his parents, that your son said he is RJ Jefferson's kid, they will try to cash in on it. They're the kind of people that seek attention. Media types would descend on this school like flies on shit. Excuse my language ma'am. I'm sorry," Mr. Tate said.

"Don't worry about it. I've heard worse, so what are you saying? Do you want me to take my son out of the school?" Lindsay asked.

"No. I wouldn't ask that. We'll just keep an eye out and see if any problems develop from this. I just wanted to know so I can be alert and prepared. Thanks for coming down. You can go ahead and take Riley home and this stays between us," Mr. Tate said.

"Thank you," Lindsay said.

Lindsay left with a new motivation and was determined that something had to change.

16

Lindsay decided that it was time to force the issue of getting RJ Jefferson to visit his son as she had outlined in the settlement papers. Lindsay placed a call to George to get the message to Jefferson in no uncertain terms.

"Hello George. I need you to get a message to RJ Jefferson that I expect him to honor my request that he meets with his son. I told my son who his father is and he has to be wondering why he's never seen or talked to him. I had to go to school today because my son got in a fight defending this invisible daddy of his. I know he wrote a big check, but being a father is more than that," Lindsay said.

"I know I signed a confidentiality agreement, but that was about the rape charge, not about his attitude towards his own son. I don't think his fans and sponsors would appreciate the story of how their hero ignored his own flesh and blood after not knowing about him for years. If I don't hear from him soon, I might be willing to give up $2 million dollars for the sake of my son and pursue those statutory rape charges. I can't make him care about his son, but I'd rather RJ Jefferson show how little he cares in person instead of letting an eight year old boy swing in the wind. You can give them my cell number," Lindsay said.

"Thank you George," Lindsay said.

Lindsay assumed that the family of the boy involved in the brief scuffle with her son decided not to dig into whether Riley was the son a professional football superstar. Two days later Lindsay was preparing lunch when her cell phone rang. Lindsay picked up her phone and it displayed "blocked number" on the screen. Incoming calls from blocked numbers were not usually answered by Lindsay, but she decided to take that call.

"Hello," Lindsay answered.

"Hello. Is this Miss Wilson?" a man on asked.

"Yes. Who's this?" Lindsay asked.

"This is RJ Jefferson," the man said.

"Yes. May I help you?" Lindsay asked.

"Well, this seems a little awkward. Should I call you Lindsay or Miss Wilson?" RJ Jefferson asked.

"You can call me Lindsay. What should I call you?" Lindsay asked.

"RJ. Most people call me RJ," he said.

"Well. What is this about?" Lindsay asked.

"Look. I'd like to set up a time to meet your son. I mean my son," RJ said.

"You mean our son. When do you want to do this?" Lindsay asked.

"Well my team has a bye week next week so we're not playing. I could come to Dallas and we could meet somewhere. Would sometime next week work for you?" RJ asked.

"Well he goes to school during the week. Are you available next Saturday?" Lindsay asked.

"Yeah. I can do it next Saturday. Where would you want to meet, and when?" RJ asked.

"Well I don't want him to meet his father for the first time in some public place. People might

160

recognize you and cause a scene. You can meet Riley at my house at eleven in the morning. Will anyone else be with you?" Lindsay asked.

"No. I'm coming by myself. I don't think anyone else should be there. Don't you think that's the best way to handle our first meeting?" RJ asked.

"Yes. I appreciate that," Lindsay said.

"I'll see you next Saturday. I'm driving down from Oklahoma City. It's not a long trip. I'll call when I get close," RJ said.

"RJ, thanks for calling," Lindsay said.

"You're welcome, Lindsay. Bye," RJ said.

Lindsay placed her phone one the table and felt she just finished the strangest conversation of her lifetime. How could talking with someone that she shared a moment that created the life of her precious son be so foreign? It became very clear to Lindsay how little it takes to become the biological parent of a child. All it took for her to become a mother was being in the presence of an older man as a teenager under the influence of alcohol. She remembered nothing about the actual act that caused her pregnancy. Lindsay recalled meeting RJ at a party, drinking and leaving with him. The next thing she recalled was waking up the next morning in that apartment. Maybe that was why she had such a feeling of emptiness and disconnection towards RJ Jefferson. There were no memories, pictures or emotional connection between Lindsay and RJ Jefferson. Lindsay would be welcoming a stranger into her home the next Saturday and introduce him to her son as his father.

Lindsay decided that she would not tell her son about his father coming to visit until Saturday morning. She didn't want Riley to go to school all week with thoughts of the impending visit from his newly-discovered father on his mind.

Time seemed to fly by as Saturday approached. Lindsay suddenly found that she was concerned with how her home looked inside before RJ's visit. Lindsay didn't know why she was worried about the opinion he would have of her and her home, but she made sure everything was as presentable as possible, including herself. Saturday morning Lindsay told her son that his father was coming to visit him. Riley could barely contain his excitement. Lindsay got a call from RJ letting her know he was on his way. Lindsay decided to wear the blue outfit she wore to the law office when she first met George in downtown Dallas. Lindsay looked in the mirror and felt the she looked as good as she could. Riley was dressed in a new shirt, pants and shoes. Riley had a fresh haircut and Jasmine wore a new dress and had a fresh hairstyle that she got when she went to the beauty salon with her mother earlier in the week.

Lindsay's phone rang at five minutes past eleven o'clock and RJ Jefferson said he was pulling into the driveway. Lindsay hurried to open the door as to lessen the odds that a neighbor would recognize the famous football star before he came inside. Lindsay opened the door and RJ Jefferson stepped into her house. He towered over Lindsay and seemed much bigger than she remembered from the law office.

"Hi. Come on in and have a seat," Lindsay said.

"Thank you. You have a nice home here," RJ said.

"Riley's in the back. Do you want something to drink?" Lindsay asked.

"Do you have a bottle of water?" RJ asked as he sat down and placed a backpack on the floor.

"Yes. I'll get the water and Riley," Lindsay said.

"Wait. Before you bring him out, can we talk for a minute," RJ asked.

Lindsay came back with the water and sat on the couch next to RJ.

"What have you told him?" Riley asked.

"I told him that you were his father and that it was a something we should keep to ourselves until after he met you. Last week he got into an argument with another little boy at school who was bragging about how tough his dad was. Riley said his dad was tougher because he was RJ Jefferson and played for the Buffalos," Lindsay said.

"Oh. He was defending me. That sounds like something I did when I was in school. Has he asked why I never came to see him?" RJ asked.

"Yes, he did ask that. I told him that you didn't know about him and I had a hard time getting hold of you since you were in California. At his age I think that sounded reasonable," Lindsay said.

"I just wanted to know where his head was before I talked to him. I guess I'm ready," RJ said.

Lindsay went to a room down the hallway. She came back with Riley and Jasmine.

163

RJ was stunned when he saw Riley because he felt like he was looking into his own face. Riley eyes, nose and cheek bone structure seemed identical to his.

"Riley this is your father, RJ Jefferson," Lindsay said.

"Hello sir," Riley said as he walked over and shook RJ's hand

"Hello son," RJ said as he shook Riley's hand.

RJ then pulled Riley to him and hugged him tightly. RJ tried to maintain his composure, but the reality that he was holding his only child in his arms unleashed a wave of emotions. This mighty man was sobbing openly in front of someone he barely remembered although she was the mother of his child. This scene was having an effect on Lindsay also, and she gave RJ a hand full of facial tissue so he could dry his tears.

"I'm sorry. I didn't expect that to happen. Something came over me," RJ said looking somewhat embarrassed.

"Riley I brought something for you," RJ said as he pulled an autographed football out of the backpack he had brought into the house with him.

"Wow!" Riley said.

"Look you can't play with that ball. You just sit it on the dresser in your room. I brought you another one to play with. This is an official North America Football League ball. You can play with that ball all day long," RJ said.

"This is my daughter Jasmine," Lindsay said.

"Hi," Jasmine said.

"Hello Jasmine. I'm RJ. Nice to meet you," RJ said.

"We will leave you and Riley alone so you can get acquainted," Lindsay said as she took Jasmine to the kitchen.

"Let me show you my room," Riley said as he took RJ down the hallway.

RJ was stunned to see a life sized wall mounted figure of himself running with a football in his hand mounted on his son's wall.

"I watch you play football every Sunday," Riley said to his father.

Riley could hardly stop talking and telling his dad about everything he liked to do and the games he liked to play.

After an hour RJ started to smell a familiar scent coming from the kitchen. He told Riley they should go up front. They walked into the kitchen area.

"Is that what I think I smell?" RJ asked.

"What do you mean? Oh, I'm cooking collard greens, fried chicken and sweet potatoes," Lindsay said.

"Really?" RJ said.

Lindsay looked at him.

"What. So you're surprised a white girl can cook that kind of food. Well, my friend's mother taught me how to cook like this when I lived with them for a while," Lindsay said.

That statement stuck with RJ, but he decided this was not the time to pursue the questions he had on his mind.

"My mother cooks like that, but I usually only get it when I visit them back home," RJ said.

"Would you like to have lunch with your son and us before you have to get back on the road?" Lindsay asked.

"Well since you asked. Sure," RJ said.

This fractured family soon sat down to eat with a strange mixture of shallow comments and small talk. RJ complemented Lindsay on the food and she realized this was the first man that had sat around her table and eaten a meal in years. After they finished eating, Riley and Jasmine went into the back yard and played with his new football. RJ and Lindsay were still sitting at the table so they could watch the children through the glass patio doors.

"Riley is a good kid. He's smart and respectful. You've done a good job with him," RJ said.

"Thank you. I did the best I could," Lindsay said.

"You said something, and it's none of my business if you don't want to tell me, but you said your friend's mother taught you how to cook when you lived with them? Why were you living with your friend's family?" RJ asked.

"Well I don't mind telling you what happened. I think it would be good for you to know. After I got pregnant with Riley, I told my father it was by a black man and he went ballistic. My whole family turned their backs on me. They called me awful names. My own father called me a nigger lover. They tried to send me to live with my aunt in

166

Houston so they wouldn't be embarrassed. I didn't want to go to a strange place for my last year of school. I asked my best friend, who is black, if I could move in with her family. Her parents took me in and treated me like I was their own daughter. I stayed there until after I had Riley and moved up here," Lindsay said.

RJ did not quite know what to say because he knew he played a major role in what happened to Lindsay even if he didn't realize it.

"I had no idea that happened to you. I really don't know what to say, except I'm sorry," RJ said.

"Didn't you ever think about what could have happened to me? I mean you didn't know me. I don't even remember everything that happened that night. It even feels weird talking to you about this because you were there, but it's like I'm telling this to a stranger. You obviously didn't use any protection when we had sex. Did you think I was using birth control? I just don't understand why you did that. Look at what happened," Lindsay said.

"It's hard for me to look at myself the way you just put it. I was an immature, selfish guy back then. I only thought about what I wanted and didn't consider the consequences and how others might get hurt. I told my dad about what happened with me, you and our son and he was so disappointed about how everything turned out. I told him about how I walked out of the lawyer's office and he said that just writing a check doesn't cut it. He said that a man has an obligation to be involved with children they bring into this world, regardless of the circumstances. I stewed over it for a while. Then

167

my father told me that if he had a grandchild out there in the world, that child deserved a whole family experience even if his parents were not together," RJ said.

"Well you're not going to disappear from Riley's life are you? Since he knows who is father is and has met you, I don't want him to be holding on to the memories of one brief meeting," Lindsay said.

"No. I'm not going to disappear, but I do have a few complicating factors I have to deal with," RJ said.

"What do you mean?" Lindsay said.

"I have to deal with my wife's feelings about my relationship with Riley becoming a threat to her," RJ said.

"How does you getting to know and spending time with your son become a threat to her?" Lindsay asked.

"Well before I knew I had a son, she had all of my attention. She feels a little insecure about me splitting my attention with someone else," RJ said.

"But, he's your son and you didn't plan this," Lindsay said.

"My son also has a mother and that means I have a connection with another woman that gave me something that she hasn't, a child," RJ said.

"We don't have any kind of relationship. If it wasn't for Riley, we would not even have a reason to cross paths. Why would she be worried about me?" Lindsay asked.

"Have you looked in the mirror lately?" RJ asked.

Lindsay was stunned by his statement and had no reply. Lindsay knew that RJ's wife didn't know what she looked like, so she was not sure what he meant by his comment.

"It's getting late. I'm going outside and throw the ball around with the kids and then I've got to head back home. Here's a phone number that you or Riley can call me on if anything comes up that you think I should know about or if Riley wants to just talk to me," RJ said as he gave Lindsay a piece of paper and went outside.

Lindsay took the phone number before turning and watching her son and daughter tackle a superstar running back as they hung on to his legs as he slowly fell to the ground. Lindsay had to snap back to reality as she caught a vision of what her life might have been if circumstances were different. A man of the house, her children and her as a wife with the perfect family, but that was a fairy tale. Lindsay lived in reality. The man playing with her children was a major reason her life imploded as a teenager and led to years of heartache and struggle. She was tied to RJ Jefferson for life because each time she looked at her son she saw him.

Within an hour RJ said goodbye to his son for the first time. Riley was not happy to see him leave and asked when he would be coming back to visit. RJ didn't have a good answer and told Riley that he would be back as soon as he could. Riley hugged his father tight and watched out of a window until his vehicle disappeared from view as he left the neighborhood. Riley walked over to his mother and she gave her son a warm embrace. Riley went to his room and stared at the autographed football his father gave him. This was the first thing Riley had received from his father and he planned to keep it as long as he could.

17

Lindsay was watching a national morning talk show when she saw a segment that caught her interest. A woman was featured as a guest and she was talking about pole dancing as a way for women to add spice to their love lives in their own homes. This subject sparked an idea inside Lindsay's mind and she drank in every word this woman said. Lindsay also decided to go to her computer and do a search on pole dancing classes in her area and she was shocked by the results that came back. Lindsay was not a computer wizard, but had become more computer literate after taking a class that was offered at her local library some time ago. As Lindsay searched the internet she discovered that there was not a major national presence in pole dancing instruction or in-home video training. Lindsay had an idea that she didn't really know how to execute.

Lindsay saw what the woman on the show was doing and felt she could do the same thing, only better. Suddenly Lindsay went from having little direction in her day to day life to trying to figure out to turn this new idea she had into a business venture. Lindsay realized she had very little business acumen and a wave of frustration washed over her. After two days of this idea eating at her, Lindsay called Robert and told him what she was thinking about. Robert told her to write her ideas down and document why anyone would take her seriously as an authority in pole dancing. Lindsay also decided she needed something different. Lindsay decided she would combine pole dancing with a fitness routine and call it Strippercise. Now all Lindsay needed was a way to put everything together and figure out how to market her idea.

Lindsay grabbed her purse and found a business card in the bottom. The card was for Masters Marketing, Inc. and the name on the card was Ronald Masters. This was the business card a man gave her in the elevator in Dallas when she was meeting with her brother-in-law at his office. Lindsay decided she would call Ronald Masters and set up an appointment to discuss her idea with him.

Trying to work on this project would take time and concentration. Lindsay decided it would be a good time to put her daughter Jasmine into a preschool program. Jasmine needed to interact with other children her own age and that had been missing since Tameka and her children moved away. Lindsay found a suitable preschool for Jasmine and felt it would allow both of them to have a little more independence.

Lindsay called Ronald Masters and reminded him of how they met. When Lindsay described what she was wearing when they first met, Ronald's memory suddenly improved and he recalled Lindsay vividly. Ronald made an appointment for Lindsay to come meet with him much sooner than Lindsay expected.

When Lindsay met with Ronald Masters, she outlined what she was thinking about and he just sat and thought for a moment before he spoke.

"So, your idea is to become the Pied Piper of pole dancing aerobics videos?" Ronald said.

"Well, I guess you could say that. I saw a woman discussing and demonstrating pole dancing on television as a way for women to put a little spark back into their relationships," Lindsay said.

"Why would they listen to you? What gives you credibility in the area of pole dancing?" Ronald asked.

"I figured you might ask that, so I made this demonstration video and had it transferred to a memory stick. Do you have a computer to play it on?" Lindsay asked.

Lindsay was dead serious about this project and she went back to The Secret Island and Jacob allowed her to use the club to make her video. Lindsay hired a videographer to record the session. Lindsay had not performed her routine in a while, but she had no trouble getting into form after a few minutes. Unlike her regular show, Lindsay did not strip down to full nakedness, but wore a tight spandex top and shorts under her top layer of clothing.

"Sure," Ronald said as he took the memory stick.

There was a 60-inch high definition smart television mounted on the wall of Ronald's office and he inserted the memory stick into into a USB port on the side. Ronald pressed a button on a remote and the music accompanying Lindsay's dance begin to play. Lindsay appeared on the screen in one of her dance costumes and she began to dance and move around the stage. Ronald was fixated as he watched this woman sitting across from him prance, entice and grind her way across the stage. Lindsay then began to work around the pole and mounted it with her handstand move. Lindsay swung around, hung upside down and slid down the pole onto the floor. Lindsay wore her six-inch heels in the video. Ronald shifted in his seat and was transfixed on the screen. Lindsay's dance ended with her crawling across the stage towards the camera and pouting her red lips in a kiss pose before fading to black.

"I was the featured dancer at one of the top gentleman's clubs in Dallas for several years," Lindsay said.

"You certainly seem to be very skilled at what you do or did in the area of pole dancing. Just how would you combine this with your exercise angle to make it a little more mainstream?" Ronald asked.

"Well I've looked into that. I could become a certified personal trainer by taking a class online. I figured if I got that certification, then I could call myself an exotic dance instructor and certified personal trainer. I think that would keep people from saying I was just some ex-stripper," Lindsay said.

Ronald was starting to become more interested in Lindsay's idea as a serious business opportunity.

"Okay. You can dance like that, but how are you going to teach some housewife with two left feet how to do what you did in that video? Ronald asked.

"Well I've thought about that. There aren't any rules for exotic dancing. I can name the moves I do anything I want. I looked at my video and took each move I did and gave it a name. I mean something as simple as how to walk towards a man. How you should point your toes and other details. Even how a woman should point her butt out when she wants to entice her partner. How to grab the pole and swing around it in a seductive way. I figure I should have a basic, intermediate and advanced lesson set so that every woman can reach her own potential," Lindsay said.

Ronald rubbed his chin.

"Something like this could be expensive. How would you fund it?" Ronald asked.

"I won't have a problem with that, but I want to find out what it would cost to put together a video instruction set. You know like all of those exercise programs I see sold on television late at night," Lindsay said.

"I have some contacts that are involved in video production, packaging and fulfillment. They can give me some direction in that area," Ronald said.

"Fulfillment, what does that mean?" Lindsay asked.

"Well, fulfillment means handling getting the product that customers order packed and shipped out. The last part would be collecting the money paid for the product," Ronald said.

"Could you ask your contacts what they think something like this would cost?" Lindsay asked.

"Sure," Ronald said.

"What do I owe you?" Lindsay asked.

"This was just an initial consultation. If we enter into an agreement, we can discuss a fee schedule then. Maybe we can meet for a business dinner next time," Ronald said.

"Well, I don't know. I would have to find someone to keep my kids if I met you for dinner. Let's just meet here in your office, if that's okay with you," Lindsay said.

Lindsay got up from the table and left Ronald's office. She thought it was strange that he didn't get up to walk her out. Ronald wanted to walk Lindsay out, but he didn't want her to notice his state of excitement over something that went beyond a pure business opportunity.

Lindsay selected a course to become a certified personal trainer and she actually felt a sense of pride when she enrolled in a class for the first time since leaving high school, even if it was online. Lindsay felt like she was resuming her personal development that was unexpectedly interrupted years ago when she became pregnant and her life took a drastic change in direction.

Lindsay was driving home from class when she had a phone call. Lindsay answered and was surprised at the voice on the other end of the call.

"This is RJ. How are you?" he asked.

"I'm fine. How about you?" Lindsay asked.

"I'm fine. How is Riley doing?" RJ asked.

"I guess you could call him and find out for yourself," Lindsay replied.

"Look, I'm sorry about that. I'll call him tonight. I was calling to ask if it was okay to invite you, Riley and your daughter to our game this weekend in Dallas. I thought he might enjoy coming and I can see him after the game. He can even come to the locker room after the game and meet some of the other players," RJ said.

"Are you serious?! He would love that. Sure we can come," Lindsay said.

"I will overnight the tickets and parking passes. You should get them tomorrow," RJ said.

"Let me ask you something. Will your wife be there?" Lindsay asked.

"Yeah, she comes to every home game and this one since it is so close," RJ said.

"How does she feel about Riley? I don't want him to feel uncomfortable or anything," Lindsay said.

"She's fine. I already told her that he would be coming to the game. It's time for everyone to know who my son is, are you okay with that because it will put your name and face out there as well?" RJ asked.

"Look, I can handle whatever comes my way. I'm worried about my son. I think he will feel so much better to be able to tell someone who his father is without them thinking he is lying to them. It's like he is some kind of dirty little secret and he won't have to feel that way anymore," Lindsay said.

"I've been thinking about that too. That's too much for a kid to be carrying around. Alright, I'll send the tickets and someone will call you before the game on how we will bring Riley to the locker room. That's for letting him come to the game," RJ said.

"He'll love it. He's crazy about football and his daddy," Lindsay said.

"I'm still getting used to that. I'll talk to you later," RJ said.

Lindsay told Riley that he would be going to see his father play football against the Dallas Posse and he could barely contain himself. Riley always wanted to attend a live professional football game and to be able to see his own father play was beyond belief. Game day could not come fast enough for Riley, but Lindsay had other things on her mind.

Ronald had called Lindsay and told her that he had set up a meeting with a video production firm at his office and wanted Lindsay to meet with them. Lindsay was very excited about moving to step two in bringing her idea to fruition. The Friday before she was to take her family to the football game, Lindsay met with the production company and they outlined a potential plan for her video and told her it would be good to create a sample to see how it played out. They also informed Lindsay that what she said to her target customers was just as important as what she showed them. Their suggestion was for Lindsay to use a script writer and public speaking coach to develop her product pitch. Lindsay realized that she was selling herself even more than her product. Then Ronald asked Lindsay a question she didn't expect.

"Lindsay what will you tell the women that you want to buy your videos that will make them pick up the telephone or go online and order your product?" Ronald asked.

"I guess I'll tell them that I will show them how to put more excitement in their love life at home," Lindsay said.

"No. That's boring. You have to say something like this. I'm the woman your men have been staying away from home for and throwing money at while you sit there alone. Let me show you how to do what I do and keep your man away from me and at home with you," Ronald said.

Lindsay sat back in her seat a little taken aback. Lindsay became a stripper to make ends meet and was not a particularly bold or boastful person. She felt that she was very good at what she did but Lindsay never thought of it in the terms that Ronald just outlined.

"So you think that is way I need to talk to make this work?" Lindsay asked.

"Look Lindsay, you are trying to give these women a reason to act. I saw your video. You're not famous with a built in fan base so you have to be in their faces with a message that makes them say yes, that's what I want. You have to be the magician that is giving away the secrets to your customers. Imagine that you were spinning around the pole and stepped down onto the stage and said something like I just did. They would be hooked, then you introduce yourself, embrace your resume as an exotic dancer and throw in the personal trainer certification and sell, sell, sell," Ronald said.

"I guess I could do that. I just never thought about what I would say. I was just thinking about how I could do those moves better than the woman I saw on television," Lindsay said.

"I know, but thousands of dancers are better than she is, but she was the one on national television. I think you have one hell of an idea, but how you present it will make or break it. You have to embrace that you are, pardon my words, the baddest bitch on the planet and will share your secrets with other women, for a small fee with shipping and handling, of course. You will be the person that turns soccer moms, businesswomen and housewives into private dancers in their own bedrooms at night. It's acting. That's all it is. Can you do that?" Ronald asked.

"Well yeah. I think I can do that. I was acting on that stage for years, pretending I was having a great time with all those men looking at me getting naked every night. It was what I had to do to survive. I guess I can do it now and keep my clothes on," Lindsay said.

Lindsay was set to start her project by first working with a script writer and public speaking coach. The next step would be to shoot a pilot video. Lindsay felt her first doubts about being able to pull off her video concept. Lindsay had no reservations about being able to perform all of the physical moves required for her video, but public speaking and talking were not her strong suit. Insecurities about everything from her education, southern accent and vocabulary all seemed to jump out at Lindsay at once. Lindsay didn't have to say anything when she was dancing because none of the men came in to hear her talk, now she had to talk women into wanting to see her dance and learn how to do the same thing

Lindsay suddenly had a full schedule to deal with involving her children, new business venture and the game that was coming up on Sunday.

18

Sunday seemed to rush up on Lindsay and she was loading her children into the car to go to the game. Riley could barely contain himself and was dressed in a football jersey with his father's name and number on the back. Lindsay decided to dress in comfortable denim clothing, but her hair and makeup were impeccable.

As she drove to the game, the huge stadium began to loom in the distance. Lindsay arrived early enough to avoid much of the traffic that would come closer to kickoff time. This was a new experience for Lindsay and her children. They walked towards the stadium past many groups involved in tailgating at an extreme level. It was obvious to Lindsay that the fans with their smokers, music and flat screen televisions outside the stadium did this regularly. Given her prior struggles in life, this was a scene that was foreign to Lindsay and she thought about how different her life was before that moment.

Riley was in awe and taking in every sight, sound and scent. Jasmine could have cared less and would have rather stayed at home. Once inside the stadium, Lindsay loaded up on soda, nachos and whatever her children wanted before they found their seats midway in the first section on the fifty yard line behind the Buffalos bench. The stadium soon filled to capacity. Music, cheerleaders and screaming fans made for a smorgasbord for the senses. Game time approached and it was time for player introductions. The visiting Buffalos' offense was introduced first. Riley stood and screamed when the stadium announcer called out the name of RJ Jefferson as the starting running back for Oklahoma.

The game started and it was much different than watching it on television. Every play seemed to move at twice the speed. It was actually much more difficult to follow than Lindsay imagined. Then during the second quarter Jasmine said something that puzzled Lindsay.

"Mommy, look you're on the big TV," Jasmine said while pointing upward.

"Jasmine what are you talking about" Lindsay asked.

"Look mommy," Jasmine said while pointing.

Lindsay looked up and saw her face on the largest television screen she had ever seen. The huge television monitor that was suspended over the field showed Lindsay and her children for everyone to see. Lindsay managed to crack a nervous smile, but she didn't realize that the same image was also on television screens nationwide along with some commentary she didn't know about from one of the announcers.

Lindsay's phone vibrated as a text message came in from Tameka.

"Lindsay what are you doing on national television? The announcer just said look at that beautiful woman. She's the mother of RJ Jefferson's son," Tameka's message read.

Lindsay was horrified. That was the last thing she expected or wanted to happen. Suddenly

Lindsay noticed a few fans seated close to her pulling out their cell phones and taking pictures of her. Luckily only a few people knew what was said on the national broadcast feed and she was able to watch the rest of the game in peace. In the end Oklahoma won the game and ten minutes before the contest ended a representative from the Buffalos came to Lindsay's seating area and took them to an a location near the locker room to wait for the team to enter so that Riley could wait on his father.

Before long the entire Oklahoma team came into the tunnel leading to the visiting team's dressing room area. RJ came over to Riley.

"You ready to go into the dressing room and meet the team?" RJ asked.

"Yeah!" Riley replied enthusiastically.

"I won't keep him too long," RJ told Lindsay.

"Okay," Lindsay said while sitting on the seat of a golf cart used to usher guests around the stadium with Jasmine leaning against her while sound asleep from being exhausted by all of the activity of the day.

"How are you doing?" a female voice asked Lindsay from behind.

Lindsay turned to see a very attractive black woman about twenty-six years old standing alongside the golf cart.

"I'm doing fine. Do I know you?" Lindsay asked.

"No, but you know my husband. I'm Monica Jefferson, RJ Jefferson's wife and I assume you're his baby mama," Monica said.

184

"I'm Lindsay and yes, RJ Jefferson is the father of my son, but I assume he told you about that before he told the world," Lindsay replied.

"Yes, he told me, but he didn't tell me anything about you," Monica said.

"It's up to your husband to tell you any details about me and my son, but I'm only here so my son can get to know his father and that's it," Lindsay said.

"Yeah. I guess that's why you arranged to get your face on nationwide television and embarrass me in front of the whole country. Everybody was texting me about how ratchet a move that was. Classic thot shit. Don't get it twisted bitch. That's my man and you better back the fuck off!" Monica said as she walked away to the other side of the tunnel.

Lindsay was stunned by the misplaced aggression displayed by RJ Jefferson's wife, Monica. Lindsay could easily see why RJ was attracted to Monica as she was a beautiful woman. Her skin was as smooth as cocoa butter with a rich medium brown skin tone. It was also easy to determine why she called herself Super Stacked during her days as a video dancer. Lindsay figured that she and Monica were about the same height, but Monica definitely had her beat in the area of bust and hip proportions. Monica Jefferson was not obese, but she was extremely solid from her shapely legs, protruding buttocks, slim waist and what Lindsay guessed to be a 38DD sized bust line. Her hair was straight and fell back to her shoulders with a crisp even straight cut. Lindsay also made note of her enormous diamond wedding ring set along with diamond stud earrings.

Five minutes later RJ walked out with Riley and he seemed surprised to see his wife, Monica standing there. He said goodbye to Riley and then Monica walked up to him and kissed him as deeply as she could in order to show Lindsay who this man belonged to. Monica then walked off with a parting glance towards Lindsay as she left. RJ looked at Monica and looked at Lindsay with a puzzled look on his face. He then walked over to Lindsay.

"I assume that you met my wife?" RJ said.

"Yes, I did," Lindsay said.

"And?" RJ said.

"My face was shown during the game on national television and the announcer told the world that I was the mother of your son," Lindsay said.

"What! How did they even know who you were or where you were sitting?" RJ said.

"Well, your wife thinks I did it to embarrass her for some reason," Lindsay said.

"Lindsay, I'm sorry. Somebody must have tipped off the press. I'm going to find out how this happened," RJ said.

"Don't worry about it. Thanks for the tickets and for taking Riley to the dressing room. We've got to get going," Lindsay said as she walked off with her children.

Riley turned around and waved goodbye to his father who just stood there as they walked away.

Lindsay was much too busy to become distracted by what took place at the football game. She continued to work on her video project and was set to meet with her script writer and public speaking coach. Lindsay had worked hard to break her dance routines into separate steps so she could teach viewers how to master each move before putting them together for a complete routine. Since her dance routine had been broken down individually, she gave each one a name and that would allow her script to be developed around each section of her instruction video.

Developing the script was not as difficult as Lindsay imagined. She actually performed each dance move to give the script writers a visual representation of what she was trying to impart to viewers. The difficult aspect of the project for Lindsay was learning to naturally deliver her script while performing the moves. Lindsay found that she was starting from scratch in learning how to speak to an audience that was unknown and unseen. Breaking bad verbal habits and projection were real challenges for Lindsay. The best thing about shooting a video was the fact that it could be shot in segments and edited together for the final product. Lindsay could work to perfect each section without being concerned about doing a flawless execution of the entire presentation.

Near the end of a hectic week of preparation for a shoot of her pilot dance video, Lindsay got a call from Tameka.

"Lindsay, what the hell is going on with you and RJ Jefferson's wife?" Tameka asked.

"Tameka, what are you talking about? There's nothing going on between us. I've only seen her one time and that was at the football game we went to here in Dallas. She came up to me, but that was only for a few minutes," Lindsay replied.

"Well she thinks that you guys have beef between you, because your face and hers is all over Blast magazine, those grocery store newspapers near the checkout counters and she's going fucking ham online," Tameka said.

"What! Are you fucking with me?" Lindsay replied.

"No. It's ugly and has big headlines about baby mama drama. Search her name online and see for yourself. It sounds like that bitch set you up. You need to handle your business with that video ho. You know I've got your back. Oklahoma's not that far. I'll go up there with you and we can beat the weave off her ass," Tameka said before she hung up.

Lindsay did as Tameka suggested and searched for Monica's name online and articles popped up immediately with reference to RJ Jefferson's baby mama situation. Lindsay rushed to the nearest supermarket and went to a checkout counter. Lindsay looked to her left and almost lost her breath. Staring back at her was an image of her face from the football game. Lindsay grabbed the tabloid and looked at the cover. In one corner there was an image contained within a circle with a far off shot of her talking to RJ Jefferson's wife in the tunnel leading to the visiting team's dressing room. The title above Lindsay's photo read RJ Jefferson's Baby Mama Drama. Lindsay placed the tabloid newspaper on the checkout counter. The grocery checkout clerk glanced up at Lindsay as she scanned the barcode of the gossip newspaper and Lindsay smiled.

Lindsay went home after she picked Jasmine up from preschool and read the article. The article was very shallow and seemed to be aimed at insinuating that drama existed between Lindsay and RJ Jefferson's wife. The brief meeting between Lindsay and Monica was portrayed as some kind of grand confrontation.

Lindsay was furious and felt she was being used as a pawn to gain attention by someone wanting the spotlight to shine on them again. Lindsay immediately felt that the encounter she had with Monica Jefferson was staged in order to generate publicity for the one time music video dancer. Maybe being in the background as the wife of a superstar athlete wasn't enough for Monica and she saw manufacturing this fake beef between them was what she needed to get her name back in play. Lindsay decided she was not going to be used again for someone else's selfish purposes and would put a stop to it as soon as possible.

Lindsay grabbed her cell phone and pressed a stored number.

"Hello. This is RJ," a male voice answered.

"RJ this is Lindsay. I went online and saw all kind of articles about your wife talking about your son's mother. Then I went to the supermarket and saw my face on some trashy gossip newspaper with the words baby mama splashed across the top, plus the story was written like I had some kind of conflict with your wife. I don't even know her, but a picture of when she came over to me at the game

189

was on the cover. What's up with that? Was I set up so she could gain some attention? Were you in on this with her? I mean I wasn't even going to that game until you called. You didn't set me up did you?" Lindsay asked.

"Lindsay I swear I had nothing to do with that. I asked Monica about what happened and we got in a huge fight about it. I wanted you to come to the game so I could spend some time with Riley and that's it. Monica found the tickets and called our public relations department and pretended that she was involved in getting you to the game. She also tipped the press off on who you were and where you were sitting, that's why the network knew where to find you. Look, I apologize for my wife's behavior," RJ said.

"That bitch! Why did she do that?" Lindsay said.

"Lindsay calm down. Monica is my wife, let's keep it respectful. This won't happen again," RJ said.

"So being the wife of a wealthy football star isn't enough for her. She decided to use me and my son to get some attention. What happened between us had nothing to do with her. I'm sorry, I've got to go!" Lindsay said as she hung up.

Lindsay decided that she was going to put all of her anger and energy into her video project and not allow Monica Jefferson to knock her off course. The production work on her video was coming along and Lindsay would soon finish her online personal trainer certification. Lindsay shot her demonstration video and one week later she

190

viewed the finished product. It was difficult for Lindsay to believe she was watching herself speak with confidence about what she believed in. By the time the video was finished, Lindsay was near tears. She never believed that she could pull off something like that given where she was in life a few months ago. Lindsay and her team made plans to shoot the final video. The production video would be shot over two weeks and would include a studio audience and three women of various ages that would serve as testimonial users of Lindsay's dance techniques along with their husbands. The women that would be involved in Lindsay's videos were taught various dance techniques by Lindsay and tried them out on their spouses.

Lindsay completed the final shoot of her video and proceeded to get an initial production run of final product completed. Lindsay also shot a commercial that would run on television late at night on cable and many of the over the air digital television channels. Orders for Lindsay's Strippercise videos would be taken over a 1-800 number that would be answered by work at home agents and the products would be ordered, billed and shipped with Lindsay's revenue share going straight into a business checking account. Lindsay Wilson had transitioned from an exotic dancer into a businesswoman within a few short months.

While Lindsay was pulling her video project together, RJ Jefferson had led his team to the Ultrabowl and he wanted his son to see him play his final professional football game. The Ultrabowl would be played in New Orleans and RJ sent tickets for Lindsay, Riley and Jasmine to attend. Lindsay decided that Jasmine would stay in Dallas with her father's parents and she invited her sister Karen to go to the game with her instead.

The game would take place in two weeks and Lindsay's commercial for her video would begin running at midnight ten days before the game. It was very late on a Thursday night and Lindsay was watching one of the digital over the air sub channels attached to one of the major networks' local affiliates.

Lindsay's infommercial was a thirty minute piece and she could hardly believe her eyes when the familiar introduction scene came onto the television screen. The introduction to Lindsay's video featured a man throwing money at the silhouette of a dancer on a stage swinging around a pole and it had a split screen of his wife at home staring at a door while checking her watch. The next scene showed the man walking through the door and an argument ensued. In the midst of the argument Lindsay stepped between the two and separated them.

"Hi I'm Lindsay W, and I'm the woman your husband was throwing money at when he was at the strip club instead of being here with you at home. I want to show you how to stop wondering why he is coming to see me instead of coming home to you. I'm going to teach you how to make him drive right by that gentleman's club and rush home by showing you how to do what I did to make him come into the club in the first place. When you finish Lindsay W's Strippercise video instruction, he will have no reason to see any woman dance except you in the privacy of your own home," Lindsay said.

The next frame of the commercial showed Lindsay in her studio with an audience and a dance floor with a pole. Lindsay then introduced herself and proceeded with her pitch, demonstration and customer testimonials. As she closed, Lindsay did a handstand mount onto the pole and ended with the words, 'Call now and change your love life forever!"

Lindsay could hardly contain her excitement. This was one of the first things that she had done on her own terms since becoming pregnant with her son. Her telephone lit up with congratulatory text messages from Tameka, her sister and from her friend Robert. As proud as she was to make it this far with her project, Lindsay knew it would be a waiting game to see how well her presentation translated into product sales.

The next day Lindsay was channel surfing and she stopped on a channel that featured material about the music and entertainment industry. To her surprise Monica Jefferson was sitting on a couch with the host of a hip hop talk show. He asked Monica how it felt to have her husband playing for the professional football championship and she gave a fairly mundane answer. The host then asked Monica how she was dealing with the public unveiling of her husband's baby's mama on national television. Monica's answer stunned Lindsay.

"You can always tell when someone comes crawling out of the background trying to come up on somebody else's fame. I'm not denying that she is the mother of his child, but where was she all of these years? Now that RJ is famous, she suddenly shows up. I'm not worried about some gold digger trying to upstage me. That move she made shows how classless and desperate some people can get. I heard she might have been a stripper or something but I don't know that for a fact," Monica said.

Lindsay was furious and could not believe the nerve of this woman. Monica had created the entire conflict with Lindsay out of thin air and was having an imaginary fight with herself, but Lindsay decided that things needed to become very real for the former video dancer.

Karen drove up from Houston to stay with Lindsay for a few days before they left for New Orleans.

"So what's going on between you and RJ Jefferson's wife?" Karen asked.

"Nothing's going on. I've only seen her one time and the next thing I know she's out there saying we have some kind of drama going on between us. She was even on television calling me a gold digger," Lindsay said.

"What's her deal? Is she crazy or does she really think you're coming after her husband?" Karen said.

"I think she misses the attention she was getting when she was doing those rap videos. Maybe she's trying to get her name out there again so she can get a reality show or something, but she's not going to do it by using me. I've got something for her," Lindsay said.

"What about you, are you dating anybody?" Karen asked.

"No. I don't have time for that. Ive been too busy," Lindsay said.

"Come on. You've got to be getting some from somebody," Karen said.

"Karen, it's not easy. I've got two kids. I'm not bringing some strange man around them and with Tameka being gone I don't have someone I can trust to watch them if I even wanted to go out," Lindsay said.

"So what do you do to relieve that tension? Do you have a few toys at least?" Karen asked.

"Karen you're crazy. Yes, I have a few personal assistants, ok," Lindsay replied.

"Well good. I thought that maybe you were becoming a nun or something," Karen said.

"Men try to talk to me, but most of them just want one thing and I'm tired of that. I would love to meet someone that isn't just trying to get into my panties," Lindsay said.

"Have you looked in the mirror lately? Look at yourself. Nothing but ass and titties in tight clothes," Karen said.

"Well what do you want me to do, get rid of them? If I got a big ass and titties, it's not my fault," Lindsay said.

"I know, but maybe you could wear clothes that will kind of cover them up a little. With all of those tight outfits the first thing any man notices is your body and he can't get past it to see the person behind the body. Of course I don't have that problem with my flat ass and chest. That's why I got my lips done. Can't you tell they look fuller?" Karen asked.

"Yeah, I did notice your lips. I thought that maybe you and George had a fight or something," Lindsay said.

"Real funny. He thinks he's king shit now since he settled your case with RJ Jefferson. All of a sudden he's the defender of the rights of single women with paternity issues. Every high profile baby mama versus baby daddy case that comes in lands on his desk," Karen said.

"Are you two doing alright in your marriage?" Lindsay asked.

"Yeah we're doing alright. We had a long discussion and decided we would try to stay together, plus, I'm pregnant," Karen said.

"What! Why haven't you said anything?" Lindsay asked.

"George doesn't know it yet," Karen said.

"Why haven't you told him?" Lindsay asked.

"It may not be his," Karen said.

"What do you mean by it may not be his?!" Lindsay asked.

"Well George got focused on career climbing and I did confirm he was fucking that bisexual bitch of a boss of his. Since he was so preoccupied, I met somebody. I was out shopping one day and this guy approached me and asked me to have lunch with him," Karen said.

"And you just went to lunch with him?" Lindsay quizzed.

"His name was Austin. He was twenty-three years old and had the most beautiful smile and blue eyes. He found me fascinating," Karen said.

"What happened?" Lindsay said.

"We ate and talked. He was in town on a business trip and was staying at the hotel attached to the shopping center. I went to his room to talk some more and we ended up in bed. He was great," Karen said wistfully.

"I can't believe you did that. You were acting like some horny cougar," Lindsay said.

"I was feeling lonely and having this beautiful young man paying all of that attention to me was what I needed at the time. I didn't want it to stop," Karen said.

"Did you ever hear from him again?" Lindsay asked.

"No. I told him I was married and didn't expect to hear from him again," Karen said.

"You didn't know him. What if you had caught something?" Lindsay said.

"It was too late for that, by the time I thought about it, I was caught up in the moment, plus, I didn't think I could get pregnant. I haven't been on birth control for years, maybe George has a problem," Karen said.

"What are you going to do?" Lindsay asked.

"I'm going to have a baby, love it and raise it as the son of my husband. It could be George's child, I just don't know and don't plan to find out," Karen said.

"Oh Karen. What if it's the guy you slept with is the father? Shouldn't he know that he has a child out there in the world? I just went through that with RJ Jefferson," Lindsay said.

"Lindsay, your situation was different. You were a kid who was taken advantage of by older people. We were both adults and knew what was going on. Even if the kid turned out to be his, I wouldn't want to ruin his life, he's so young. My child will know George as his its father and I will just deal with it," Karen said while biting her lower lip.

"Okay. That's your choice. I'll respect it and not say a thing. You know I can keep a secret. That's for sure," Lindsay said.

"Let's go shopping. I want to spend some of your money and make you over. Let's see if we can make you look good and cover up some of your natural assets," Karen said.

"Alright, but you're just jealous," Lindsay said.

"Honey to be jealous, I would need to at least have an ass to begin with," Karen said as they walked out.

On the way to the shopping center Lindsay got a call from Ronald.

"Lindsay. I got a call from the fulfillment company. Your videos are flying off the shelf. They have run out of the initial run and are now producing additional sets to meet orders as they come in. It looks like you have a hit on your hands. You still have the login information so you can track your sales don't you?" Ronald asked.

"Yeah, I have the user id and password," Lindsay said.

"Good. When you get a chance go online and look for yourself," Ronald said.

Lindsay could hardly contain her excitement and started to scream.

"What the hell is wrong with you?" Karen asked.

"That was Ronald, the guy at the marketing firm that helped put my video together, and he said my video is selling like crazy. I'm so excited," Lindsay said.

"Lindsay do you know what that could mean? You could become famous," Karen said.

"Famous. Why would I become famous?" Lindsay asked.

"If this thing becomes a huge hit, people are going to recognize you and want to talk to you in person," Karen said.

"I don't know about that. How could I become famous when I don't even have any friends up here? I realized that when Tameka moved out, I was alone with no connections. We had always depended on each other for all of those years. When she left I realized I didn't know anyone else I could trust or talk to about anything. It's kind of scary. I don't really trust anybody," Lindsay said.

"Lindsay you have to let your guard down. You can't go through the world alone. You're too young for that," Karen said.

"I know, but I feel so insecure about everything. Before, when I had no money, I knew what was coming in and what was going out. I had less, but I felt better about managing things. Now I have all this money in the bank, but I'm always thinking that I'm going to lose everything and end up in worse shape than I was before. Every time I spend something I'm thinking, 'There goes more money that I'll never be able to replace', Lindsay said.

"Lindsay you have to relax a little. I know you feel like you suddenly got shot out of a cannon, but you have to accept that you deserved what you got from RJ Jefferson for what he did to you," Karen said.

"Karen, I know, but one day I was stripping in a club to survive and the next day I had millions of dollars in the bank. I felt like, what did I do to deserve that. Suppose my son's father was like Jasmine's and had nothing," Lindsay said.

The sisters arrived at the shopping center and were in a boutique looking at clothes when a woman in her forties approached Lindsay.

"Ma'am, I don't mean to bother you, but you look like that woman I saw on television last night that does that Strippercise video, Lindsay W.," the woman asked.

Lindsay was totally unprepared to be recognized and just stood there for a second before she responded.

"Well ma'am, I am Lindsay W. I'm surprised you recognized me," Lindsay said.

"I thought it was you. My name is Joan and I ordered your video and can't wait to get it. I could use a little more excitement in the bedroom and I think your video will help. I won't bother you much longer, but could I get your autograph on this pad?" Joan asked.

Lindsay signed the woman's pad with her first name followed by the capital letter w.

"Thank you. It was nice to meet you," the woman said as she walked away.

"Well sis, you officially have fans now. How did it feel to be recognized?" Karen asked.

"It was really strange. I never thought about people coming up to me and asking for my autograph. I'm just a regular person like they are," Lindsay asked.

"No you're not. You're someone with an informmercial that comes into the home of thousands of people every week across the country. Somebody was going to recognize you sooner or later, get used to it," Karen said.

After spending several hours shopping it was time for Lindsay to leave and pick Jasmine up from preschool. Lindsay had not lost focus on what Monica Jefferson did to her and had plans for the former video dancer that revolved around the Ultrabowl. Lindsay had researched the past of Monica Jefferson aka Super Stacked. The Ultrabowl attracted a traveling circus of entertainers and groupies. Monica Jefferson's favorite rapper would be in New Orleans throwing a huge pre-game party at a rented mansion. Monica once had a long running stint as the main video dancer and side chick of Mason Jones who went by the industry name of Little Assassin. Lindsay felt that Monica would not be able to resist hanging around her old environment and Lindsay planned to exact her revenge in a most unexpected fashion.

19

Lindsay Wilson was a multimillionaire and had never been on an airplane. Lindsay was seated with her sister and son in the boarding area at Love Field airport about to board her first airliner to fly to New Orleans for the Ultrabowl.

"Lindsay, relax! You didn't tell me that you have never been on an airplane before," Karen said.

"I really never thought about it until now. I didn't have the time or money to fly off somewhere before. Since I've been living up here I hardly go more than thirty miles away from home. Going home when daddy got sick was the longest trip I've taken since I left from down there," Lindsay said.

"Don't worry. It's just like riding the bus, only faster," Karen said.

Riley was busy looking out at the runway as airplanes took off and landed. The announcement to board came and Karen grabbed Lindsay by the hand like she did when they were small children as they got in line to board. Once onboard they seated themselves in a row with three seats. Riley sat by the window with Lindsay occupying the middle seat while Karen sat next to the aisle.

With a jolt the aircraft was pushed back from the gate and was soon moving under its own power as the powerful jet engines spooled up and moved the Boeing 737 onto the runway. The airliner stopped momentarily before power was applied by the pilot to accelerate the airplane to takeoff speed.

Lindsay pressed her back into the seat and she had a death grip on the seat handles. Karen placed her hand over the hand of her younger sister as they streaked forward. Lindsay got an unfamiliar feeling in her stomach as the airplane tilted upward and left the ground. Soon the sound of the landing gear retracting into the wheel wells transformed the hulking machine into a machine meant to fly at maximum efficiency.

Lindsay survived her first flight and before she knew it they were checking into their hotel in New Orleans. Bourbon Street was a necessary stop and Lindsay could not wait to get there. Karen had been to New Orleans before and she could tell that it had been a long time since her sister had truly enjoyed herself without a laundry list of worries on her mind.

Once back at the hotel room, Lindsay pulled out a ticket and showed it to Karen.

"What's that," Karen asked.

"This is a VIP pass to Little Assassin's Ultrabowl party," Lindsay said.

"Why are you going to that?" Karen asked.

"I could be wrong, but I'm betting that Monica Jefferson will be there. She was his side chick when she was dancing in those rap videos before she became Mrs. RJ Jefferson. If she's like I think she is, she won't be able to resist," Lindsay said.

"I don't get it. What are you going to do, whip her ass?" Karen asked.

"No. I'm going to see if she has left that world behind or if she is the same old video groupie she was before. If she is, then I'm going to catch her in the act. If she's not there then I'll leave and come back here," Lindsay said.

"Isn't that kind of risky? What if she recognizes you, plus what are you going to get out of catching her?" Karen asked.

"I'll get her off my back for one thing. I don't think she would want her husband to know that she was partying with her old boyfriend before the biggest day of his career. I didn't do anything to her and she went out of her way to embarrass me. I'm just not going to let her get away with it. Plus this is New Orleans, I bought this little Mardi Gras mask and that will be my disguise," Lindsay said.

"Okay. I'll have fun with Riley while you're play detective. You just be careful. Some of those guys can play pretty rough.

Hey did you ever look up your video sales information?" Karen said.

"No, I didn't. I'll log in on my phone and check it now," Lindsay said.

Lindsay logged into her video distributor's account and her eyes could not believe what she was seeing.

"Oh my God!" Lindsay exclaimed.

"What is it?" Karen asked.

"I've sold 30,000 video sets in a week. We only produced a thousand ahead of time," Lindsay said.

"How much do you make of each one?" Karen asked.

"Ten dollars," Lindsay said.

"You just made $300,000!" Karen said.

"Holy shit," Lindsay said.

"You're a hit," Karen said.

"You know what; I came up with this idea on my own. Sure, I was able to produce the video with the money, but this was my idea. I can't believe people are buying something I came up with. Karen you don't know how good this makes me feel. I never thought I could do something like this," Lindsay said.

"Well congratulations sis. You are officially a successful business woman," Karen said.

"Yeah, I guess I am. Riley, come here," Lindsay said.

Riley came over to his mother and she planted a big red kiss on his cheek and left a pair of red lipstick lips on his face.

"Mama, yuk," Riley said as he ran to the bathroom to wash the lipstick off his cheek.

It was the Friday night before the game on Sunday and Lindsay was dressed and prepared to go to rapper Little Assassin's private pre-game party.

"How do I look?" Lindsay asked Karen as she stood in the middle of the floor.

"I guess that depends on the look you are going for. You look like a hoochie mama. I hope you have underwear on, because if you make one wrong move or sit down too fast, that little black dress will be damn near around your waist," Karen said.

"I've got to fit in, besides this dress is too tight around my legs to slide up over my butt. How about my shoes?" Lindsay asked.

"Are you going to fight Romans with all of those straps on those things?" Karen asked.

'It's the gladiator style. It's hot right now," Lindsay said.

"Okay. You're ready. Your hair looks good, Go out there and skank it up," Karen said laughing.

"Funny," Lindsay said.

"Mama, where are you going?" Riley asked.

Lindsay pulled out her mask and put it on.

"I'm going to a costume party," Lindsay replied.

"You mean like a Halloween party? Can I go?" Riley asked.

"No. This party is for grownups. You can stay with your aunt Karen. She's going to order some pizza and you guys can watch one of your favorite movies on television. Okay," Lindsay said.

"Okay mama," Riley said.

"Riley we're going to have so much fun," Karen said as Lindsay kissed her son and left.

Karen watched anxiously as Lindsay closed the hotel room door.

Lindsay took a taxi to the party that was in a mansion that Little Assassin had rented and transformed into a club for the night. Lindsay was very familiar with Little Assassin's music as he made songs that were considered strip club anthems. Little Assassin's music had often boomed in the background when she was dancing on stage, but she never thought about going to one of his events. This night was not about being a groupie, but it was about taking care of an issue before it spiraled out of control if her instincts were right.

The taxi stopped in front of a stately looking southern style mansion and Lindsay stepped out of the vehicle. The bass backed music could be heard outside as she approached the entrance. Two huge muscular black men stood by the entrance and were checking everyone entering the venue. Lindsay had her silver mask on that only covered her eyes as she approached the entrance. Lindsay handed her pass to one of the men and he placed a gold toned band around her wrist and ushered her in. Lindsay had an all access pass that cost one thousand dollars and gave her the right to enjoy all the amenities the party offered including sitting in Little Assassin's private VIP area if she wished. Lindsay figured if she didn't catch Monica Jefferson there she would still have a good time and go back to the hotel. Lindsay walked in and the unmistakable scent of marijuana hit her nostrils and she was not surprised, but it was not a smell she encountered daily.

Others at the event knew what the colors of the wristbands meant and Lindsay's gold wristband attracted attention as she moved between levels in the three story house that others could not access. White bands allowed first floor access; silver allowed second floor entry and gold included all three levels. There was one other floor in the home that only Little Assassin could go on or invite someone to and it was the master bedroom suite that was above a short staircase. A guard stood watch at the bottom of the master bedroom staircase.

The place was packed with people out to have a good time. Young women were everywhere with their goods on display. Lindsay fit right in although she did elicit a fair amount of stares as she was in the minority as the majority of the attendees were black, although not exclusively, because hip hop music was mainstream from a consumer standpoint.

Lindsay eventually made her way to the third floor and walked down to the cordoned off area that comprised Little Assassin's private VIP section. Lindsay was granted entrance and she walked in and sat across from the rapper and a few members of his entourage. Little Assassin was dressed in leather and Lindsay could see the LA tattoos on each side of his neck. The rapper was not as tall as Lindsay thought he was compared to how he looked on his videos and he was sporting his signature long braids.

"Glad you came. What's your name?" the rapper asked with the diamonds in his grill showing.

"My name's Melanie. I'm a big fan of yours," Lindsay said.

"You must be. You dropped a grand for that pass. What do you like about my music?' Little Assassin asked.

"I like the raw lyrics and the beat. It's good to dance to," Lindsay replied.

"Really, you can dance? What kind of dancing can you do?" he asked.

"I can twerk a little," Lindsay said.

"Oh shit! Big Ron, she said she can twerk," Little Assassin said to one of the other men.

"Well, I can a little," Lindsay said.

"You want to give me a sample," Little Assassin asked.

"No, I don't think so," Lindsay said.

Big Ron looked at his smart phone and leaned over to Little Assassin.

"Hey, you know who is upstairs. She took the back elevator," Big Ron told Little Assassin.

"Awright. Look, take her some food and shit. Tell her I'll be up there in about thirty minutes," Little Assassin told Big Ron as he left.

"Hey, I understand if you don't want to dance right now. Come with me. I'm going downstairs to meet everybody. You can be my escort," Little Assassin said.

"I'd love to," Lindsay said.

They left the area and made their way downstairs to the first floor. The crowd tried to mob the rapper and women were pushing towards the front. Two burly body

211

guards pushed through the crowd ahead of Lindsay and the entertainer.

"Who the hell is that bitch with him?" Lindsay heard one woman in the crowd say as they passed.

Little Assassin then stood on the stairs and took a microphone.

"I want to thank everybody for showing up and showing love. It's time to set this mutherfuckin party off. I'll be back in a little while. Everybody have a good time. DJ, light this mutherfucka up!" Little Assassin said as the speakers blasted one of his most popular hits as the lights went down.

Lindsay went back to the third floor with the rapper and sat at a table overlooking the levels below her.

"Hey Melanie thanks for coming. I've got to go take care of something. Hang out here and have a good time. If you're still around maybe we can hook up later," Little Assassin said as he left and went upstairs to the master bedroom level.

Lindsay was dying to know who was in that room waiting on him, but with the guard standing watch, there was no way she could find out. After sitting there thirty minutes she noticed a big commotion going on downstairs out by the pool area. It seemed that a fight had broken out. Lindsay walked over to the guy standing watch at the stairs and told him something was going on.

He walked over to where she was sitting and looked outside.

"Damn, it's fucking Sub Zero and his crew. What the fuck are they doing here," he said as he rushed downstairs.

Lindsay didn't care what was happening as she took that opportunity to hurry up the stairs to the bedroom area. Lindsay walked slowly and heard music coming from the room with the door slightly open. With her heart pounding, Lindsay took out her phone and turned the video camera on. Lindsay slowly peeped into the room and the sight before her eyes stunned her for a moment.

Little Assassin was standing on the floor with his pants around his ankles and was drinking from a red plastic cup. A woman was kneeling on the bed in front of him rocking her body back and forth with her rear end slapping against his pelvic area with her face resting on her folded arms. The woman had her eyes closed with her face towards the door. Lindsay could clearly tell it was Monica Jefferson. Lindsay pushed the record button on her phone and nervously captured thirty seconds of action. Monica Jefferson opened her eyes and looked towards the open door but Lindsay was gone. Monica closed her eyes again without ever realizing she had been video recorded in the most compromising of positions.

Lindsay put her phone away in the small clutch purse she was carrying and hustled down the stairs. The guy that was guarding the upstairs bedroom was still out by the pool and Lindsay wasted no time exiting the premises. As Lindsay walked out the front door, she passed by two police cars pulling up to the scene. Lindsay jumped into a taxi stationed outside and told the driver to take her to the hotel. Lindsay still had her mask on because she didn't even want to run the risk of a cab driver recognizing her. Lindsay felt frightened, excited and a little ill all at the same time. Although Lindsay was sure no one at the party knew who she was, she still felt a sense of apprehension. Lindsay bought her party pass with cash at a radio promotional event in Dallas so that she would not leave a credit card trail.

It was possible that the video would be useless given the low light in the bedroom, but her cell phone was designed to have good low light video recording capabilities. Lindsay would wait until she was back at the hotel before she even tried to play back what she captured on her phone. A wave of emotions came over Lindsay as she considered the effects of what she saw could have on others. Monica Jefferson was a low life in Lindsay's opinion to betray her husband on the eve of his greatest professional achievement. Lindsay had mixed feeling towards RJ

Jefferson. Lindsay hated him for what he did to her when she was a teenager, yet he was her son's father and if he loved his wife he would be crushed by her actions. Lindsay knew that the release of something like the video she recorded could ruin RJ Jefferson's post-football career.

Lindsay finally arrived back inside the safe confines of her hotel room and still felt like she was out of breath. Lindsay was careful not to wake her son who was sleeping on the pull out sofa bed in the living room area of the suite she had rented. Once inside the bedroom she was sleeping in, as part of the two bedroom suite, Lindsay went into the bathroom and closed the door. Lindsay pulled out the earphones for her phone and plugged them into the headphone jack. Lindsay turned on the phone and pressed the small icon that activated the video camera. The last video recorded was displayed at the bottom and with a press of one finger it played. To Lindsay's surprise the images were crystal clear. Monica's face was very recognizable as the open door allowed more light into the room than Lindsay thought. Little Assassin's face was visible but it was from a side view and not as clear. Even the sounds were clear and the moans coming from Monica were audible as well as other sounds from the encounter. Lindsay's phone's sensitive microphone picked up something she was too shocked to hear in person while the video recording was being made.

"Oh shit!" came from Monica's mouth in response to Little Assassin's attention.

After thirty seconds the video ended and Lindsay could hardly breathe. The mission Lindsay embarked upon yielded more than she expected, but now she didn't know what to do with her evidence.

Lindsay went to Karen's room and opened the door.

"Karen. It's me, Lindsay," Lindsay announced.

Karen reached over and turned on the lamp on side of the bed and looked at the digital clock.

"Lindsay, it's one in the morning. You made it back. I was getting a little worried, but I had to get some sleep. What happened?" Karen asked.

Lindsay just looked at Karen and sat on the bed with her cell phone. Lindsay pressed the play button and Karen's eyes became as wide as the moon.

"Oh my God! Is that his wife?" Karen asked.

"Yes, that's RJ Jefferson's wife with her ass in the air and that's her old rapper hookup from when she was a music video dancer behind her," Lindsay said.

"What are you going to do with this?" Karen asked.

"I don't know," Lindsay said almost breaking into tears.

"I thought that you wanted to bust her in the act," Karen said.

"Yeah, I thought I would find her at the party, but there she is fucking this guy. I'm not crazy about RJ Jefferson, but this could destroy that guy. He is my son's father," Lindsay said.

"But Lindsay, this woman is making an ass of him. Wouldn't you want to know if you had a husband and he was doing that to you?" Karen said.

"He could get pissed at me and take it out on my son and stop seeing him. That would kill Riley to find his father and then lose him all over again," Lindsay said.

"Look. I've been through this shit before. If someone had caught George's ass on video screwing that bitch boss of his, I would want to know. You can't keep all of this to yourself. Every time you see or talk to Riley's father from now on would make you a fraud, so you need to figure out what to do. You can't put the horse back in the barn now, it's too late," Karen said.

"I thought I would just see her there in his VIP suite or something and use that to get her to back off," Lindsay said.

"Well you got a lot more than you bargained for," Karen said.

Lindsay left Karen's room and went to bed with her mind racing.

All too soon the day of the game arrived and Lindsay, Karen and Riley walked into the Megadome for the world championship of professional football contest. Once again Lindsay had prime seats and this time they were near the player's family section. Lindsay spotted Monica Jefferson as she walked to their seats. Lindsay swore that Monica stared her down as she walked by with Karen and Riley.

"I'm going to the concession stand to get some nachos and drinks," Lindsay said.

Lindsay walked up the steps to the first concession level and while she was on her way to get in line she heard someone call her name.

"Lindsay," the voice called again.

Lindsay wondered who could be calling her name in New Orleans and she turned around and Monica Jefferson was standing there walking towards her.

"Your name is Lindsay, isn't it?" Monica said.

"Yes, my name is Lindsay and how do you know that?" Lindsay asked.

"I saw your name in that other phone my husband bought so you could call him about your bastard son," Monica said.

Lindsay and Monica were standing in an area off to the side out of the flow of foot traffic. Lindsay felt a flash of anger rush over her and snapped. Before Monica could react Lindsay had slapped her across the face with her right hand.

"I've been trying to ignore you bitch, but if you say one more thing about my son, I'll whip your gold digging ass right here!" Lindsay said.

Monica stood there in shock as she held the side of her face.

"You got anything else to say to me, bitch?" Lindsay asked as she stood there with her fists clenched.

Monica didn't say anything and hurried to the bathroom. Monica wanted to look at her face and try to cover any marks with makeup before she returned to her seat. Lindsay continued to the concession stand before going back to join her son and sister.

"What took you so long?" Karen asked.

"I had a little incident on the way. I ran into Monica Jefferson and ended up slapping the shit out of her," Lindsay said.

"What!" Karen said.

"She walked up behind me. I heard somebody calling my name and turned around and it was her. Then she called Riley a bastard and I just snapped on her ass. That bitch can burn in hell," Lindsay said.

Riley was sitting alongside Lindsay and had no idea about the drama taking place around him.

"What are you going to do?" Karen asked.

"I'm going to burn her ass. I can tell she's not going to stop harassing me and now she's dragging my son into it. The chips can fall where they may," Lindsay said.

The game was a classic and RJ Jefferson went out with a bang as his team became world champions. RJ Jefferson was named most valuable player and ended his playing career on top, he knew nothing about the upcoming turmoil in his personal life.

20

Two weeks after the end of the championship game, RJ Jefferson travelled to Dallas to visit his son. Lindsay decided that this would be the time she would reveal to RJ what she found out about his wife in New Orleans.

"Riley, could you go play with Jasmine in your room for a little bit? I need to talk to your father, okay," Lindsay said to her son.

The children left the room and RJ Jefferson had a puzzled look on his face.

Lindsay checked to see that the children were out of the area and she beckoned for RJ Jefferson to come into the living room.

"What's going on?" RJ Jefferson asked.

"Look, RJ, I've been struggling with something I found out in New Orleans before the game," Lindsay said.

"What's that? RJ asked.

"I went to a pre-game party at a mansion thrown by this rapper named Little Assassin. Have you heard of him," Lindsay asked.

RJ sat straight up on the couch and seemed to become very attentive to what Lindsay was saying.

"Yeah, I know the name, go on," RJ said.

"Well, I ran into somebody you know there," Lindsay said.

"Who was that?" RJ asked with anticipation.

"Your wife, Monica," Lindsay said.

RJ stood up with a visibly upset look on his face and walked back and forth before sitting back down.

"Are you sure it was her?" RJ said.

"Yes, I'm sure and that's not all," Lindsay said.

"What do you mean that's not all?" RJ asked.

"Brace yourself," Lindsay said as she pulled out her cell phone and hit the play button.

RJ watched the scene on Lindsay's phone with his mouth hanging open. He handed the phone back to Lindsay and just sat back on the couch with his head turned towards the ceiling.

"What the fuck! How did you get this?" RJ asked.

"I wanted her to leave me alone and thought if I went to the party and saw her there she would back off out of fear that I would tell you. I didn't expect to see this. I walked up on it. I didn't know who was in that room and it turned out to be Monica," Lindsay said.

"Did she see you?" RJ asked.

"No. She didn't see me. Her eyes were closed the whole time," Lindsay said.

"We just came back from a vacation after the game. She was there telling me how much she loved me. The whole time she was lying through her teeth. How could she do this shit right before the biggest game of my life, and my last game? She was being a slut and cheating on me with that piece of garbage. Didn't she think someone would see her in there?" RJ said.

222

"Apparently that place has a rear entrance that she used to enter without anyone else seeing her. I'm sorry RJ, but I thought you needed to know," Lindsay said.

"She told me she was through with that life. I've been played for a fool all these years. She was probably fucking that guy when I was on the road for out of town games and training camp. Damn!" RJ said.

"What are you going to do?" Lindsay asked.

"Look, can I have a copy of that video. I know it's a lot to ask, but I need it to make some things happen," RJ said.

"You're not going to come after me for recording it, are you?" Lindsay asked.

"Oh no, I should be thanking you. I had my doubts about Monica, but I'm crazy about her and you don't know how much this hurts me. That's my wife and I wanted to have children, build a family and grow old with her. I love her and I guess it was just a bullshit game she was playing. I was just her fucking dumbass sugar daddy,"

"RJ, I'm sorry," Lindsay said.

"We signed an airtight prenuptial agreement with one exception, proof of infidelity. I've been fighting off groupies left and right and she's just wide open with this guy. I'll tell her I hired a private detective. Your name won't come up at all. I love her but I can't trust her anymore, at all. I almost feel sick from being with her for the past two weeks after seeing that," RJ said.

"Sure, I'll save a copy to a thumb drive, I'll be right back," Lindsay said as she walked over to her laptop and transferred a copy of the video to a memory stick after taking it from her phone.

Lindsay walked back over to RJ and he had tears running down his face. Lindsay didn't quite know how to react. Lindsay sat on the couch and hugged this huge man and he sobbed into her shoulder like a baby.

"I'm sorry about that. I tried to hold back and be strong, but I can't get that image out of my mind of her with that scum and coming back to me like nothing happened. If that's the life she wants, she can have it, but it won't be behind my back. God I feel like an idiot," RJ said.

"I was really afraid and didn't know what to do after I recorded this. Look, I almost didn't even tell you about this until she confronted me at the game in New Orleans," Lindsay said.

"What! What happened at the game?" RJ asked looking totally confused.

"I was going to get food at the concession stand and heard someone call my name. I turned around and it was your wife. She made some comments about getting my name off your phone and then she called Riley a bastard. I lost it and slapped her. I figured for her to say that meant that she was not going to leave me along and was now dragging my son into this. That's when I decided I had to tell you. What if Riley came to visit you and she felt that way about him. I had to let you know what was going on," Lindsay said.

"That's our son. He's my son too. I know we're not together, but since I'm through with playing football I want to spend more time with

Riley, and yes I want him to spend some time with me at my house. I can't believe she said that. That's the icing on the cake for me. If she can't be faithful to me and accept my son, it's over. I accepted a lot of her past baggage when we got together because I loved her and she said she loved me, I decided the past was just in the past. I guess I didn't really know my own wife," RJ said.

Lindsay had no words and just patted him on the shoulder.

"You're not upset with me for what I did, are you?" Lindsay asked.

"Why should I be upset? Everybody in that rap music world probably knew Monica was still fucking that gutter rapper. I'm the big football star with a thot wife sneaking around behind his back with this Assassin guy and lord knows who else. They were probably laughing at me when I thanked her for being there to support me when I accepted the MVP award at the Ultrabowl. All you did was open my eyes so I can stop being a joke. If I was young and crazy like I was in college, I'd probably kill that guy, but I'm not like that anymore. I have my future and a son to think about, plus he didn't make Monica do this, she's a grown ass woman and chose to lie down with dogs," RJ said.

RJ cleaned his face up, said goodbye to his son and went back home.

Lindsay felt very uneasy about what could happen when RJ Jefferson got back home. She felt no sympathy for Monica, but wondered if he could keep his emotions under control. If he became unhinged things could go very badly for Monica. It turned out that Lindsay had nothing to worry about as RJ Jefferson's first stop when he got back to Oklahoma was not at his house, but at his lawyer's office. Jefferson never let Monica know that anything was going on until she was served with a petition for divorce that included no payout under terms of the prenuptial agreement. When Monica protested, she was presented with the video recording of her having sex with Little Assassin and she broke down in tears. She tried to claim she had been drugged without her knowledge, but could not explain why she was there to begin with. Monica finally admitted that she had been sleeping with the rapper and a few others throughout her time of being married to RJ Jefferson. The divorce happened very quickly and Monica moved back to California and was attempting to land a role on a reality show about ex-wives of celebrities and get back into the rap video game.

Lindsay read about the split of RJ Jefferson and Monica and felt a bit of sadness. Lindsay felt that RJ Jefferson really loved Monica and her betrayal wounded him on every level. Although she had no romantic feelings for the father of her son, she could tell he was not the same impulsive person she met as a teenager. Lindsay had something else on her mind as Tameka was due to arrive any minute for a weeklong visit. They hadn't seen each other since she had moved back home. The doorbell rang and Lindsay ran to the door.

"Tameka!" Lindsay screamed when she opened the door and they embraced.

Tameka's children ran into the house. Lindsay's kids joined them and it became a screaming reunion. After catching up on events the two old friends sat down on the couch.

"I heard about RJ Jefferson and Monica splitting. Did you have anything to do with that?" Tameka asked.

Lindsay told Tameka the whole story.

"I knew it. I knew she couldn't leave that life alone. She was too deep in it before she met him. That's just low down and ratchet. How do you do that to your husband?" Tameka said.

"It tore that man down. Think about it. He must feel like those years he was married to her never happened, because it was all bullshit on her part," Lindsay said.

"She was addicted to that low life type of environment and just used him for his money," Tameka said.

"Well, what about you, are you dating or anything?" Lindsay asked.

"I am seeing this guy I met at church," Tameka said.

"Church! You're going to church?" Lindsay asked.

"Well my mother told me that my kids needed to be in church so they could know about the bible. She thought it would instill some discipline in them. I gave it a try and I think she was right. So anyway, this guy named Terrance starts to talk to me every Sunday before service starts, he's the son of one of my father's friends. He works for the county, so he has a good job. He's tall, dark and

227

has a big smile. He asked me out to dinner and I went out with him," Tameka said.

"What about your kids. Did he say anything about you having three children?" Lindsay asked.

"I told him I have three children and he said that he knew that. He said they were cute children, but not as cute as their mom," Tameka said.

"He sounds like a smooth talker. Have you, you know, with him yet," Lindsay asked.

"No. I'm holding back on that, as bad as I want to, but I want to really get to know him better. He's going to have to put in some work to get in these panties. I learned my lesson on dropping my drawers too fast and there they are running around your back yard," Tameka said laughing.

"What about you? Men must be hanging off you with your video blowing up like it is," Tameka said.

"I might as well be a nun. I'm not seeing anybody. It's pretty sad," Lindsay said.

"So, what about your friend, you used to drop in on every once in a while?" Tameka asked.

"Robert. I kinda drifted away from him. He was nice to me and we had fun, but it wasn't going anywhere," Lindsay said.

"So you're not doing anything, with anybody?" Tameka asked.

"No. That thing has cobwebs on it by now," Lindsay said.

"What about RJ Jefferson?" Tameka asked.

"RJ Jefferson! Why would you bring him up?" Lindsay replied.

"Well, you do have a connection with him," Tameka said.

"I just don't get any kind of vibes from that guy. We still seem to be strangers in the same room together just because we have to be there. It's really strange," Lindsay said.

"Maybe it's because you still see him as the guy you met when you got pregnant and you can't get past that. Have you ever talked to him about his past or yours? Have you even sat down and even had a deep discussion about how you two will raise your son so you are on the same page. What if both of you are telling little Riley to do totally opposite things about the same situation? You at least need to talk to that man about that or you could have a mixed up kid," Tameka said.

"I guess you're right. I haven't talked to him since he got divorced," Lindsay said.

"You need to call him and make the first move. He is probably walks on eggshells around you because he knows what he did to you was so wrong when he was younger, plus you could explode his whole world if you went to the police about the statutory rape charge," Tameka said.

"I never thought about it that way. Okay, I'll call him. I don't hate the man. I just have a hard time looking at him knowing how I was treated," Lindsay said.

"Lindsay, I know, but for the sake of your son you have to try to talk with this guy and get a better understanding of how you will raise your son together. Why don't you see if he can meet you while I'm here and I can watch the kids," Tameka said.

"What do you mean? You think I should ask him out or something?" Lindsay asked.

"It's not like it's a date. It would be a meeting in a more relaxed setting to talk about your son and how you would work together," Tameka said.

"Okay. I'll do it," Lindsay said.

Lindsay picked up her phone and dialed RJ Jefferson. She felt nervous about calling without really knowing why. Lindsay invited RJ to meet her for dinner at a restaurant in Dallas that would give them enough privacy to have a meaningful discussion about their son while Tameka looked after her children.

Lindsay met RJ Jefferson at an upscale steakhouse in north Dallas that featured booths that would allow for private conversations. Lindsay was seated when Riley arrived and the waiter escorted him to her seating area.

"Wow. You look nice," RJ said.

"Well, thank you," Lindsay replied.

"Look. I wanted to meet with you so we could relax and talk about how we were going to, you know, handle how we deal with our son. It sounded strange for me to say our son, but that's the reality. I feel like we kind of tiptoe around each other and I don't think that's good for us or Riley," Lindsay said.

"I'm glad you said that, because I've been really uncomfortable around you. I don't know what to say or how to react. I don't want to make you angry and I feel a lot of guilt about what happened between us. I know we went through the legal and money thing, but that doesn't change what I did and it's hard for me to accept that I could do that given how I try to be now," RJ said.

"Well, how do you try to be now?" Lindsay asked.

"I try to be honest, straightforward and a man of my word. I worked hard over the years to tone down that "look at me" attitude. That's why what happened with Monica hit me so hard. I was ready to build a family with her and she just flushed everything down the toilet," RJ said.

"I'm sorry. I should have asked how you are doing after all of that happened," Lindsay said.

"It was horrible. I laid everything out to her and she still tried to lie about what happened. She came up with some story about something being put in her drink and that she didn't remember what happened. Once she figured out she was trapped, she just exploded on me. She told me that I was too boring and she missed the excitement of the rap music world. Monica said she never stopped seeing those guys and she was going to become a star on her own. It was pathetic. My whole marriage was a sham. She thought she could marry me and cash out on the prenup once I was through playing and launch her entertainment career and that Little Assassin guy was going to be her sponsor. The only problem was that she violated the agreement, she didn't get anything," RJ said.

"I can tell that it is still an open wound," Lindsay said.

"Yeah it is and it will be for a while. What about you? Are you seeing anybody special?" RJ asked.

"No. I'm not seeing anybody. I have a hard time letting anybody get close and I don't want to bring different men around my children," Lindsay said.

"Well you probably have to fight them off," RJ said.

"Why do you think that?" Lindsay said.

"Look at yourself. You're a beautiful woman," RJ said.

"Well, thanks, I think. That sounds strange coming from you for some reason," Lindsay said.

"Why. It's true, plus your video is selling like hotcakes," RJ said.

"You know about my video?" Lindsay asked.

"Well I wasn't sleeping very well after Monica and I broke up. I was channel surfing late one night and I stopped on a station and had to do a double take. It was you pitching your Strippercise video. I was shocked," RJ said.

Lindsay turned red at the idea that RJ had seen her video commercial.

"Why are you acting embarrassed? I think it's great that you did that," RJ said.

"Really?" Lindsay said.

"It took having an idea and following through on it to make something like that happen. Everybody can't do that,' RJ said.

Lindsay proceeded to tell him how she got the idea and what it took to bring it into reality.

"I'm impressed. Now let's talk about raising Riley," RJ said.

"Oh yeah. That's the reason we are here," Lindsay said.

They then proceeded to discuss what they wanted to achieve in raising their son. When the dinner was over and the food had been taken away, RJ Jefferson walked Lindsay to her car to say goodnight. Lindsay felt a strange tension in the air as she neared her vehicle.

"Lindsay I had a good time tonight. This is the first time I've really relaxed since splitting with Monica. This was a good idea," Riley said.

"I had a good time too. I hardly ever go out and even then it's with my children. It felt different to be with another adult," Lindsay said.

Lindsay and Riley just stood and looked at each other awkwardly. Riley suddenly grabbed Lindsay by the shoulders, hugged her and planted a kiss on her forehead.

"You're a good woman Lindsay Wilson. I'm lucky my son has you for a mother," Riley said as he started to hurriedly walk away before Lindsay grabbed him by the shoulder.

"Hey. RJ you're going to be a good father. You're not the same guy I met all those years ago," Lindsay said.

"Thank you. Lindsay, can I ask you something?" RJ asked.

"Sure," Lindsay replied.

"Would you consider going out with me again. I mean, I know this sounds odd, since we have a child together, but I would like to get to know you better," RJ said.

"RJ, are you asking me out on a date?" Lindsay asked.

"Well, I guess I am. How about it?" RJ said.

"Okay, but nothing too fancy," Lindsay said.

"How about next Friday, that will give you time to arrange for a babysitter and I'll pick you up," RJ said.

"So you're going to drive from Oklahoma to my house to take me out on a date?" Lindsay asked.

"Sure," RJ said.

"I'll go out with a man that's going to drive three hours to pick me up," Lindsay said.

"Great. Thank you. I'll call you," RJ said.

Lindsay drove home wondering what she was getting herself into by going out with this man. Lindsay got home and it was just like old times with Tameka waiting for an update.

"Well how did it go?" Tameka asked.

"We came to an agreement on what we wanted to do with Riley and I'm going out with him next week," Lindsay said.

"Excuse me. Did you say you were going out with him next week? I don't get it. How did that happen?" Tameka asked.

"He's not as bad as I thought. I just had to get past what happened before. He's different. He asked me out. I thought about it and said yes," Lindsay said.

"I hope you know what you're getting into," Tameka said.

"What's that supposed to mean?" Lindsay said.

"I mean you have a lot of emotional baggage built up with him. How are going to just get past that. I couldn't do it, but you're grown," Tameka said as she went to bed.

Lindsay just sat there for awhile and thought about what Tameka had said.

The next day Lindsay's teenage neighbor served as a babysitter so she and Tameka could spend some quality time together shopping. The friends were walking along the concourse of one of the most exclusive malls in Dallas catching up with each other's activities since they had been apart. Suddenly Tameka froze in her tracks.

"Tameka, what's wrong? You act like you've just seen a ghost," Lindsay observed.

Tameka suddenly turned her back and faced Lindsay.

"I did see a ghost. Do you see that man, the black guy with the woman and children walking towards us? The woman has on a red blouse," Tameka said.

"Yeah, I see them. What about it?" Lindsay asked.

"That man is my old lawyer sugar daddy, Calvin, and his family," Tameka said.

"Are you serious?! Did he see you?" Lindsay asked.

"I don't think so. Let's go into this clothing store," Tameka said.

Once they were inside the store, Tameka turned to Lindsay.

"I can't believe I ran into that asshole in here with his perfect little family. He still calls me, but I never answer. I didn't know his wife was a Becky," Tameka said.

"A Becky? What's a Becky?" Lindsay asked.

"That means she's white. Now I feel even worse for having ever been with him that way. He made her his queen and me his whore," Tameka said.

"You said you knew what the deal was, so why does her being white make it feel worse?" Lindsay asked.

"Lindsay, I love you, but you will never be able to understand. Trust me. Let's get out of here," Tameka said.

"Tameka, I thought that was you. I recognized you, even from behind," a man said as they stood by a rack of clothes.

Tameka turned around and was looking Calvin right in the face.

"What are you doing in here? Where's your wife and kids?" Tameka asked.

"They went to a children's store on the second floor. I'll catch up with them. Aren't you going to say hello after everything we shared together?" Calvin said.

Lindsay moved around behind the rack of clothes and listened.

"No Calvin. You need to get back to your family. What we had is over. I don't even live here anymore," Tameka informed.

"I'll call you later. I can sweeten the deal. I miss what we had together," Calvin said.

"Calvin, listen to yourself. You're pathetic! Your family is right downstairs in this same building. If you want to buy some pussy, find someone else and get a therapist to listen to you bitch about your wife. Calvin, lose my fucking phone number. Lindsay let's get out of here!" Tameka said.

Calvin just stood there with his mouth open and watched Tameka walk away almost dragging Lindsay behind her as she had grasped her by the hand.

All too soon it was time for Tameka to leave and go back home. Lindsay hated to see her friend leave, but knew their lives had taken different paths. Lindsay had already secured a babysitter for her upcoming date with RJ the next week. A teenage neighbor would come over and look after the children while she went out with RJ.

Lindsay had no idea that her prior dinner with RJ to discuss Riley didn't go unnoticed. A photographer captured Lindsay and RJ exiting the restaurant together. He also took a picture of Lindsay and RJ in the parking lot from an angle that made RJ's kiss to Lindsay's forehead seem like something else altogether. Lindsay did not keep up with celebrity gossip websites, but they were abuzz with talk of how RJ Jefferson kicked Monica "Super Stack" Jefferson to the curb to be with his baby mama. Monica Jefferson was furious to the point of becoming borderline unstable. Monica now hated Lindsay with a passion. Humiliated on social media, Monica was boiling with rage inside.

Friday night came all too soon and Lindsay went all out on her clothes, hair and makeup. She felt that she looked pretty hot by her own estimation. RJ arrived and drove up in his Red Range Rover and met Lindsay with a bouquet of roses. Lindsay was really surprised and her son was confused as to why his mother was leaving with his father to go out somewhere, although Lindsay had told him they were going somewhere to talk. RJ had selected a dinner club with a live band and dance floor.

"Thank you for the roses. I didn't expect that," Lindsay said.

"Well you look better than those roses," RJ said.

"Well thanks. I don't go out that often so I decided to fix myself up a little," Lindsay said.

"Well you did a good job," RJ said.

Once at the club they ordered dinner and begin to find out things about each other that they never knew before. Lindsay even went into what happened with her family after she got pregnant.

"Lindsay, I'm sorry that happened. Like I said before, I had no idea," RJ said.

RJ asked Lindsay how she went from being a country teenager to become a big city exotic dancer.

"That's an interesting story. I was with my daughter's father, Trey, who is in prison by the way for drug distribution. Well, Trey liked to go to strip clubs and I went with him to make sure he wasn't taking someone else home, if you know what I mean. One night I wondered how much those women made. I mean men were just throwing money at them. I was shoving burgers at people out of a drive through window and that wasn't cutting it. I bought a lap dance from their top dancer and asked her what she made. I was shocked at what she told me. I talked to Trey and he thought it was a great idea. He seemed to think that having a stripper girlfriend gave him more street cred or something. I went back to that club after screwing up all the nerve I could and auditioned. I was a nervous wreck. I think I danced with my eyes closed the first time, but I needed to make more money to survive. They hired me on and I gradually worked my way up to being the featured dancer. That's it," Lindsay said.

"With everything I've done in life. I don't think I would have the confidence and nerve to stand in front of other people totally exposed. How did you do that and get comfortable with people looking at you like that?" RJ asked.

"It wasn't easy. I had never done anything like that. I talked it over with my friend, Tameka, and we even prayed about it. After weighing my options it was the fastest way for me to make the kind of money I needed to support my kids. I never imagined myself doing that, but I wasn't embarrassed or ashamed. I was proud that I could overcome my personal fears and do what I needed to do to survive as a single mother. My children still don't know what I did to make ends meet. They just knew that their mama kept food on the table and a roof over their heads," Lindsay said.

"Lindsay, you did a great job. Riley and Jasmine are great children. They are smart and respectful. They say yes sir and yes ma'am to adults. Children are like sponges and they soak up what the adults responsible for their upbringing pour into them. You have poured good things into your kids. I know this is going to sound strange coming from me, but I'm proud of the job you've done. You could have easily fallen apart," RJ said.

"Thank you. Women in my situation get plenty of criticism, but not too many pats on the back," Lindsay said.

After they finished their meal the band started to play a slow song and RJ asked Lindsay to dance. Lindsay accepted and felt a little unsure in the beginning, but soon she was leaning her head into his shoulder. Lindsay's six inch heels compensated for their height difference enough that they were at ease on the dance floor. Lindsay told RJ that she needed to get back home so the babysitter could go home.

Lindsay and RJ left the club and walked to his vehicle. RJ came over to Lindsay's side of the vehicle to open the door for her. Before he opened the door he pulled Lindsay up against his body, leaned down and kissed her on the lips. Lindsay hesitated slightly and then she put her arms around his neck and they indulged in a long, deep kiss that lasted for at least one minute.

"I didn't expect that, but I liked it," Lindsay said with a smile.

"I loved it," RJ replied as he opened the door.

Lindsay got inside while RJ went to the other side.

RJ was about to start the engine when and audible click came from the rear of the vehicle.

"So you kicked me to the curb so you could get with this white bitch!" a female voice said.

RJ and Lindsay snapped their heads around and were looking into the barrel of a gun in the hands of RJ's ex-wife Monica.

"Monica, what the fuck are you doing in here?!" RJ exclaimed.

Lindsay was stunned and thought about what her children would do without her if she died that night.

"I still had a set of keys motherfucka! I guess you forgot about that," Monica said.

Lindsay didn't dare say anything to this woman who was obviously mentally unstable. Monica had a wild look in her eyes and Lindsay felt that she also had drugs in her system. This was not the well put together woman Lindsay had encountered before. Monica looked like she was running on almost no sleep. Her eyes were bloodshot with dark circles underneath. Monica's usually neatly trimmed and smooth hair was unkempt and uneven.

"Ain't that a bitch! RJ, it hasn't even been two months and you already fucking this ho. Baby, I know I fucked up. I shouldn't have done what I did, but RJ please, not with this bitch baby," Monica said.

"I drove all the way down here to see you baby. I went to our house. I waited outside, but I was too afraid to come to the door, so I parked down the street. Then I saw you leave and I followed you. I followed you all the way to this white ho's house. How could you baby? I saw you get out of the car with roses in your hand. You gave this bitch red roses. You used to send me red roses when you were on the road, remember. You said you loved me. RJ, you promised to stay with me for better or worse, didn't you baby," Monica said sobbing.

Monica then pointed the barrel of the gun right at Lindsay's face.

"Ho, I know it was you. You did it. I talked to Little A, he said a white woman was there that he didn't know with a mask on. It was you, wasn't it? Bitch, you set me up didn't you? You took that video. I should smoke your ass right now," Monica said.

Lindsay didn't make a move and knew this woman was on the edge.

"Monica you need to put the gun down, before someone gets hurt," RJ said.

"I just saw you kissing that bitch right in front of my face. Why did you kiss her in front of me? You took her out last week too, didn't you? I saw the pictures online of you with her. Come on baby! She can't fuck you better than I can. She can't suck your dick like I can?" Monica pleaded.

"Monica, calm down. You don't have to do this," RJ said.

"I know baby. I came ready for you. I didn't even put any underwear on. Look baby. This is for you. This pussy is all for you. Just throw this white bitch out of here and I'll show you I can make you happy again right now," Monica said as she pulled her short skirt up to her waist.

Monica held the gun in her right hand and used her left hand to show RJ what he had been missing as she ran her fingers between her thighs and over her exposed vagina. Although it was late at night it was still almost eighty degrees outside. Conditions quickly became uncomfortable inside the vehicle as a mixture of perspiration, fear and human aromas filled the cabin. Monica hadn't showered in days due to her state of mind. The combination of Monica's pungent odor combined with Lindsay's perfume and RJ's cologne to produce and almost indescribable scent cocktail laced with anxiety. The heat and humidity seemed to almost steam the trio as they sat there immersed in near unbearable tension.

Monica ranted for thirty minutes while shifting her aim of the gun back and forth from Lindsay to RJ. She told of how she was rejected by her former rap music industry associates since she had fallen on hard times. Monica even told in detail of how she was used, abused and tossed aside by her former lover Little Assassin. Suddenly red and blue lights flooded through the interior of the vehicle as two police cruisers stopped in the parking lot of the club. A binding white spotlight lit up the inside of the Range Rover.

"Ma'am, please put the gun down," blared from police speakers.

Lindsay thought about how she ended up in a full blown hostage situation simply by going out for a dinner and dance date. Monica lost all sense of rationality when she realized the police had arrived as she was alternately sobbing and cursing in the back of the vehicle.

"I'm not letting you go RJ! I'm going to stay here until you promise me that you will take me back. I didn't mean to do that to you. I've learned my lesson baby. I'm going to stay right here until you give me an answer," Monica said.

The tension inside the vehicle was near unbearable. Time wore on and an hour passed and then two hours. Lindsay could hear the sound of helicopters from local television stations flying over the scene. The live video stream had gone nationwide with reporters on the air from the scene reporting on the ongoing hostage situation.

Monica had grown fatigued and could barely keep her eyes open. Near the three hour mark, RJ turned and looked at Monica and she had placed the barrel of the gun up to her mouth.

"Bye RJ. I'm sorry. Till death do us part. I meant that!" Monica said between sobs.

"Monica, no!" RJ screamed as she pulled the trigger with the barrel of the gun in her mouth.

Lindsay screamed as the sound of the gunshot seemed to continue to reverberate throughout the cabin of the Range Rover.

Monica's body fell backwards and disappeared behind the rear seat. The bullet exited the back of Monica's skull and shattered the rear glass of the vehicle. Police officers slowly approached the sports utility vehicle with their guns drawn. RJ and Lindsay held their hands up so the officers could see they were unarmed.

Lindsay was shaking so badly that she could not stand up once she stepped out onto the parking lot. RJ told the detective that Monica was his ex-wife and had hidden behind the back seat until they came out of the club. RJ went over to Lindsay and she was still shaking. The detective walked over to Lindsay to take her statement.

"I've met you before," the detective said.

Lindsay looked up at him. He was the same detective from the doctor attack incident several months earlier. Lindsay gave her statement and they waited for the coroner to arrive and take Monica's body away. RJ walked over to the gurney and positively identified Monica's body and told the detective that they were married for three years. RJ walked back over to Lindsay, sat down on the curb and cried like a baby with his hands over his face. Lindsay put her arms around him as she knew he still had feelings for Monica and was broken in two after witnessing her take her own life. The police informed RJ that his Range Rover would be taken to the police impound until the investigation of Monica's death was complete.

"Take it. I don't ever want to see it again," RJ said.

The police called a taxi to take Lindsay and RJ wherever they wanted to go. A taxi finally arrived and took Lindsay and RJ to her house. Her babysitter saw what happened on television and stayed until they got home.

"Look, RJ it's too late to do anything now. Why don't you stay here and get some sleep? This is a sofa sleeper and I'll get some sheets for you. I'll take you to get a rental car after you wake up. How are you doing? That was horrible," Lindsay said.

"I don't understand what happened to her that quickly. Why did she kill herself? She was so young. I knew the divorce was rough on her, but I felt I had no other choice after what happened," RJ said.

"Listen, I didn't know her or how her mind worked, but I can relate to part of her life. I danced in strip clubs for years to survive and take care of my children. She danced in rap videos. We were both looked upon as objects to fit someone else's fantasies. Monica found you and you fell in love with her and she became your wife. Maybe Monica felt like she disappeared when she became Mrs. RJ Jefferson and missed being known for what she did on her own," Lindsay said.

"But that wasn't a good life for her. When I proposed to her, I told her that part of her life was over and she wouldn't have to degrade herself dancing half naked with those guys treating her like a piece of meat anymore. I guess she couldn't stay away from that life," RJ said.

"RJ you have to understand that she was proud of what she did before. It might not have been what many people would want for their daughters, but she built her name and made a decent living doing that. I danced in a club where I would strip down until I was naked. I did it to survive and didn't let it consume me. Am I proud of what I did before, yeah, I am proud of it because it supported my family. I didn't have a college education or some other natural talent. I made it the best way I could. How long have people been telling you that you were great because of your football talent," Lindsay said.

"Every since I was in the seventh grade," RJ said.

"That's not the way it is for most people. We have to find something that we can do well enough to make ends meet. Maybe she felt lost when you got divorced and found out her old life was gone also. We're lucky to be alive. She was not the same person and could have shot us instead of turning the gun on herself," Lindsay said.

"You're right. I didn't know her tonight. That was not the Monica I knew, and loved. She should have called me. I was so mad when we broke up that I just cut her off. What she did cut me to the core, but I never thought she would do what she did tonight," RJ said.

"What about her family. How will they find out?" Lindsay asked.

"This will kill her mother. She's a sweet woman and we got along great. She was so happy when we got married because she knew Monica would be away from that whole music video scene," RJ said.

"Are you going to call her or let the police let her know?" Lindsay asked.

"You're right, I should call her," RJ said.

RJ took his cell phone out and dialed. He went into the bathroom so he could talk in private. After thirty minutes he emerged visibly shaken.

"She's in a state of shock. It seems that Monica's been gone for a week and they didn't know where she was. Apparently Monica went off the rails when she got back to California, was partying every night and not coming home until the next day sometimes. Her mother can't believe what happened. I wish I had known she was acting that way, maybe I could have done something or got her some help," RJ said.

"You can't put this on yourself. She had some problems before this happened. She was living a double life. By day she played your faithful wife and she was leading another life with those people she hung out with in the music business, when everything came out, she just lost it. Think about the idea of driving from California, to Oklahoma and the following you to Texas. Then she hid in the back of your truck waiting on us. That's insane," Lindsay said.

"You need to get some sleep," Lindsay said as she left RJ.

Lindsay went to her room, but there would be no sleeping that night. The ordeal that took place kept playing through Lindsay's mind. She could still see the blood that splattered on the back of the shattered rear glass of RJ's vehicle and hear the sound of the gunshot.

The next day Tameka called and woke Lindsay out of a sound sleep.

"Lindsay, are you ok?" Tameka asked.

248

"Yeah. I'm fine," Lindsay said.

"What in the hell happened. It's all over the news that RJ Jefferson's ex-wife held him and a woman hostage before then she killed herself. Was that you in the car with him?" Tameka asked.

"Yes, it was me and it was horrible. She was hiding behind the back seat until we got inside and then she pulled a gun on us. It was just crazy. Look, I'll call you back later. I hear the kids," Lindsay said.

Lindsay took RJ to get a rental car and he drove back to Oklahoma. The next week was a somber period as Monica's body was flown back to California and funeral arrangements were made. RJ paid for the expenses of the funeral, but was not going to attend, but Monica's mother insisted that he be there and he agreed to her wishes. Her funeral service was simple and elegant. Monica's mother did not want any of her enablers or users to be in attendance at the final home going and she personally turned rapper Little Assassin away from coming into the sanctuary with RJ Jefferson standing right behind her. Instead of causing a scene he quietly left the area.

Paparazzi photographers were all around the funeral services, and had staked out RJ Jefferson's home in Oklahoma the prior week. Lindsay even saw someone in a car with a camera parked on her street when she took the trash out one morning. The next morning after Monica's tragic death, gossip websites were full of cell phone images of the event. Social media simply exploded. Even photos of Lindsay, RJ and Monica in the vehicle were published online. Lindsay hoped that things would settle down after the funeral was over.

Lindsay didn't know where things would go with her and RJ Jefferson's personal relationship after Monica's death. She thought about the irony of their first kiss and his ex-wife's death occurring together. It was not a memory that would make the foundation of a solid relationship. Lindsay thought that maybe this was an indication that any personal relationship between her and her son's father was cursed.

21

RJ Jefferson came back from California a changed man. He spent a lot of time reflecting on his life and what had been going on around him that he had been ignoring. RJ thought about all of the cities, parties and clubs he had been to over the years. He thought about the women that followed the team, hooked up with players and the multiple mothers of children that some of his former teammates had. Then RJ Jefferson thought about the mother of his own son, Lindsay Wilson and his ex-wife Monica. That when it hit him that his behavior with Lindsay when he first met her was no different than what Monica was involved in with Little Assassin except that Lindsay was a teenager at the time and that made it worse.

RJ called Lindsay and asked her if she would come visit him in Oklahoma with her children. RJ said he would arrange for them to fly there, but Lindsay said she preferred to drive because she wouldn't have to deal with any photographers that might spot her in the airport.

Lindsay drove to Oklahoma on a Saturday morning and finally arrived at the gated entrance to RJ Jefferson's home. The gate was open and she drove up to the front entrance and parked in the circular driveway. This was a very large home with acres of rolling grounds surrounding the main house. Lindsay walked to the front door and pressed the doorbell. A housekeeper answered and welcomed Lindsay and her children inside.

Lindsay saw RJ coming down a spiral staircase.

Riley ran to his dad.

"Dad, is this your house?" Riley asked his father.

"Yep," this is it.

"Wow," Lindsay said as RJ hugged her and greeted Jasmine.

"Let me show you around," RJ said as he took them on a tour.

At the end of the tour RJ asked the kids if they wanted to watch a movie in the home theatre room and they readily agreed. He ordered up a pay-per-view showing of a popular children's movie and they settled in their seats with popcorn and drinks. RJ and Lindsay sat in an area right outside the movie room so that they could talk.

"How was the funeral?" Lindsay asked.

"It was a sad deal. A young woman felt she had nothing left worth living for and took her own life. It has caused me to think about a lot of things in general and about myself," RJ said.

"What do you mean?" Lindsay asked.

"I feel like Monica got used up and spit out by the world. I mean this modern culture we live in has an element that will exploit and consume women and throw them aside like garbage. I was a part of that for a while. I treated you that way. I get it now," RJ said.

"RJ, I know you get it now, but women also have to have enough strength to look out for themselves. Monica made some bad choices in the end. When I was stripping, there would be some man there every day telling me what he could do for me if I spent time with him. I knew it was all bullshit. I made my money and went home to my kids," Lindsay said.

"You had something more than yourself pushing you. Your children brought you home. Some of these young girls I see out there don't have a chance. They've bought into the idea that their way to the top is through their bodies and a man. I've lived it. Some of these young women are nineteen and twenty years old and they will do anything to be with a guy with a little money. They end up with no education, alone and with kids with no fathers around to help. It's almost like some of them expect it to happen, like it is just a normal part of life," RJ said.

"Look, I've lived that reality and I don't want to piss you off, but while you were living like this, I was struggling and barely hanging on while living in a rundown apartment. So what do you want to do, save the world now? Some of these women live that lifestyle by choice. I know because I've met them. There are some that got into a bad situation because they made an early mistake in life and would love the opportunity to put in work to do better. Those are the women that need help and a second chance," Lindsay said.

"Hey, I'm glad we can talk to each other like this now. After what we went through with Monica we should be able to say anything to each other. I think we have a self esteem problem with young women, especially in the black community. We have to get them to think beyond their idea that their best assets are their bodies and sex. Can you relate to what I thinking on that. I think that was one of the things that took Monica down," RJ said.

"RJ, I supported my family with my body for years by working in a strip club. They didn't come in there to see my brains. I'm white and I've been white all my life, but I think it's more about who has money and who doesn't. When you're broke and have few options, you look at what you have that is of value and men have placed value on a woman's body. Why do you think prostitution is the world's oldest profession? Women are trading their bodies to get a few bills paid these days, you know that. You can't just work on the women and girls to change things. Some of the young men have an attitude that they don't have any responsibility for the children they are bringing into the world. I can't point my figure at you, because you didn't know you had a child and you stepped up when you found out, but your behavior when you got me pregnant is what I'm talking about. You dropped into that little town, left your sperm behind and were gone. That's what's going on all over the place now. Am I right about that?" Lindsay asked.

"You know, you're right. You can't attack just one side of the problem. The attitude of irresponsibility among young men has to change too. How do you change that, there is an army of guys like Little Assassin promoting sex, drugs and partying as a lifestyle," RJ said.

"The only way to slow it down is to raise responsible young men and women and that takes both parents showing their children that doing the right thing pays off. When I was stripping I would always take a shower when I got home so my children would not smell the smoke from the club on me. I wasn't ashamed of what I did for a living, but I didn't have to expose them to it. There was a time when a girl getting pregnant meant there would be a meeting between the fathers of the girl and boy involved and often times a shotgun wedding would follow. It didn't mean that the marriage would last, but the general knowledge that was the way things went back then made those young men a lot more careful than they are now. Some kids today are three generations without a father in the house, so who's showing the boys how to be responsible men. They think that a woman being the single head of the house is the way it's supposed while the father just goes on his way. The girls think that raising children without the father in the house is normal, so where does it end," Lindsay said.

"How do you plan to handle that in your own household? You're raising a son and daughter on your own," RJ said.

"Wow! Ok, you went for the kill didn't you? I'm aware that I'm raising my kids alone. You know the situation with our son and I have managed to get his father involved in his life. My daughter, who I love to death, came about when I was making questionable choices in men. I never claimed to be perfect. Her father is in prison for a long time right now for selling drugs. I decided early on that I would not parade men in and out around my children, because it too dangerous and you don't know what these people will do now days. When you stayed over at my house the night everything happened with Monica, it was the first time a man has stayed under the same roof with my children, and you slept on the couch," Lindsay said.

"Who am I to judge someone else's choices in people? I badly misjudged what was going on with my own wife. I still can't wrap my head around what happened," RJ said.

"I still think about it every day too. I'm always questioning myself about showing that video to you," Lindsay said.

"No, you did the right thing. What happened after that was the result of a series of bad decisions on her part. If you hadn't told me, how would you even look me in the eyes knowing that she was making a fool out of the father of your son? What happened was not your fault. Monica made her choices and they didn't turn out well for her and that's why she was exposed. If Monica hadn't been in that bedroom with that scum, there would have been nothing to video and she could still be here alive, as my wife. I feel terrible and still had love for her. We were married. Things will get better with time," RJ said.

"Thank you. I've been carrying around this feeling of guilt for my part in this and I needed to know that you didn't blame me," Lindsay confessed.

"I don't blame you at all. Let it go and concentrate on the future," RJ said.

"Okay, back to what we were discussing. So, what are you thinking about doing?" Lindsay asked.

"Well I'm thinking about trying to start some kind of organization to take back the community and help at risk young women, but what you just said before let me know that including young men has to part of the solution. I'm thinking that I want to do more than just sit in some television studio every Sunday talking about football. I can use my fame or whatever influence I have to at least try to make a difference in somebody's life. You can go online and see teenage girls shaking their butts for the camera and putting it online for the world to see," RJ said.

"Everything that happened with Monica really shook you up didn't it?" Lindsay asked.

"Yes, it really shook me up. Maybe it woke me up," RJ said.

"Well how would you pay for something like that? I know you have money, but something that big could drain you quick," Lindsay asked.

"I figured I would get my sponsors involved. They make a lot of money off young people and they could use the good pr in giving back, plus, I've got a lot of high profile friends that I think would put their weight behind something like this. Back in the day, professional athletes got involved in politics and social causes. Now they are too concerned about not offending anyone so they can remain marketable, all they do is buy big homes, fancy cars and party. I'm going to see if I can change that," RJ said.

"Have your sponsors said anything to you about what happened with Monica. Did it hurt you with them?" Lindsay asked.

"They're all sticking with me. My ads will be pulled for a while and then they will slowly put them back on the air as time goes on. Well what do you think about what we just discussed?" RJ asked.

"I think that it's a great idea. It won't be easy, but it's a great idea. I'm impressed that you even came up with it," Lindsay said.

"Well, I try to be more than just a big dumb jock," RJ said while laughing.

"That's the first smile I seen since Monica died," Lindsay said.

They got up and went into the theatre room to check on the children and sat down and watched the rest of the movie with them.

It was getting late and Lindsay thought about heading back to Dallas when RJ made a surprising request.

"Why don't you spend the night and go back tomorrow?" RJ asked.

"Spend the night. I didn't bring a change of clothes or anything. I wasn't expecting this," Lindsay said.

"It's just one night. I've got six bedrooms in this place and I can spend some time with Riley. There's a shopping center about three miles down the street and I'll get you and the kids a change of clothes," RJ said.

Lindsay just looked at him for a long time and saw the pleading look in his eyes.

"Okay, we will spend the night," Lindsay said.

RJ smiled and got his car keys and drove down to a local shopping center and bought a change of clothes for Lindsay and the children. Lindsay was taken aback because RJ was addressed as Mr. Jefferson every time they entered a store and he signed many autographs for the short time they were out. RJ had also instructed his chef to prepare a meal for dinner and to have it ready to serve when they returned.

They ate out by the pool and watched the sun slowly sink behind the horizon. The children went to bed in bedrooms next to each other on the upstairs level. Lindsay would sleep in a guest bedroom down the hall from the master suite.

Lindsay was sitting in an upstairs mezzanine area off the master bedroom that faced an open window that had a view of downtown Oklahoma City.

RJ came in with a bottle of wine and proceeded to pour a glass for him and Lindsay. RJ sat alongside Lindsay and he pressed a button and music begin to play from speakers built into the ceiling. One side of the room feature a large fish tank with brightly colored tropical fish swimming about and the other side had a waterfall structure with water trickling down with multicolored backlighting.

"This is so relaxing," Lindsay said.

"Lindsay I wanted to talk about what happened that night before we knew Monica was in the car. We kissed," RJ said.

"Yes, we did kiss," Lindsay replied.

"How did you feel about that?" RJ asked.

"Well, I was surprised, and it didn't suck," Lindsay replied.

"Well, I'm glad it didn't suck," RJ replied.

"That's not what I meant. I was just surprised that you kissed me and I kissed you back. I have so many mixed up feelings about you because of how we first met. I don't know if I can truly forgive and let go of my anger, even after all of these years," Lindsay said.

"I know. I think that's one reason I kissed you. I wanted to see if there was anything there. We have a son together and if there was any small chance we had a connection I wanted to find out, but that entire night was taken over by what happened after that?" RJ said.

"Can I ask you a personal question?" Lindsay asked.

"Of course," RJ replied.

"After you found out what Monica was doing with the guy, did you get tested? I mean she was your wife and I imagine you weren't using protection. Why would you?" Lindsay asked.

"Yes, I did get tested and I was scared to death. I didn't know who all she had been with and definitely did how many people that guy had slept with. I think that may have made me the angriest of all. It just showed me that she didn't care about me or my well being at all. I was so disappointed in her for that," RJ said.

"It's getting late. I need to get to bed so I can make that drive tomorrow," Lindsay said as stood up to go to her room.

As Lindsay stood RJ grasped her right hand and pulled her down to his lap and kissed her softly.

Lindsay kissed him back and looked him in the eyes.

"What are you doing? Don't you think this is too soon?" she asked.

RJ didn't answer and kissed her again and Lindsay wrapped her arms around his neck. RJ stood up and lifted Lindsay in his arms and walked towards the bed.

"No, not there. That's her bed. I can't go there," Lindsay said.

RJ understood and carried Lindsay back over to where they were before and laid her down on the oversized curved seating unit they were in before. RJ slowly peeled off Lindsay's clothing and kissed each area of flesh as it was uncovered like he was christening new territory. Lindsay's mind was in a fog and her senses were spinning out of control. She felt pleasure, guilt and passion all coming down on her at once. Lindsay felt conflicted to be with this man who derailed her life all those years ago and somehow felt she was betraying herself. Guilt washed over Lindsay for being in the bedroom of RJ's deceased ex-wife who she exposed as a fraud and eventually led to her divorce and breakdown. Pleasure flowed through Lindsay's body that she had deprived of carnal release for the sake of her children.

Lindsay was stretched out over the leather of the chair without a stitch of clothing on her body. RJ looked up at Lindsay and she stroked his forehead before pulling him up to her body. RJ positioned his body over hers and Lindsay let him know what she wanted with a slight smile. Lindsay gasped as she touched this man who felt like he was made out of solid muscle. RJ slowly joined with Lindsay and it was a new experience for both of them. Although it was true that their son shared their DNA it did not happen out of love, but out of one sided lust. Lindsay looked deep into RJ's eyes before feeling his strength and power move her entire body. Lindsay gasped before wrapping her legs around his thighs, her arms around his neck and meeting him movement for movement. As they made love Lindsay could feel a welling up of emotional residue that she had been holding onto for years. With her eyes tightly closed she found a release that was beyond physical. Lindsay began to shake uncontrollably with tears running down her face. RJ joined Lindsay in releasing his own form of pain as he was scarred from the unexpected end to his marriage and the tragic death of his ex-wife.

Afterwards they looked at each other as Lindsay reclined against the chest of her son's father.

"What do we do now?" Lindsay asked.

"We can't go back since we just made love," RJ said.

"Did you invite me up here hoping that would happen?" Lindsay asked.

"Well. I'm going to completely honest with you. I was really suspicious of your motives when I first found out about the whole paternity thing at first. I figured that you were some woman I had an encounter with in the past trying to blackmail me into settling to protect my reputation, but I was wrong," RJ said.

"Why did you storm out of the office when you found out that Riley was really your son?" Lindsay asked.

"I was angry at myself. I didn't know you then. I figured, well. I thought. Okay this is what I thought. How stupid could I be to get some little dumb, country white chick pregnant and risk my entire future," RJ said.

Lindsay was stunned by his words and sat up and looked him in his eyes.

"That's what you thought? Oh God," Lindsay said wiping a tear.

RJ could see that she was visibly hurt by what he said.

"Lindsay, that was before I knew you or our son. You're beautiful, smart and a great mother," RJ said."

"Well, I thought you were a totally insensitive asshole who had no interest in getting to know your own son. I hated you, but I insisted that you get to know Riley and be a part of his life. I think it's important for a boy to be with his father," Lindsay said.

"I'm glad you did that or I would not have gotten to know you too," RJ said.

"So, you don't think I'm just a little dumb, country white chick anymore?" Lindsay asked.

"Well, you're still country," RJ said.

"You're still an asshole. RJ, I was a kid when I got pregnant with Riley. I told you how my family treated me. It wasn't funny. It was hell," Lindsay said.

RJ looked at Lindsay like he just began to understand how much she went through while he moved on to a prosperous career playing professional sports. RJ pulled Lindsay close to him and hugged her.

"I'm sorry," RJ said.

"RJ, maybe we made a mistake by sleeping together. It was good, but I don't know if you really get me. I'm not some dumb bimbo and I don't take a back seat to any man. RJ, do you really respect me?" Lindsay asked.

"Yes, I respect you and I respect you even more now. You aren't like most women I've been around who are just saying what I want to hear," RJ said.

"That's because I'm not like those other women. You are my son's father and I look at you that way first. I'm not a celebrity groupie trying to come up on your fame or money. What happened in that law office was strictly business. I don't know how you really felt about all of that, but I was advised to do what I did. I want to clear the air so that there is nothing hiding in the background if we decide to see each other as more than co-parents. How did you really feel about the settlement?" Lindsay asked.

"Well, I thought it was excessive and the part about keeping quiet about the statutory rape charge seemed to be extortion to me. It felt like I was being bribed," RJ said.

"RJ, I was sixteen years old. My so-called friend, Cindy, set me up and invited me to that game and I was excited to go and be around college

264

kids. I didn't find out until later that her boyfriend had promised you that he would have a girl there for you to do your business with. I wasn't used to drinking and don't even remember what happened," Lindsay said.

"Hold up. You're telling me that you were at that party because Mark told Cindy he promised me that he would get a girl for me. Mark told me that you wanted to talk to me and were a big fan of mine," RJ said.

"I'd never heard of you before that game. I heard your name being called at the game and that was the first time I'd ever heard of you," Lindsay said.

"Mark never told me he was getting a girl for me. I'm confused," RJ said.

"That's what Cindy told me the next day when she drove me back home," Lindsay said.

"Something's not right, here. It sounds like you got set up and I was just stupid, but somebody's lying. I'm going to find out who's lying, do you want to help me?" RJ said.

"Yes. I do want to help you, because I want the truth. Cindy stuck to her story when I confronted her at her real estate office in Nacogdoches," Lindsay said.

"You know I haven't seen my old buddy Mark in a while. Maybe I should invite him and his wife up for a visit," RJ said.

"Lindsay, I want to apologize again for being insensitive. I want to continue to see you as more than just Riley's mother and find out where this can go. I have feelings for you, but I don't want to move too fast. How about you?" RJ asked.

"I want to keep seeing you too, but we have to go slow. We have so much bad history between us and have to see if we could even function as a couple without hitting each other over the head with something from the past, but this is nice right now," Lindsay said as she kissed RJ again.

22

Lindsay went back to her life in Dallas, but she spoke with RJ on the phone every day and without any notice, flowers or some other gift would appear at her door. This was a new experience for Lindsay as she had never been pursued or courted by any man and the fact that it was this man made it more unique. Lindsay's experiences with men had been a series of brief encounters with mostly unexpected and often unpleasant outcomes. Plans were in the works for Lindsay to start shooting her follow-up to her successful Strippercise video. She had become somewhat of an underground celebrity and even conducted a session at a local fitness club that was full of excited attendees. Then an unexpected call came in from RJ.

"Lindsay, I've got a date for Mark and Cindy to come up and visit next Saturday. Would it be possible for you to come up here the night before?" RJ asked.

"Sure. I want to find out what really happened that day that changed my life," Lindsay said.

"What about the kids," RJ asked.

"It will be the start of spring break, and they will be visiting their grandparents, so I'll be there," Lindsay said.

"Great, I can't wait to see you again," RJ said.

Lindsay was wrought with anticipation. This visit by Cindy and her husband should answer a lot of questions and either RJ was lying or Cindy was covering something up that she didn't want known.

Lindsay flew to Oklahoma City and RJ picked her up at the airport. Cindy and Mark were scheduled to arrive at RJ's home before noon the next day. Given that they were alone for the rest of the day, RJ and Lindsay indulged in each other and made plans for how they would handle the visit with Cindy and Mark.

Mark and Cindy drove into RJ's driveway around eleven thirty on Saturday morning. RJ gave them the grand tour of the house and grounds before they sat down to talk. Lindsay stayed in the closet as they briefly looked into the master bedroom. As RJ showed Mark and Cindy the outside of the home, Lindsay moved down to the theatre room. RJ said he would come over to the area near the theatre room to talk with Mark and Cindy.

"RJ your place is amazing," Cindy said.

"Thank you," RJ said.

"RJ, it's been a hell of a year for you. I mean you won the championship, got divorced and then that stuff with your ex-wife, I just couldn't believe it," Mark said.

"Yeah, there've been a lot of highs and lows. Let's not forget, I also found out I was a father, and you guys had something to do with that," RJ said.

"Well, yeah and that too. Weren't you with your son's mother when your ex took her life?" Mark said.

"Yes, I was. Lindsay, that's her name. We went out to discuss our son and joint parenting, but things took an unexpected turn. Cindy you knew Lindsay from before, right?" RJ said.

"Yeah. We were casual friends when I was younger. You know, high school days," Cindy replied.

"Mark you told me that Lindsay wanted to talk to me when we were at the club after the game all those years ago in college. Did you know her too?" RJ asked.

"Well, you know, I had met her through Cindy, but we weren't like friends or anything," Mark said.

"I guess I really stepped in it that night and it came back to bite me in the ass, big time," RJ said.

"Well she told me she thought you were hot and wanted to talk to you. I had no idea she was that young. Sorry man," Mark said.

"Hey man, I did what I did. Nobody made me take her over to your place," RJ said.

Cindy was shifting uncomfortably in her chair as that conversation continued. Cindy's eyes widened when she saw Lindsay emerge from the theatre room.

"Hi Cindy, aren't you going to introduce me to your husband?" Lindsay asked.

"What are you doing here? What's going on?" Cindy asked as she looked around at RJ puzzled.

"That's what I want to know. Mark, I thought you said you already knew Lindsay," RJ said.

"Well, maybe I got her mixed up with somebody else. It was a long time ago," Mark said.

"Okay. Cindy you told me that Mark asked you to find a girl for RJ to be with when he came to town. Mark just said something different. Could it be that Mark has a different story because he never said anything to RJ about getting him a girl before the game, did he?" Lindsay said.

"I don't have to answer to you," Cindy said.

"Okay Cindy, I'm tired of lying about this. Just tell them what happened," Mark said.

"Mark!" Cindy said.

Cindy looked at her husband and looked down at the floor.

"Okay! I was pledging to a sorority and needed to do one last task to go over. I had to sleep with a player from a visiting football team or get someone else to do it in my place. We called it a sacrifice. I wasn't going to do it because of Mark, so I found a sacrifice and it was Lindsay. I had to have proof, so when RJ and Lindsay were in the apartment bedroom, I came in with one of the sorority sisters and confirmed that the sacrifice happened. We watched you go in and waited before we went in to see that it happened," Cindy said.

Lindsay just stood there with her face blank and her fists clenched as waves of anger washed over here. Without warning Lindsay exploded.

"You fucking bitch!" Lindsay said as she lunged at Cindy.

Mark went to make a move to defend his wife, but RJ put a stop to that.

"Mark! Don't you move a fucking muscle!" RJ said as he stood up blocking Mark.

Lindsay had pinned Cindy against the floor and was pummeling her with wild blows to both sides of her head as Cindy tried to shield her face with her hands. Both women were wearing short skirts and both garments were bunched at their waist levels as they struggled on the floor.

Lindsay ripped Cindy's blouse from her body as she tried to crawl away. Lindsay pinned Cindy against the floor again and was straddling her back while Cindy was face down. Lindsay grabbed Cindy's head in both hands and was poised to begin pounding it against the black marble floor face first when suddenly; Lindsay was lifted into the air by the waist. RJ had pulled Lindsay off Cindy before she seriously injured her.

"You two need to get out of here now!" RJ said to Mark and Cindy.

Cindy grabbed the remnants of her blouse and left with her husband.

"I'll kill you bitch if I get my hands on you! I'll monkey stomp your ass bitch!" Lindsay screamed while sobbing.

Lindsay was still clutching a fistful of Cindy's hair extensions in her hands when Mark and Cindy drove off.

"Put me down," Lindsay said to RJ.

RJ put Lindsay down and she proceeded to straighten her clothes and hair.

"Remind me to never piss you off," RJ said.

Lindsay started crying and collapsed into RJ's arms.

"She did that to me to join some stupid group! That's just sick!" Lindsay said.

"I know. I'm actually shocked about what really happened that night. We were both deceived, but you really paid a high price," RJ said.

"I'm sorry. It was like I just blacked out. I wanted to kill that bitch. She lied through her teeth and pulled her weak ass husband into it. She probably has his balls in a jar sitting on a counter," Lindsay said.

"Now, what do you know about monkey stomping somebody? You didn't grow up in the hood," RJ said.

"I may not have grown up in the hood, but I've lived there for a long time," Lindsay said.

RJ just looked at her and smiled.

"What?" Lindsay said.

"If you could have only had my view. All I saw was ass and elbows," RJ said.

"What? Was my dress up around my waist or something?" Lindsay asked.

"Neither one of your dresses were covering what they were supposed to be covering," RJ said.

"Oh well. At least her husband got to see what a real ass looks like. The next time he grabs that boney butt he can think about this donk," Lindsay said.

"Maybe I was wrong about you, so you didn't set me up with your buddy Mark as a target, you just were dumb and irresponsible after you got there," Lindsay said.

"Well yeah, I guess you could put it that way. They thought their lie would never be uncovered because the only people that knew the two different versions were you and me. I guess they figured we would never get together and come up with two versions of what happened that didn't match," RJ said.

"Did you see the look on her face when I walked out? She knew she was trapped. It's amazing what people will do to another person to get what they want. I could never do that to some young girl," Lindsay said.

"Well at least we know what kind of people they are and lengths they will go to get what they want. Those kind of people are dangerous if they get too much power in their hands," RJ said.

"So in the middle of all of that commotion, you were looking at my ass. Were you looking at her skinny ass too?" Lindsay asked.

"There wasn't much to see, you know in comparison," RJ said.

"You men are such dogs. You know considering your choice in women, you must be an ass man. Your ex-wife had plenty butt. She had more than I do. Is that your weakness?" Lindsay asked.

"Well, I do appreciate a woman with curves in all of the right places," RJ said.

With that Lindsay started walking upstairs and she dropped her skirt along the way. Halfway up the staircase she slapped her own butt with her hand and RJ followed her as if on cue.

Lindsay began to see RJ in a different light after finding out that he didn't willingly conspire with Mark and Cindy to set her up as a sex toy for one night. Her trust in him grew over the months to follow as they spent more time together. RJ also grew closer to Lindsay's daughter, Jasmine, who was young and would not understand why RJ would spend time with her brother and not with her. Jasmine had never met her father who was sent to prison before she was born. Jasmine's father told Lindsay that he did not want his daughter to see him for the first time while he was behind bars.

Then one night while Lindsay and RJ were sitting out by the pool after the children had gone to bed, RJ looked over at Lindsay.

"What?" Lindsay asked.

"I love you," RJ said.

"You do?" Lindsay replied.

"I've been waiting on you to say that. I fell in love with you a long time ago, but I wanted to hear you say it first," Lindsay said as they kissed.

"Why didn't you tell me?" RJ said.

"I didn't want to get rejected, so I waited," Lindsay said.

"I think you didn't say anything because it would have meant that you had to admit to yourself that I am really a good guy who showed poor judgment and did a bad thing. You don't like to be wrong. I've learned that about you," RJ said.

"Really? You've learned all of that about me. I'll keep letting you think you're the smart one. Men like that," Lindsay said.

"You know how to cut a brother to the quick," RJ said.

"When I was working in those clubs, every man walking in there thought they were God's gift to women. They had this idea that the dancers were all just brainless bimbos. One guy called me a thot baby mama because I wouldn't let him have his way with me. He didn't know me, but he just assumed I was some woman that would do anything for money. He tried to put his hands on me and I hit him with a bottle. Later on he stalked me and sabotaged my car so it would stop running. This guy was a doctor. He attacked me and tried to rape me in a parking lot. One of the other dancers came along and saved me. That happened on my last night working in the club and I think about how close I came to never seeing my children grow up. What I'm saying is, a lot of my experiences with men have not been that great, but for some reason the world looks at some women in the position I was in and call us ratchet, thots and baby mamas, most of the time we're just trying to survive. We had help getting in positions like I was in. Those babies had fathers, but most of the time the women were the ones trying to raise them the best way they could. Most mothers won't walk away from their kids like a lot of guys do. How do some men just have kids and move on like they had no part in it. I'm not talking about you because you didn't even know you had a son," Lindsay said.

"You had a hell of a life back then didn't you? I'm glad all of that is over and you don't have to live that way anymore. You know I've thought about how someone can have a child or even multiple children and move on like it didn't happen. I don't understand that. I've played with guys that had four of five children by different women and they really had no relationship with them or their mothers. Society seems to have given men a pass while they pile on the women. When I started thinking about doing the foundation, I did a little research. Almost all of the research is on how many children are born out of wedlock to women and on how many households are headed by women without a man in the house. I started thinking about why is everything focused on the women like it's all their faults. Then it occurred to me that most of these reports are from government agencies. The government is going to measure what is measurable. Okay, a woman has a child; it gets reported to the government. The census is taken, they record who the head of the household is. The father doesn't have to be there when the baby is born, but the woman has to be there because she is the one giving birth. I don't think they can measure how many children some random guy has when he is walking down the street, but people can see a single woman walking with her three kids with no man around. The women with multiple children are visible and the men hide in plain sight," RJ said.

"Maybe those guys need a big sign on them like, I have five kids by four different women," Lindsay said.

"Here's the kicker. Some of those same guys I know that have children spread all over the country, will go into a club and call some woman a ratchet ho or thot at the drop of a hat. It's crazy. I'm thinking, no, you're the ratchet one," RJ said.

"Hey, football season starts in a month. Oklahoma is going to retire my number at halftime,

I would like for you to be there. Can you make it?" RJ asked.

"Sure, I can come. I'd love to be there," Lindsay said.

"There's only one thing," RJ said.

"What's that?" Lindsay asked.

"I want you to go home with me and meet my parents before the game," RJ said.

"Meet your parents! Why?" Lindsay replied in surprise.

"They want to see Riley, he is their grandson and they've never met him. Since we're serious about our relationship, I want them to meet you too. I've wanted to ask you to let me take him down there to meet them, but thought you might be uncomfortable letting him go with me alone. After just telling each other how we feel, I thought it was the perfect time for this to happen. I always visited them every year before the season started and even though I'm not playing anymore. I wanted to keep up that tradition," RJ explained.

"Okay. We can do that. I mean, RJ, no man has ever taken me to meet his parents before. I'm nervous already, what if they don't like me?" Lindsay fretted.

"You'll be fine. They don't bite," RJ said.

23

Two weeks before RJ was to be honored by his former team, he drove up the driveway of his parent's home in east Texas about forty miles from where Lindsay grew up. Lindsay and her two children were also inside his Cadillac Escalade sports utility vehicle. Lindsay was very apprehensive about meeting RJ's parents, especially his mother.

RJ's father, Harold Jefferson, was outside looking under the hood of his Cadillac Coupe Deville.

"Hey old man," RJ said as he got out and walk over to his father.

"Who you calling old?" Harold said as he hugged his son.

Harold was a big man who stood six feet two inches tall. Lindsay could see who RJ inherited his physical size from.

"Who is that standing behind you?" Harold asked.

"Riley, this here is your grandpa," RJ said.

"Come here and give me a hug," Harold said.

Riley shyly walked over and felt the welcoming embrace of his paternal grandfather for the first time.

"This is Riley's sister Jasmine and this is Lindsay," RJ said as he introduced everyone.

Jasmine got a hug just like her brother did.

"It's nice to meet you Mr. Jefferson," Lindsay said as she held out her hand.

"It's good to meet you too Lindsay. Jeremiah didn't tell me how pretty you were," Harold said.

"Thank you, but who's Jeremiah?" Lindsay asked.

"That's my middle name. Riley Jeremiah Jefferson. For some reason down here they tend to call people by their middle names sometimes," RJ explained.

"That's right. Me, his mother and everybody else that really knows him calls him Jeremiah. That RJ stuff is for everybody else. Come on inside. Your mama is in the kitchen cooking," Harold informed.

The group walked up to the house and entered the front door.

"Harold! Why didn't you tell me they were here?" Evelyn Jefferson asked as she turned around.

"Well, I brought them up here didn't I?" Harold said.

"Look at those pretty babies. Come give Granny a hug," Evelyn said as she stooped down with her arms open wide.

Riley and Jasmine both went to Evelyn and she gave them a big hug. Although Jasmine was not her biological grandchild, Evelyn knew a small child would not understand being treated differently. In Evelyn's mind she would treat both of them equally in her home. After showering affection on her grandson and his little sister, Evelyn stood and hugged her son.

"Mama this is Lindsay," RJ said.

"It's nice to meet you Mrs. Jefferson," Lindsay said.

"It's good to finally meet you. We need to talk later, but I've got to finish cooking," Evelyn said.

"Can I help?" Lindsay asked.

"You know how to cook?" Evelyn asked.

"Yes ma'am. What are you fixin?" Lindsay asked.

"Did you say fixin. You are a country girl aren't you? Well, I'm going to fry some catfish. Make some cornbread and cook some black eyed peas," Evelyn said.

"Black eyed peas. Do you have any fat back? I like to use it for flavor," Lindsay said.

"You know about fat back? Here girl, put this apron on and show me what you got. You men can get out of this kitchen and out of our way. We'll call you when it's ready, but it's going to be a while," Evelyn said.

Lindsay looked at RJ and smiled.

"Okay mama. Me and daddy are going to take a little ride," RJ said as he left the kitchen with his father.

Evelyn took the children to the living room and found a children's channel on television and before long they were asleep on the sofa. Both children were tired from the trip from Oklahoma. Evelyn and Lindsay shared cooking duties in silence until RJ's mother decided to bring up a subject that had been on her mind for a while.

"Lindsay, you seem to be a nice person. Jeremiah is my son, but I'm not foolish enough to think he's perfect just because of that. On behalf of my family, I want to apologize for what he did to you when you got pregnant with my grandson. He was raised better than that," Evelyn said.

"Mrs. Jefferson, you don't need to apologize to me. RJ was a grown man and he made the choice to do what he did, not you," Lindsay said.

"I know he did, but we've always told him a person's behavior reflects either good or bad on their family. If Riley in there got into a fight at school, what the first thing that happens. They call you to find out why he's acting that way. They always say it mama's fault. You know I'm right about that," Evelyn said.

"Yes ma'am," Lindsay agreed thinking back on when she was called when Riley got in a fight at school.

"How are you doing? You know, with how you feel about that whole situation," Evelyn asked.

"I've made my peace with it. RJ has told me over and over again about how sorry he is for treating me like that. He said he's a different person now. I believe him. I believe people can change once they get a clear understanding of how their actions affect the lives of others," Lindsay said.

"The question I have, is can you forgive him. I'm not just talking about forgiving him for his sake. I'm talking about forgiving him for your sake. Lindsay, you need to release this weight from your soul," Evelyn said.

"What do you mean?" Lindsay asked.

"I want you to think of all the things you had to do over these years that you probably would not have done if that had never happened to you. You had to take care of your children, make a living the best way you could and, God knows, maybe even do some things you never would have done if things were different. I don't judge anybody, because that's not my job, but you had to be strong to everybody on the outside and not show weakness for the sake of your children. Tell me whatever you want to unburden yourself," Evelyn said.

Lindsay looked into Evelyn's eyes with an almost fearful gaze.

"Come on. It's safe in here," Evelyn said.

"I was so scared when I found out I was pregnant. I was just a kid and thought I was worthless for someone to do to me what happened that night. It was like what happened to me after that didn't matter to anybody. Nobody cared about how I felt. Everybody was worried about what they wanted, even my family. Once my folks found out I was pregnant by a black man, they disowned me. They were more concerned about what other people would think about them than about what happened to me. I was their blood and they threw me away. I went to live with my best friend's family, but I was always thinking they would get tired of me and put me out. It was really hard when I started to show, you know. There I was walking around school with my pregnant belly sticking out and the other kids talking about me. They called me names and were so mean to me. It got out that a black man was my baby's father and all the white kids turned their backs on me. I was so scared when Riley was born. Tameka and her family were there with me, but my own mother wasn't there. I felt awful and then I had this little baby in my arms. Me and my friend, Tameka, left for Dallas when Riley was just a baby. It was so hard. There were times when we didn't have enough to eat at first because we were too broke to buy food. If I had any extra food I would give it to Riley and go to bed hungry. It was so hard," Lindsay said as she started to sob and break down.

"Come here baby," Evelyn said as she held Lindsay in her arms.

Lindsay sobbed into Evelyn's shoulder like a baby.

"It's okay. I know it was hard, but you came through it," Evelyn said.

"I'm sorry," Lindsay said as she stood up.

Evelyn gave Lindsay a paper towel to dry her eyes.

"You don't have anything to be sorry about. Mamas need hugs and shoulders to cry on too. I know. Jeremiah doesn't realize it, but I married his father when he was one year old. I was a single mother myself. I guess the young folks call it a baby mama now days. Well, I was a baby mama too," Evelyn admitted.

"I had no idea," Lindsay said.

"Jeremiah doesn't know, so please don't tell him, but I know where you're coming from. I was judged by family and friends alike. I was called all kind of names and some men thought I was an easy target just because I was a single mother. Harold finally grew up some and we got married. We moved here and started our family life together. As

283

far as people around here knew, we were just a family of three without that other baggage," Evelyn said.

"You really do get it. I've never had anyone ask me what I went through because of how my life changed so fast. I feel so much better to just let it come out. I felt embarrassed to know I was in that situation and ashamed, but it was real. Thank you," Lindsay said.

"Don't thank me. I don't know what you and Jeremiah are to each other, but you are my grandson's mother and that makes you family. I care about and for my family. Besides, us baby mamas have to stick together," Evelyn said with a wink.

Lindsay laughed and kissed Evelyn on the cheek.

"Hey Evelyn come here!" Harold called from the front door.

"Harold, what is it?" Evelyn said as she walked to the front door.

Lindsay and Evelyn looked outside. Harold and RJ were standing next to a new black Cadillac CT6 Platinum sedan.

"What in the world!" Evelyn exclaimed.

"I finally talked him into getting rid of that old car. I just bought this for him," RJ said.

"This is the first new Cadillac they've come out with in a long time that I think is a real Cadillac. I wasn't gonna drive those little ass cars they were making with a Cadillac name slapped on them. I'm a big man and I need a big car," Harold said.

"Good lord. You two get cleaned up. We can eat in about thirty minutes," Evelyn said.

Lindsay was taken aback by the fact that RJ spent eighty thousand dollars without blinking an eye to buy his father a new car. After thirty minutes they all sat down around the dining room table. Everyone held hands while Harold said a prayer and enjoyed a family meal. Lindsay looked around and realized that environment had been missing from her life for years.

That night three of RJ old friends came by and they were engaged in a game of dominoes on the deck behind the house. RJ had a big cigar in his mouth and beer in his hand. RJ's friends Albert, Michael and Paul were having quite a time while slapping the dominoes down so hard that the table shook.

"When those four get together to play dominoes I don't go around them. Why do they have to do all that cussing to just play a game?" Evelyn commented.

Lindsay was looking on in fascination, because she had never seen RJ that way with old friends around him. Lindsay decided she would go out on the deck and meet RJ's companions. Lindsay was wearing a pair of tight white jeans, a snug blue top and sneakers. Lindsay walked out of the back door.

"That's fifteen on yo ass!" Paul yelled as he slapped a domino down on the table.

"Hey RJ. Hi guys. So are you going to introduce me to your friends?" Lindsay asked.

The raucous domino game fell silent.

"Ahh yeah. This is Paul, Albert and Michael. Fellas this is, ahh, my girlfriend Lindsay," RJ said.

"It's nice to meet all of you. I'll let you get back to your game," Lindsay said as she turn and walked back to the door.

Lindsay didn't believe what she just heard. RJ introduced her to his oldest friends as his girlfriend, not simply as his son's mother, but his girlfriend. Lindsay went inside, but stood there with just the screen door closed and could still hear the men outside.

"Damn man. That's your baby mama. She's fine as fuck!" Paul remarked.

"You don't see white women, built like that every day with an ass like that man. So you're going with your son's mother. Damn!" Michael said.

"Hey dogs! I'm sitting right here! Don't look so damn hard. Yeah we have a little something going on and it's nice you know," RJ said.

"Look man. You've gone through hell with what happened with your ex-wife. I'm happy for you," Michael said as he placed a domino on the table.

"I'm glad you're happy for me. I hope you're happy for this twenty-five I'm putting on yo ass. Game!" RJ said as he slapped his domino on the table.

"Damn! How did I miss that?" Michael said.

"You got distracted. That's why I had her come out here," RJ said with a laugh.

"Man, now I know you're lying," Albert said as they all got up from the table.

"Us regular folks have to go to work tomorrow," Paul said as they said their goodbyes.

RJ went inside the house and it was getting late.

"Alright, we have plenty of space since Jeremiah insisted we add on to the house after he started playing pro football. Everybody has their own room. Lindsay your room is on the left side of the hall and Jeremiah on the right. The kids have these two rooms up front with the bathroom in the middle," Evelyn said.

"Mama, I'm going to stay up for a little while and watch TV," RJ said.

"Your father is already asleep and I'm joining him. Those kids wore me out," Evelyn said.

"I'm going to put Riley and Jasmine to bed. I'll be back," Lindsay said.

Lindsay came back and sat across from RJ.

"RJ what was that outside tonight?" Lindsay asked.

"Oh we always carry on like that when we get together," RJ said.

"I'm not talking about that. You introduced me as your girlfriend. Did I miss something?" Lindsay said.

"I didn't know you were coming out there and when I told them who you were, I used the closest description of how I feel about you. How do you feel about that?" RJ said as he held Lindsay's hand.

287

"Well, it sounded strange to hear it announced to your oldest friends, before we discussed it, but I'll be your girlfriend if you will be my boyfriend," Lindsay said with a smile.

"Okay, now we sound like two teenagers," RJ said with a laugh.

"It's getting late and I'm going to bed," Lindsay said as she kissed RJ on the cheek.

RJ went to his room thirty minutes later. About two o'clock in the morning Lindsay felt her bed shift and her eyes flew open.

"It's me," RJ said in a whisper.

"What are you doing in here?" Lindsay asked also in a whisper.

RJ didn't answer, but instead slid under the sheets and wrapped his arms around Lindsay from behind. RJ snuggled up to Lindsay and she lay there with her eyes wide open.

"You don't think you're getting some tonight, do you? RJ, this is your parent's house. They are right down the hallway," Lindsay said quietly.

"Their bedroom is on the other side of the living room," RJ informed while talking into Lindsay's ear.

Lindsay was trying to resist RJ's advances, but he was pushing all the right buttons by kissing the back of her neck and using his hands to massage all of her pleasure points. Although RJ locked the bedroom door when he came into the room, the potential of being discovered added to the excitement of the moment. Lindsay's willpower was weakening as her breathing began to quicken. Lindsay turned to face RJ and kissed him deeply.

"We have to be quiet and quick," Lindsay said to RJ in the darkness.

Lindsay turned on her side and pushed her butt into RJ. RJ pulled Lindsay's panties down from behind and she soon gasped as he slowly mated their two bodies together. There in the darkness Lindsay and RJ performed a silent and sensual dance. Lindsay was building to a monumental climax, but knew she didn't dare scream out loud. Lindsay grabbed the pillow her head was resting on and bit down on it to muffle her sounds of bliss. RJ directed his vocal exclamation internally as he squeezed Lindsay tightly. As they slowly disengaged, RJ rolled onto his back and Lindsay rested her head on his shoulder.

"RJ, you were so bad, but that was so good and so hot," Lindsay admitted in a low tone of voice.

"Yes it was. I love you Lindsay Wilson," RJ said.

"I love you too. I meant to ask you, do you want me to call you Jeremiah like everybody does down here?" Lindsay asked.

"No, call me RJ," RJ said.

"I thought I would ask," Lindsay said.

"You know what I just thought about?" RJ said.

"What's that?" Lindsay asked.

"I never brought a girl over to the house when I was growing up. My friends used to tell me about girls they brought over to their folks house when they were gone, so you are the first girl I got some from in my parent's house and I did it with them at home. I win," RJ boasted.

"RJ, you're ridiculous. You'd better go to your room before we get caught," Lindsay said with a kiss.

RJ slid out of bed and tip toed across the hallway to his room. Lindsay rested her head on the pillow with a smile on her face and a feeling of contentment that she hadn't felt in years. Lindsay slowly drifted off to sleep with the calls of night birds in the woods bordering the field behind the home serenading her. Although Lindsay didn't know where her relationship with RJ was going, she was pleased with the direction it had taken.

The next day RJ took Lindsay for a walk in the woods behind his parent's home. They walked hand in hand down a tree lined trail until they came upon a flowing creek and RJ stopped. Lindsay and RJ sat at the base of a huge tree on one of its partially exposed roots.

"Why did you stop here?" Lindsay asked

"This is where I used to come when I was growing up to hang out with my friends. We would fish or just talk. It's where I would wonder what I would do when I grew up and left from down here. I could think about things here," RJ said.

"What did you think about?" Lindsay asked.

"I thought about where I would end up as I watched the water flow by and this was before I even started playing sports. My dad worked for a utility company. He operated this huge machine called a dragline that dug coal out of the earth and made good money. Down here everybody knew how well you were doing based upon who you worked for. I thought I could do that too when I grew up and then I started playing sports. My dreams changed and I changed," RJ stated.

"You changed? How did you change?" Lindsay asked.

"I went from being big, awkward Jeremiah and became RJ Jefferson. Girls started paying attention to me. People told me how great I was and I didn't even have to do as well in school to pass to the next grade. I believed the hype and became the asshole you met in that club after that football game down here. I became the guy that could get a young girl drunk, have sex with her and leave town without a second thought, because I was the fucking great RJ Jefferson and she was another piece of pussy," RJ said as he hung his head.

"RJ, you said you aren't like that anymore, so why are you beating yourself up about that now?" Lindsay asked.

"Until you showed up I never really had to look myself in the mirror and face the consequences of my past actions. I thought I had got lucky and there was nothing left behind from my reckless behavior, but there was. You and Riley paid the price for what I did while I moved on and was living a dream life. I'm glad that you had the guts to slap me upside my head with reality. I was living a lie. My marriage was all bullshit and I was pretending to be Mr. Squeaky Clean. The truth is, I just never got caught," RJ admitted.

"I understand about me and RJ, but is there something else I should know about. Do you have another child out there somewhere or is it something else?" Lindsay asked.

"No. I learned to be more careful about that, but when I first got into the league I didn't miss an opportunity to party. I indulged in a few mind altering substances during the off season and as many women as I could handle. Sometimes it was two or three at a time. I was young, rich and beautiful women were putting it in my face every time I turned around. I was out of control," RJ said.

"RJ, I get it. I'm not stupid. I'm surprised about the drugs, but there are plenty of women out there chasing rich and famous men. They love the excitement of being around someone like you even when they know it's not going anywhere. Some of them just want to be able to brag about all the famous dicks they've ridden. It's sad, but it's true, but there's one thing I don't understand, how did you go from doing all of that to where you are now. You should be broke, dead or out of the game a long time ago if you kept living that way," Lindsay said.

"My hero sat me down and snapped me out of it. I was going into my second year and we were about to play Miami. I was in a club and the last person in the world I expected to see showed up. Terrell Taylor, the record holder for career rushing yards walked into that strip club and sat down across from me while I was getting a lap dance. There he was and I had a woman bent over with her naked ass two inches from my face. I was in shock.

He introduced himself and asked me to take a walk with him," RJ said.

"What did he say to you?" Lindsay asked.

"He told me I was on the verge of being thrown out of the league because of my off field behavior. Basically he told me I was about to blow the greatest opportunity I would ever have in life by thinking with my ego and dick. That's exactly how he put it. He told me that just gravitating towards everything that felt good would lead me to destruction and a short career. He said he didn't want to see me labeled as just another dumb black athlete who couldn't control his social habits, sexual appetite or finances and end up washed up and broke. It snapped me out of it. He got me in contact with his advisors and here I am today," RJ said.

"I'm glad he showed up, but what I don't understand is why did he even care? He didn't know you," Lindsay said.

"I found out one of my offensive linemen, who is now my best friend, Datron Jenkins, was his cousin. He saw what I was doing a decided to call Terrell Taylor to step in. It was a good move. Datron told me what he did a couple of years later. I thanked him for doing it. So, do you still want to be the girlfriend of a former drug taking manwhore?" RJ asked.

"Nobody's perfect and we all have a past. I'm glad you thought enough of our relationship to tell this to me. I can tell it's not something you're proud of. I'm in love with the man you are now. I met the old you and didn't like him. I'll still be your girlfriend if you will still be the boyfriend of a former stripper baby mama," Lindsay said.

"That's a deal," RJ said as he kissed Lindsay.

RJ looked around.

"You know we could get in a quickie out here. There's nobody around," RJ said.

"You are so horny, but RJ, there could be snakes out here," Lindsay said.

"You're right. There are snakes out here. There goes one now," RJ said as a water moccasin swam by.

"Oh my God! Let's go back to the house," Lindsay said as she stood quickly.

"But, baby it's gone now. We can still..." RJ said.

RJ's pleading was to no avail as Lindsay started walking back to the house while leaving him behind.

Lindsay enjoyed the rest of her visit with RJ's parents, but she was ready to return home and see what the next steps in her life's journey would bring.

24

It was the day of the first game of the season and halftime had arrived. The general manager of the Oklahoma team was standing in the middle of the field with RJ Jefferson announcing that the franchise was retiring his number and unveiling his name on the honor circle of players that was posted between seating sections in the stadium. Lindsay, her children and RJ's parents were standing on the sideline watching. Suddenly the stadium announcer asked everyone to turn their attention to the large monitor hung over the stadium. Lindsay looked up with the rest of the fans. She was confused at first. The screen had an image of RJ on the screen and then she realized it was a live feed of him on the field. RJ dropped to one knee and his voice came blaring through the speakers.

"Lindsay Wilson. Will you marry me?" RJ said.

Lindsay froze and had an out of body experience before running onto the field to meet RJ half way and said yes. They kissed and the nation saw Lindsay Wilson get engaged on national television as this was the featured game of the week. The entire stadium erupted in cheers. Lindsay couldn't believe she had no idea that RJ was about to propose to her in front of the world. RJ slipped the largest diamond ring Lindsay had ever seen on her finger. RJ then scooped her up in his arms and carried her to the sidelines.

Lindsay, RJ and the rest of the group went to an elevator that took them up to a suite that RJ had reserved for the game. It became clear to Lindsay that he had been planning this for a while.

"Riley and Jasmine, I'm getting married to RJ. We are going to be a family. Isn't that great news?" Lindsay said.

Jasmine just looked at Lindsay and could care less because she had no idea what that meant.

"RJ told me he was going to ask you to marry him when you were at our house. I told him I thought you were a good woman and would be good for him," Evelyn said.

Lindsay looked at Evelyn in surprise that she never gave her a clue that she knew anything.

"He told me too and I think that's the way it should be for a boy to be raised by both his parents together," Harold said.

Evelyn leaned over to Lindsay and whispered in her ear.

"I heard him sneaking over to your room that night. He's too big to be that quiet and I hear everything that goes on in that house. This is between us don't tell him I know," Evelyn said.

Lindsay's cheeks turned read.

"You knew?" Lindsay said in a whisper.

Evelyn just looked at Lindsay and winked one eye at her.

"Are we going to live with daddy at his house in Oklahoma?" Riley asked.

"We haven't figured that out yet, but aren't you excited that your mom and dad will be together with you all the time?" Lindsay asked Riley.

"Yes! Dad can I get a dog after you and mama get married?" Riley asked RJ.

"Riley, I didn't know you wanted a dog," RJ said.

"Well, I didn't, but Tommy, my friend that lives down the street has a dog and I like playing with him, so I thought it would be fun to have a dog too," Riley said.

"Yes, you can get a dog, but a dog is a lot of responsibility and you will have to take care of it," RJ said.

"I'll take good care of it," Riley said.

"Okay. When we figure everything out, we'll get you a dog and you can pick it out yourself," RJ said.

"Thanks dad," Riley said.

Lindsay walked over to RJ while looking at her ring.

"I can't believe you did this. How long have you been planning this?" Lindsay asked.

"I've known I wanted to marry you for a while. I've been planning this for a couple of months. I called your father last week and asked for his permission to marry you," RJ said.

"Wait a minute. You called my father, Clyde Wilson, and asked for my hand in marriage. Are you serious?" Lindsay asked.

"Well, I thought it was the right thing to do since you've never been married before," RJ said.

"What did he say?" Lindsay asked.

"He gave me his blessings to and said I was a lucky man," RJ said.

"That's hilarious. Although I've made up with him, the idea of him giving you his permission to marry me makes my stomach turn, but I'm not going to let that get me down. I've got a wedding to plan," Lindsay said.

"Where do you want to get married," RJ asked.

"Back home in east Texas," Lindsay said.

"Okay. I'm cool with that. Why there?" RJ asked.

"I left there with my head down. I was embarrassed, broke and had a new baby that my parents didn't even want to see. I don't want that version of Lindsay Wilson to be the last image of me that everyone has in their head. I want to get married there so people can see that I survived and didn't stay down or crash and burn. I want them to see that my children are nice, decent kids. I also want them to see the big, handsome man I'm getting married to," Lindsay said.

"Lindsay, I don't want to wait too long. My dad is not in the best of health. He has diabetes and high blood pressure and I want him to be there at the wedding while he's still feeling good. Do you think you can pull it all together in three months? How does November or December sound?" RJ said.

"I think I can pull that off. I'm not planning a royal wedding, but I want it to be nice," Lindsay said.

"I'll set up a bank account to pay for everything and we can talk about other details later. Lindsay, I want this to be your dream wedding," RJ said.

26

Lindsay was excited to begin planning her wedding and designated her sister and Tameka as the planning committee. The second Saturday in December was settled on as the wedding date and all planning details revolved around that time, but there was one other less than romantic detail that had to be attended to.

RJ Jefferson was not one of those professional athletes who had been frivolous with his money over the years. Riley had surrounded himself with sound advisors and had a net worth approaching thirty million dollars. RJ's financial team insisted that Lindsay sign a prenuptial agreement and RJ was bringing the subject up as delicately as he could one day when Lindsay was sitting with him in his home office in Oklahoma.

"Lindsay you know I love you, but my advisors want you to sign a prenuptial agreement. I personally don't like them, but that is kind of the way things go today given the divorce rate out there today. How do you feel about that?" RJ asked.

"RJ, you know I don't need your money. After the settlement and with my videos, I'm fine. I'm not marrying you for money. I could do fine on my own. I'm marrying you because I fell in love with you. I never would have imagined this would happen, given our history," Lindsay said.

"I know, but this is to protect you as much as it is to protect me, because I don't want anything you have to be at risk based upon what I do. I want your assets, money and property that you have when we get married to be protected from anything I do. Suppose I get in some involved in some business or something else that goes south. I don't want them to come after what you have just because you're my wife. I would be responsible for all of our expenses and solely liable for any debts we incur as a family. Your money would be yours to do with as you like. The settlement we had before will stay the same," RJ said.

"That doesn't that make any sense? You will be paying child support for your own son when he will be living in the same house with you," Lindsay said.

"Lindsay, it's best to leave it like it is. I plan on us living the rest of our lives together, but what if two years from now we break up for who knows what reason and the agreement has been broken, that would not be good. I'm not getting married to you as a way to get out of something. Riley's my son and the heir to whatever I have. I'm also going to send Jasmine to college. Jasmine will not be my stepdaughter; she will be my daughter as far as I'm concerned. I know I'm not her biological father, but he's not here. I'm not going to make her feel any different than Riley. What do you want her to call me?" RJ asked.

"I want her to call you daddy. I'm not one of those women that will tell you not to do this or that with my child because you're not her blood father. After we say I do to each other, you are my husband, the head of the household and I will consider you to be the father of both of my children.

We will be one family, not one and a half of a family," Lindsay said.

"The fact that you are willing to allow me to lead your children into adulthood shows me how much you love me. You have been doing this on your own forever and I will be new at raising children, so I'm not saying I know everything. I'm going to need you every step of the way to show me what I should do. Sometimes I might be talking, but it will be your words coming out of my mouth, you know what I mean. Why are you crying," RJ asked.

"I've just been doing this by myself for so long. It's going to be hard to let go of some of the responsibility, but I know you're a good man and I trust you," Lindsay said while wiping away tears.

"Now, you got me all emotional. Okay, the last thing I wanted to talk about and I hope we don't have to discuss this financial thing again. I don't want you to have to ask me about spending money on things you want or for you to have to spend your money every time you want to get something for yourself. You will have an account with two hundred thousand dollars in it per year that will be your personal account. So when we get married that account will have your name on it," RJ said.

"RJ isn't that too much. I mean we will be living together and I have money already," Lindsay said.

"Lindsay, I'm worth about thirty million dollars and I've started my television analyst job already. There will be a network cameraman at our wedding. We might be at an event with the President of the United States at some point. You will probably meet all kind of actors, celebrities and even politicians, so you might need to buy a gown that costs two or three thousand dollars to attend an event. You will need to find a stylist to help you select clothing for certain occasions. That account will come in handy," RJ said.

Lindsay's eyes got as big as the moon.

"The President! You mean I could meet the President? What would I do around all of those kinds of people? I would probably make a fool of myself. I could say something stupid or use the wrong fork or something. I'm just a dumb little country white chick, remember," Lindsay said.

"Stop bugging out on me. I'm from Nacogdoches, Texas, just down the road from where you're from. I'm just a big dumb country black guy. I got here because I was big, fast and didn't get badly injured. The first time I went to a five course dinner, I asked the guy sitting next to me why they were bringing out the food one item at a time because I was ready to eat. I figured out that I went to fancier events every year as the amount of yards I rushed for and touchdowns I made increased. Before I knew it, I was sitting at that dinner in Washington where all of the reporters come together and eat while the President tells jokes. Sitting at the tables around me, were Oscar winning actors, Grammy award winners and Senators. I decided if I was going to keep going to those types of events, my dumb ass needed some help. I took an etiquette class that taught me what to do in different social situation and I'm glad I did," RJ said.

302

"Okay, I won't stress out about that kind of stuff," Lindsay said.

"Don't worry about it. People will show you how to do anything, for a fee of course," RJ said.

"Draw up the prenup paperwork and send it to my lawyer. Your guys have his contact information," Lindsay said.

"Okay, they will work it out," RJ said.

"What about my videos. How do you feel about your wife doing a Strppercise, video series?" Lindsay asked.

"Is it making money?" RJ asked.

"Yes it is," Lindsay said.

"I might want to invest in that. You can try out your new moves on me," RJ said.

"You're so nasty," Lindsay said.

"You know it," RJ replied.

"Have I shown you my desk dance?" Lindsay said as she climbed on top of his mahogany wood desk.

RJ rushed over and closed the office door just in case prying eyes might wander by the office.

With plans for her wedding coming together like she wanted, Lindsay was taking a break at home and watching the midday local news broadcast when the name of the apartment complex she used to live in was mentioned by a field reporter. Lindsay sat down on the couch and watched the report. The reporter proceeded to tell what took place the night before at the property.

"Sadly, the sound of gunfire erupted during the early hours of the morning in this parking lot. When the shooting ended a young man in his early twenties was dead. Latron Williams, whose photo is shown here, was found dead lying between two cars. The investigation is ongoing," the reporter said.

Lindsay was frozen and couldn't believe her eyes. She watched Latron grow from a boy to a man and she recalled that early morning conversation she had with him when she first found out that he was selling drugs. A wave of sadness washed over her and she shed tears for another young black man lost to the violence of the streets. Lindsay knew Latron's mother and had talked with her often when he was younger. Lindsay had not been back to those apartments since she and Tameka moved out all of those months ago. Two days later Lindsay drove up and parked in the parking lot of the place that she had called home for years.

After being gone for so long, Lindsay viewed the apartment complex with new eyes. It looked so much older, smaller and stark than before. There was no softness to that place with concrete, sharp angles and tan stucco dominated the structure. For all its shortcomings it was home and served as a safe haven for years to Lindsay and Tameka's combined families.

Lindsay looked up to the door where she once lived and a young woman was standing outside leaning on the walkway railing. Flowers adorned a makeshift memorial in the parking lot at the location where Latron's body was found. Lindsay saw the apartment where Latron's mother lived and a wreath was hanging on the door. Lindsay walked up the door and carried food she had brought with her to leave with the family. Lindsay knocked on the door and someone opened it and let her in.

"Hello, Mrs. Williams," Lindsay said.

"Lindsay, is that you?" Latron's mother, Mercedes Williams, said.

"Yes ma'am," Lindsay said.

"Girl, come over here and give me a hug," Velma said.

"I'm so sorry. I saw what happened on the news," Lindsay said.

"Thank you baby. Have a seat. I told Latron that he needed to change his ways. I've seen this happen too many times, but he thought he was different. It finally just caught up with him. I've just about cried out all of my tears. I'm putting it in God's hands," Mercedes said.

"Have you set the funeral arrangements yet?" Lindsay asked.

"Not yet. We're trying to scrape the money together to just put him away decent, but dealing drugs don't carry no insurance policy when something like this happens," Mercedes said.

"Who's handling the arrangements?" Lindsay asked.

"Heart of Heaven Funeral Home. They're down off Highway 67. They've buried most of the people in our family. They're nice people and helping us the best way they can," Mercedes said.

"Maybe they can work something out," Lindsay said.

"You know I saw a football game a little while ago and I was telling Latron that the woman

RJ Jefferson proposed to had to be you. I kept saying how did Lindsay from upstairs end up with RJ Jefferson. How did that happen?" Mercedes asked.

"It's a long story, but he is the father of my son, Riley. We weren't married or anything when I got pregnant and really didn't have a relationship at all. We got together over how to raise our son and we kind of fell for each other," Lindsay said.

"That's good. A boy needs his father around to show him how to be a man. I did the best I could with Latron, but he just wouldn't listen when he got to a certain age. Me and his daddy, we got married, but it didn't last. We were just too young to know how married folks were supposed to treat each other. He's been gone for years. What happened to your friend, the black girl, Tameka?" Mercedes asked.

"She moved back home to be close to her folks and is going to college. Her parents are helping with her kids," Lindsay said.

"Praise the lord. I didn't know what happened to ya'll. You had been here for a while. Then, when I saw you run on that field, I was like, you go girl. Get that man," Mercedes said laughing.

"Latron was a good guy. I could tell whenever I talked to him. You take care of yourself. I'm praying for you," Lindsay said.

"Thank you, baby. Thanks for coming by to see me. Most people that get out of here don't ever come back so it means a lot to me that you thought enough of me and Latron to come show your respect. You take care of yourself baby," Mercedes said.

Two hours later Mercedes Williams got a call from Heart of Heaven - Funeral Home and the director informed her that someone paid for the rest of Latron's funeral expenses in full. Mercedes asked who paid for it and he said it was a blonde white woman, but she didn't want to give her name. The funeral home director said she called wanting to know how much was needed to cover the services. The woman said was a friend of the family who wanted to make a donation and he told her the amount. One hour later she walked in with five thousand dollars cash and paid for the services. She viewed the body, sat in the chapel for about ten minutes and then left. Mercedes thanked the funeral director and she knew it was Lindsay who paid for Latron's funeral. Mercedes was thankful and attributed it to someone that had a big heart.

Lindsay called Tameka and told her about Latron and they also discussed how plans for the wedding were progressing. They called Karen and patched her into the conversation. Karen was busy taking care of her young daughter who looked just like her mother. Karen never said anything to George about her encounter with a young man before she got pregnant and was going to raise her daughter as his in any event.

The big day was one month out and everything was in place, including the prenuptial agreement that George got sweetened to the tune of two hundred thousand dollars for each year of marriage deposited directly into an account for

Lindsay. If Lindsay and RJ's union made it past three years, Lindsay would walk away with three million dollars if it ended in divorce regardless of reason or fault. George thought that RJ's feeling for Lindsay were genuine, but he felt lawyers put Riley up to soft peddle his future wife into signing an agreement that left her to walk away with nothing if the marriage failed.

The venue for the wedding would be the largest church in Henderson, Texas and the couple was set to honeymoon in Hawaii. Within one month Lindsay Wilson would become Mrs. RJ Jefferson and time seemed to be flying.

27

Lindsay and the wedding party had arrived in east Texas and the entire area was buzzing. The watch was on to see if someone could catch a glimpse of a professional football player or other celebrity from out of town. This wedding would draw professional athletes, entertainers and a few other media celebrities. Due to the curiosity surrounding this event it was necessary to maintain a tight guest list. Since Lindsay was not a member of a church, RJ's pastor from Oklahoma would perform the wedding ceremony. RJ Jefferson was a superstar, but he went to a church in the heart of the black community in Oklahoma City. RJ felt that his presence in that community was important because other young black men needed to see that you could be successful and still maintain a common touch. Reverend Joseph Franklin was already in town because the wedding rehearsal and dinner were taking place the Wednesday night before the ceremony.

The wedding rehearsal went off without a hitch and the entre party gathered at the civic center, which was the same place that the wedding reception would be held, for the rehearsal dinner. The head table was reserved for those of special importance in the lives of the bride and groom. Tameka and her parents were seated on the same side as Lindsay's family. RJ's parents, family and best man were seated on the other side of the table.

Reverend Franklin said a prayer to set the tone for the dinner. Food and drink were flowing when RJ stood to give a toast.

"I would like to thank everyone for coming, because it means the world to me. I haven't always been the way I am now. There was a time when I believed everything people would say about me. When you are constantly being told how great you are, you might start to believe it and that can be a big mistake because you might believe that you are better than other people. That attitude might cause you to treat someone in a way that you won't be proud of later in life. I was like that once and it caused me to miss years of the life of my son. It also caused a lot of pain for a wonderful woman that I finally found again and in a few days she will become my wife. I just want to say before God and everybody here, Lindsay, I'm not that guy anymore. I'm glad we found each other again and I love you," RJ said.

Lindsay was moved to tears and kissed her husband to be. After drying her eyes Lindsay stood and took the microphone.

"Ya'll I'm not a big public speaker, but I'm better than I was. I want to say that it's been a long road for me to get back home. I left here a long time ago and it was not under the best of circumstances. I was young, scared and had a new baby to take care of. One thing I have learned is in life you can be down and get knocked down, but as long as you keep getting up there is still a chance to come out on top. For a long time I didn't trust men very much. I didn't want them around my children and I

310

pretty much took them out of my life. Now, this man right here, that I'm going to marry in a couple of days, I tried hard not to like him because of a memory I had of him from the past. I went in saying I don't like this guy and found out that I didn't like who I thought he was, but I fell in love with who he is now. RJ, I love you," RJ stood and kissed Lindsay.

"I'm not done yet," Lindsay said.

"I want to thank my best friend, Tameka Davis. I would not have made it if it was not for you. We were like two people in a lifeboat hanging on to each other and we looked after each other's children while we worked and survived. Mr. and Mrs. Davis, Tameka's parents, allowed me to come into their home when I really needed help and I can't thank you enough for what you did for a scared young girl," Lindsay said as she took her seat.

Lindsay's father, Clyde Wilson, stood up and everyone that knew him held their breath in anticipation of what he might say. Clyde walked with a slight limp from his stroke, but his mind and speaking ability remained strong.

"I'm Lindsay's father Clyde Wilson. I want to apologize to my daughter for being a closed minded fool years ago. I said and did some things that a father should never do or say to their child when they are in a position of need. I want to steal something that my future son-in-law said before. I'm not that guy anymore either. The world has changed and I found out that you either keep up or get left behind. I love you Lindsay and I'm proud of

311

the woman you've become and Mr. Davis, thank you for looking out for my daughter when she needed someone," Clyde said as he sat down.

Lindsay walked over and hugged her father.

The rest of the week went without incident and finally the day of the wedding arrived. Lindsay was sitting in the back of the church in a dressing room and her nerves were on edge. Tameka and Karen were with Lindsay trying to calm her down.

"Why are you so nervous?" Tameka asked.

"I've never done anything like this before. I'm getting married. After tonight, my life won't be the same. I will be RJ's wife. I'll be waking up in his bed and in his house. I've been on my own for so long. I hope I can get used to being with someone else all the time," Lindsay said.

"You know what's happening to you? It's called cold feet. It will pass," Karen said.

"How do I look?" Lindsay said.

"You look great and that is a dress that only you could wear," Tameka said.

"I'm glad that you had a dress made that tells the world who Lindsay Wilson is before you become Lindsay Jefferson," Karen said.

"Is it too much? It's not slutty is it?" Lindsay asked.

"No, it's perfect," Tameka said.

"It's time," someone said that opened the door.

"Okay, I've got to get these two little girls down the aisle," Karen said.

Lindsay's daughter Jasmine and Tamika's daughter Tasha were the flower girls. Tameka was the Maid of Honor. Karen and Tameka's cousin Angela from Dallas were bridesmaids. Riley's best friend, Datron Jenkins, an offensive lineman for the Buffalos served as his best man. RJ's two younger brothers were groomsmen. A live band began to play processional music and Lindsay's son Riley, who served as ring bearer, walked behind his little sister and Tasha who walked ahead of him spreading flower petals. The parents were seated before the attendants marched in and took their place at the front of the church under a large golden toned metal arch covered with red roses. The groom was already standing in front of the pastor waiting for the bride to walk in. Riley had not seen Lindsay's wedding dress and had no idea what to expect. Finally, there was only one person left that needed to walk down the aisle, the bride.

The band stopped playing and the church sanctuary fell silent. Suddenly the sound of the church organ cut through the silence like a knife with the opening of Felix Mendelssohn's Wedding March. Suddenly Lindsay walked into view and an audible gasp came from the assembled guests. Lindsay wore a wedding dress like none of them had never seen before. Lindsay's dress was solid white silk with lace borders. The dress clung to Lindsay curves like a glove and the front hemline of the dress ended just above her kneecaps. The dress had a second layer that flowed downwards and formed a train, but it gave the appearance that it was one piece so the side and front views were completely different. As Lindsay took each step her exposed forward leg and shoes were clearly visible, but the trailing leg would disappear into the second layer of the dress. The top of the dress featured a heart shaped opening that allowed her ample cleavage to show, but the opening was covered by a thin layer of lace. Lindsay walked alone until she was halfway down the aisle and then she paused. Lindsay's father Clyde Wilson walked from his seat with a slight limp and escorted his daughter the rest of the way until she was facing her future husband, RJ Jefferson. Lindsay smiled at him through the lace veil covering her face. RJ was struggling to suppress a mischievous grin.

The Pastor stated that they were gathered to join this man and woman in holy matrimony and he uttered some words that held more weight than he ever knew.

"Who gives this woman to be wed?" Reverend Franklin asked.

"I do," Clyde Wilson said.

Clyde Wilson took his daughters hand and walked her two steps and moved her hand to place it in Riley's hand.

Lindsay cut her eyes to watch her father take her hand and move it to RJ's. Lindsay did not make any effort to assist much in her hand movement to RJ's hand. Lindsay wanted Clyde Wilson to know that he using his power to physically place his daughter's hand in the hands of the same black man whose seed he cursed when she was pregnant. Lindsay did not resist her father's effort to place her hand in Riley's, but she needed for him to exert himself a little to make it happen. When Lindsay saw her hand, her father's and RJ's all together for the briefest of moments she smiled. Her father had used racial slurs towards her when he discovered that she was carrying the child of a black man and wanted to hide her to avoid embarrassment. Now, before God and the world, Clyde Wilson, willfully gave his daughter over to a black man who would become her husband and his son-in-law. The entire episode of Clyde placing Lindsay's hand in Riley's took mere seconds, but to Lindsay it helped to ease years of pain.

Lindsay and Riley exchanged vows and even said brief words they wrote to each other about being two broken pieces that created a whole person. Finally the culminating moment arrived.

"I now pronounce you man and wife. You may kiss your bride," Reverend Franklin said.

Riley lifted the veil that covered Lindsay's face, kissed his new wife and they turned to face the church full of well wishers.

"I now present Mr. and Mrs. Riley Jeremiah Jefferson," the minister announced to the world.

Applause and cheers rang throughout the sanctuary and the newly minted husband and wife walked out together with their children in tow.

After seemingly endless photographs, it was finally time to go to the reception and Lindsay rode over to the civic center in a limousine with RJ and they went to a back dressing room to get ready for their grand entrance as husband and wife. Lindsay shed the outer layer of her dress and that left the other portion that was perfect for dancing.

"I loved that wedding dress. You looked awesome," RJ said to Lindsay.

"I thought you might get a kick out of that. I hope I didn't give anyone a heart attack," Lindsay said.

"You almost gave me one," RJ said as he grabbed Lindsay and began to kiss her deeply and ran his hands over her rear.

"I know you don't think you are about to get a quickie in here. That has to wait until we get to Hawaii," Lindsay said.

"Hawaii!" RJ said.

"That's right. The next time you get some of this, I want to hear the ocean in the background," Lindsay said.

"Alright, but you might get weak before then," RJ said.

"I might get weak? Please," Lindsay said laughingly.

"Well, Mrs. Jefferson, it's time to kick this party off," RJ said as they walked out to have their first dance as husband and wife.

Later when things were winding down, Tameka excitedly came over to Lindsay.

"Lindsay, guess what? Terrance proposed to me. We're engaged," Tameka said excitedly.

"Congratulations, I'm so excited for you. He's crazy about you. I can tell," Lindsay said looking at Tameka's ring.

"Girl, we have come a long way from where we started," Lindsay said.

Lindsay stood up and hugged Tameka.

"I missed you and your kids so much when you left, but you did the right thing by coming home. Now you are going to school again and found a man that loves you and is all yours," Lindsay said.

"I missed you too. My kids cried all the way down the road the day we left. They missed you and your children so much. We need to make sure we stay close and don't drift too far apart, but your life is about to change. You are going to meet all kind of new people and go to places you never dreamed of," Tameka said.

"I know it's kind of scary," Lindsay said.

"Don't say that. After what you've been through, you don't have anything to worry about," Tameka said.

Everything was about over and RJ and Lindsay were being driven to D/FW International Airport to board their flight for their honeymoon in Hawaii. Once onboard the jetliner Lindsay felt that her new life had really started when they left the ground and finally touched down in Honolulu. RJ and Lindsay then took a short flight over to the big island of Hawaii where they would spend one week for their honeymoon in a luxury resort where they had reserved a private bungalow with beach access.

Lindsay felt that she was in a different world as she watched the sun set as if it was sinking into the ocean while she was wrapped in the arms of her new husband. RJ took Lindsay by the hand and they walked from the beach to their honeymoon cabin. Once they were inside RJ turned to Lindsay.

"Can you hear the ocean?" RJ asked.

"Yes. I can hear the waves coming onto the beach," Lindsay said.

With that RJ scoped his wife up in his arms and carried her into the bedroom to consummate their marriage. Lindsay hung onto RJ as they made love with the sound of the waves crashing in the background. There was no mood music or dim interior lighting needed. Soft moonlight lit the room. Lindsay welcomed the strong embrace of this man who promised to love and protect her forever. Lindsay felt her long journey from the ultimate of rejection to the height of acceptance was complete because only death would break that bond.

Their week in Hawaii was a wonderful way for them to really get to know each other without any other distractions. RJ had been to Hawaii before to play in all-star games, but he had not visited the big island of Hawaii. Lindsay loved the natural beauty and variety. For some reason one of Lindsay's favorite places was when they were on top of the hardened lava flows of the Kilauea volcano far above the area where molten lava flows into the ocean. It was a quiet and desolate place with a roaring wind constantly blowing. Lindsay said she could hear herself think in that place and that was a rare occurrence.

Everything comes to an end and so did the time for this honeymoon. RJ and Lindsay flew back to their new reality of starting a life together as a family. The couple made a drive down to Lindsay's parents to collect their children and unopened wedding gifts.

They got back to RJ's home and realized that the job of merging two separate households had not begun yet. After they recovered from travel and time zone changes Lindsay and RJ sat down and opened their wedding gifts. They really didn't need anything, but Lindsay ran across an envelope that caught her attention. The name on the envelope was Mercedes Williams. Lindsay opened the envelope and pulled out the card that was inside. The card had the words thank you written in gold embossed letters. Lindsay removed the card and read what was written inside.

"Lindsay thank you for what you did for my family. I have no proof that you paid for the rest of Latron's funeral, but the description of the person let me know who it was. Plus, I saw your name on the guest registry. You have a good heart. May you have a blessed life. Love, Mercedes Williams."

RJ saw the expression on Lindsay's face.

"Hey, what's wrong," RJ said.

"This young guy in the apartment complex I used to live in, named Latron, got killed a few weeks ago. He was selling drugs and someone shot him. He was young when I moved in there and to hear about him dying got to me. I saw him selling drugs when I came home one night, that's when I decided I had to get in touch with you. I could see Riley ending up the same way as Latron if he didn't have his father in his life to help guide him. I went to see his mother after he was killed and they didn't have enough money to pay for the funeral and I finished paying for it, but I didn't tell her I did it, but she figured it out," Lindsay said.

"You did that? You're really something," RJ said.

Due to the timing of their wedding, Christmas was approaching fast and there was a big Christmas tree in the family room with plenty of presents under it for everyone. This was a very new experience for everyone as this was their first holiday together as a family. Lindsay and the children were attending church with RJ and their lives together seemed to be off to a promising start. Lindsay only hoped that this was an omen of better things to come.

28

One year into her marriage Lindsay was happier than she had ever been and thought that Tameka was right when she told her not to worry about taking on new experiences. Lindsay had met a variety of new people over the past year of varying levels of fame and importance and found most of them to be fairly normal with a few eccentric exceptions. Three months prior Lindsay had served as Tameka's Maid Of Honor at her wedding to Terrance who Lindsay found to be a nice man who really loved her best friend.

The conversation that Lindsay and RJ had before they got married about doing something to help young men and women who stumbled early in life had born fruit. Two organization were up and running with the help of funding dollars from some of RJ's sponsors. There were two facilities in Oklahoma City that served as prototypes for a nationwide rollout. The Lindsay Center For Young Women was dedicated to giving young women a second chance to achieve their dreams and the Riley Institute did the same thing for young men. Both organizations had outreach programs dedicated to preventing teen pregnancy and it included educating young men and women. It was not easy to push an agenda of self respect and responsibility in a climate that was drenched with messages flowing from the popular entertainment culture glorifying irresponsibility for the sake of self gratification.

Lindsay was out on a shopping excursion and stopped in a quaint café for a light lunch. While she was eating she noticed a teenage black girl sitting at a bus stop. Lindsay thought it was odd for her to be there as it was a school day and she had allowed two buses to pass without getting on either one. When a third bus passed and the girl was still sitting there, Lindsay decided to take a chance. Lindsay walked out and sat on the bench alongside the girl.

"It's a nice day for December, isn't it?" Lindsay said.

The girl glanced at Lindsay, but she didn't respond.

"Where are you going?" Lindsay asked.

"What do you want lady?" the girl asked.

"Listen, I just saw you sitting here for a while and I just wanted to see if you needed anything," Lindsay said.

"What business is it of yours? Why you trying to get in my business? You don't know me," the girl said.

"Look if you're in trouble maybe I can help you. It's the middle of a school day. What are you doing down here?" Lindsay asked.

Lindsay pulled out a business card and was about to give it to the girl and leave. The girl read the card and called to Lindsay.

"Miss!" the girl said.

Lindsay turned and sat back down alongside the girl.

"Yeah, honey what is it?" Lindsay asked.

"I'm pregnant. My mama kicked me out," the girl said.

"My name is Lindsay. What's yours?" Lindsay asked.

"Shemeka," the girl said.

"How old are you Shemeka?" Lindsay asked.

"Fifteen," Shemeka said.

"Oh God! Was it your boyfriend that got you pregnant?" Lindsay asked.

"No," Shemeka said almost bursting into tears.

"Honey what is it?" Lindsay asked.

"It was my mama's boyfriend. It started by him saying I was pretty and could be an Instantchat model with the body I had and become famous. He bought some clothes for me to wear that didn't cover me up a lot and took pictures of me, you know thongs and stuff like that. I posted them and people started following me and I thought it was working. Then he told me I should take some naked pictures, because if people liked me with clothes on they would like me even more with my clothes off, so I did it," Shemeka said.

"Where was your mother when all of this was going on?" Lindsay asked with a pained look on her face.

"She was at work. She is a nurse's aid and works the night shift at the hospital," Shemeka explained.

"So she didn't know this was happening?" Lindsay said.

"No ma'am. I believed what he was telling me because people online were commenting about how much they liked my photos and how good I looked. Then one night he told me if I really wanted to blow up, I should do a sex video. I told him I didn't think I should do that, but then he starting talking about all those reality stars who got famous or became even more famous after doing one and it sounded like it made sense. I asked him how I would find somebody to be in the video with me, because I didn't know anybody that would do that because they would be too afraid their family or friends would see it. Then he said if I didn't know anybody then he would do the video with me and block his face out after it was done so nobody would know who he was. I thought about it and said okay, so he set his camera up one night and we did it. I was nervous at first, but he gave me a pill and I felt better," Shemeka said.

"So, your mother's boyfriend talked you into letting him make a video of both of you having sex. How old is he?" Lindsay asked.

"I don't know. I guess he's twenty something. My mama is thirty-two and I think he's a little younger than she is," Shemeka said.

"What happened after the video was finished?" Lindsay asked.

"I got scared and told him not to post the video because I thought it would get back to my mama. I asked him to delete it, but he wouldn't and told me I better not tell anybody about it. The next night he came into my room and got in bed with me and I told him to get out. I told him I only had sex with him to do the video. He told me if I didn't do what he wanted he would post the video and tell my mama it was all my idea. I was scared and didn't know what to do, so I did what he wanted. We stated having sex almost every night and he made me do all kind of things I didn't want to do. Then, when I missed my period I was so scared and confused, but I didn't say anything to anybody. I took one of those home pregnancy tests and it said I was pregnant, but I kept having sex with him. Then one night my mama came home early from work because she wasn't feeling good. She heard us, opened my bedroom door and saw him on top of me," Shemeka said.

"Oh my God," Lindsay said with a gasp.

"Mama started screaming at us. He told mama I led him on and threw myself at him. He said he did what any real man would do if a woman put it in his face. I told mama I was pregnant and that he was lying. Mama said it was my fault for being too fast. I told her it was his fault for taking advantage of me and she got really mad at me. She called me a little slut and kicked me out. He's still there living with her," Shemeka said through tears.

Lindsay embraced Shemeka and hugged her tight.

"I'm going to get you some help. I know some people that will help you and I'm going to help you. Do you want me to help you?" Lindsay asked.

"Yes ma'am," Shemeka said.

"Come on baby. Let's get you something to eat first," Lindsay said as she took Shemeka into the café for a hot meal.

An hour later, after making a few phone calls, Lindsay Jefferson drove off with Shemeka with the mission of preventing another girl from traveling the same hard road she had gone down years before. Lindsay knew she couldn't save the world, but maybe she could change a few lives for the better one at a time.

Lindsay helped Shemeka and many other girls like her and the justice system dealt out punishment to Shemeka's mother's boyfriend for what he did to her. The center for young men had an active outreach that centered on mentoring about the importance of practicing socially responsible behavior. One of the main focuses for the program for young men was enforcing the idea of consequences for actions they took that affected others, including fathering children. RJ and Lindsay felt they were making a difference, although they were fighting an avalanche of negative forces moving in the opposite direction.

Lindsay continued her personal development by enrolling in college and was in her second year of a business administration major that she took mostly online to allow her travel and schedule flexibility. The Strippercise video business was going great and she was preparing to roll out the fourth edition that included a new offering that Lindsay thought would take the business to the next level. Lindsay remembered something RJ told her a long time ago about her business and she was going to take him up on his offer.

RJ walked into his bedroom and there was a chair sitting in the middle of the floor and a platform with a pipe of some kind protruding from it.

"Lindsay, what is this in the middle of the floor?" RJ asked.

Music suddenly burst forth from the speakers in the room and Lindsay walked out from the mezzanine area and RJ sat down in the chair and watched. Lindsay was wearing one of the ensembles that she used when she worked at The Secret Garden Club. Lindsay walked up to the compact platform and grabbed the pole that was about eight-feet tall and she did a handstand mount. Lindsay then started to spin around the pole and landed on the platform. RJ was mesmerized as he had never seen his wife dance like this. Lindsay had her heels on and she grabbed the pole with both hands with her back towards RJ who had moved his chair up close to the small platform.

Lindsay squatted down until her butt touched the surface of the platform and she started to bounce her rear end rapidly up and down to the bass beat. RJ was amazed and then as the music ended, Lindsay bent over and looked at her husband through her legs.

"What do you think?" Lindsay asked while breathing hard as she turned around.

RJ didn't say anything. He threw his wallet, car keys and house keys onto the stage.

"That was awesome," RJ said.

"This portable stage is a new product for my video set's platinum option. You told me to try out new stuff on you," Lindsay said.

"Sold!" RJ said as he threw Lindsay over his shoulder and carried her to their bed.

About The Author

ESSENCE® bestselling author D.T. Pollard lives in the Dallas/Fort Worth, TX area. He is married and has one son.

Other works
By
D T Pollard
Rooftop Diva – A Novel of Triumph
After Katrina (fiction)
Fools' Heaven – Love, Lust and
Death Beyond the Pulpit (fiction)
TARP TOWN U S A – The
Recession That Saved America
OBAMA GUILTY OF BEING PRESIDENT
WHILE BLACK
Vampire Sapien
The Mark Unmasked
Publish Free For Kindle Today
Sell Worldwide Tomorrow
World Wide Nuclear Power Plant Guide
Unemployed But Not Destroyed
Vulture Capitalism
Whitney Houston – Poems for Whitney
Whitney Amy Michael Elvis
The Good Old Girls Club
President Obama – Diary of Disrespect
Who
Who Moved My Ocean – Avoid The Shrinking Job
Trap

Mitt Romney's America – No Trespassing By The
47%
Romnesia – How Dangerous Is It
Obama 2.0
Carnage Control
Gold Digger's Grave
Things You Can't Tell Mama – The Pastor's Wife
Things You Can't Tell Mama – Her Man Was Once
Yours
Things You Can't Tell Mama – Her Blond Best
Friend
Things You Can't Tell Mama - Mr. Taboo
Things You Can't Tell Mama – The Prophetess
Affair
Things You Can't Tell Mama–Your Best Friend's
Mother
Things You Can't Tell Mama – The President's Sex
Tape
Things You Can't Tell Mama – Anthology
Confessions of a Single Black Woman
Tiberius – Rap's Rainmaker
Things you Can't Tell Mama – The Pastor's Wife 2
Mommy Porn
Jacob's Cabin
The Pastor's Lover
Side Piece
Side Piece 2 – Amber Alarm
Hero In The Hood
The Pastor's Lover 2
She Twerks Hard For The Money
The Pastor's Lover 3
Forget Big Brother We Tell DAD Everything
The Pastor's Wife 3

Hoe Hoe Hoe Merry Christmas
Ghetto Tony and White Trash Tina
Fifty Shades of Plaid
Grandma Does It Better
Keisha's Mama Is So Fine
Less Pretty
Pretty For A Dark Skinned Woman
Massive Monroe
The Pastor's Lover 4 – The Pastor's Wife 4
The Obituary of Gut Bucket Johnson
Forget Big Brother – We Tell DAD Everything
Unreal Housewives of South Dallas
Liquid Memories: You Can Live Forever
Gold Digger's Game
Ebola – Partying With Grace
THOT On The Beach
What Would Dr King Think About Today's Black America
Your Best Friend's Mother 2 – Lust In London
Donald Trump –The Big White Man Returns
Secrets of a Baby Mama 2